PRAISE FOR LEXI BLAKE AND MASTERS AND MERCENARIES...

"I can always trust Lexi Blake's Dominants to leave me breathless...and in love. If you want sensual, exciting BDSM wrapped in an awesome love story, then look for a Lexi Blake book."

~Cherise Sinclair USA Today Bestselling author

"Lexi Blake's MASTERS AND MERCENARIES series is beautifully written and deliciously hot. She's got a real way with both action and sex. I also love the way Blake writes her gorgeous Dom heroes--they make me want to do bad, bad things. Her heroines are intelligent and gutsy ladies whose taste for submission definitely does not make them dish rags. Can't wait for the next book!"

~Angela Knight, New York Times bestselling author

"A Dom is Forever is action packed, both in the bedroom and out. Expect agents, spies, guns, killing and lots of kink as Liam goes after the mysterious Mr. Black and finds his past and his future… The action and espionage keep this story moving along quickly while the sex and kink provides a totally different type of interest. Everything is very well balanced and flows together wonderfully."

~A Night Owl "Top Pick", Terri, Night Owl Erotica

"A Dom Is Forever is everything that is good in erotic romance. The story was fast-paced and suspenseful, the characters were flawed but made me root for them every step of the way, and the hotness factor was off the charts mostly due to a bad boy Dom with a penchant for dirty talk."

~Rho, The Romance Reviews

Perfectly Paired

OTHER BOOKS BY LEXI BLAKE

EROTIC ROMANCE

Masters and Mercenaries
The Dom Who Loved Me
The Men With The Golden Cuffs
A Dom is Forever
On Her Master's Secret Service
Sanctum: A Masters and Mercenaries Novella
Love and Let Die
Unconditional: A Masters and Mercenaries Novella
Dungeon Royale
Dungeon Games: A Masters and Mercenaries Novella
A View to a Thrill
Cherished: A Masters and Mercenaries Novella
You Only Love Twice
Luscious: Masters and Mercenaries~Topped
Adored: A Masters and Mercenaries Novella
Master No
Just One Taste: Masters and Mercenaries~Topped 2
From Sanctum with Love
Devoted: A Masters and Mercenaries Novella
Dominance Never Dies
Dominance Never Dies
Submission is Not Enough
Perfectly Paired
For His Eyes Only, Coming February 2017
Treasured, Coming April 25, 2017

Lawless
Ruthless
Satisfaction, Coming January 3, 2017
Revenge, Coming June 20, 2017

Masters Of Ménage (by Shayla Black and Lexi Blake)
Their Virgin Captive
Their Virgin's Secret
Their Virgin Concubine
Their Virgin Princess
Their Virgin Hostage
Their Virgin Secretary
Their Virgin Mistress

The Perfect Gentlemen (by Shayla Black and Lexi Blake)
Scandal Never Sleeps
Seduction in Session
Big Easy Temptation
Smoke and Sin, Coming Soon

URBAN FANTASY

Thieves
Steal the Light
Steal the Day
Steal the Moon
Steal the Sun
Steal the Night
Ripper
Addict
Sleeper, Coming Soon

Perfectly Paired

Masters and Mercenaries~
Topped, Book 3

Lexi Blake

Perfectly Paired
Masters and Mercenaries, Topped, Book 3
Lexi Blake

Published by DLZ Entertainment LLC

Copyright 2016 DLZ Entertainment LLC
Edited by Chloe Vale
ISBN: 978-1-937608-57-6

McKay-Taggart logo design by Charity Hendry

This is a work of fiction. Names, places, characters and incidents are the product of the author's imagination and are fictitious. Any resemblance to actual persons, living or dead, events or establishments is solely coincidental.

Sign up for Lexi Blake's newsletter
and be entered to win a $25 gift certificate
to the bookseller of your choice.

Join us for news, fun, and exclusive content
including free short stories.

There's a new contest every month!

Go to www.LexiBlake.net to subscribe.

ACKNOWLEDGMENTS

Thanks to my whole team. To my editor and general chief accessory in multiple endeavors, Kim Guidroz. To Stormy Pate, Riane Holt, Kori Smith, and Liz Berry for the feedback. To my husband who manages to hold us all together.

Top is obviously a product of my imagination but the struggle of wounded veterans coming home from war is very real. Please support business that make a practice of hiring and training our veterans for jobs that will secure their futures—as they secured ours.

CHAPTER ONE

Sebastian Lowe watched as his boss, Sean Taggart, settled into the chair behind his desk. Unlike other offices where Sebastian was forced to stuff his big body into some miniscule but suitably expensive chair designed more for fashion than comfort, Taggart offered up a large, masculine seat across from his perch. Too often Sebastian felt like a massive bear attempting to fit on some delicate work of art and fearing he was about to break it. He would end up on the floor and it would take a couple of the line chefs to drag him back up to his artificial feet.

He hated being vulnerable.

"Thanks for coming in on your off day," Taggart said.

Yes, despite the comfortable seating, he was definitely still vulnerable. He should have taken Chef up on his offer to go with him to New York to meet with the producers of the new show Taggart was hosting. Instead, he'd put it off claiming he had to stay behind to oversee the installation of the new refrigerator in the wine cellar. He'd been unhappy with the reliability of the old one. He should have taken that plane ticket and pretended like he was comfortable with the prospect of being on television. He should have known that a place like Top would grow and likely need a sommelier who would look good on camera.

A sommelier who didn't spend half his life merely trying to stay on his feet.

"Not a problem." He'd been packing and readying himself for the temporary move to Fort Worth. The exercise had been a bit depressing since it forced him to acknowledge he hadn't spent much time turning his apartment into a home. It was furnished and bland, with no spark of his own personality and very few comforts. He'd made the decision that when he returned, he would find a better place. He'd been planning on becoming a settled adult and trying to find a condo or a small house to invest in. He'd been ready to give up the vagabond existence he'd found himself in since that terrible day when he'd realized Alicia wanted nothing more from him.

It looked like he might be moving on from Dallas in a permanent fashion, but one thing was for certain. He wouldn't be returning to Georgia. There was nothing left now. No restaurant. No family. Not even redemption.

"I called you in because I need to talk about something that will affect your work situation," Chef said.

Fuck. He hadn't realized until this moment how much he wanted to settle down. He'd worked in some amazing places, but he loved this small restaurant in Dallas. In the restaurant world, Dallas wasn't much of a blip on the map. It wasn't even a Michelin-rated town, but Top had something he'd never found before. It had a magic most places didn't. Family. God, it felt a little like he'd had a family again.

Even if he was the weird uncle who wore a three-piece suit everywhere and rarely went to parties.

"Of course," he began, pleased his voice was so even. He wasn't going to beg. He didn't beg for anything. Well, not since the day he'd begged and pleaded with God to take his life instead of Gary's. He knew it wasn't really God's fault. It had been the damn SAM that had taken down the helo they'd been riding in. Fate had taken Gary's life and left Sebastian with no legs. Modern technology had sort of given them back.

Chef leaned toward him. "You know how much I appreciate what you're doing to help with the opening of the new restaurant. I can imagine that being forced to move to Fort Worth for eight weeks is a pain in the ass."

"I don't mind." Not if it meant he got to keep his job. Not if it meant he wasn't getting kicked aside for some snotty-ass som who'd never done anything in his damn life but study for his master's level and get his hair done so he could squawk about the finest Cab on cable TV. "I've looked at the apartment. It's more than suitable."

The Fort Worth apartment Taggart was offering to let him stay at was nicer than his place, but then he was only now getting to the point that he had some extra cash to spend on things like an apartment with more than one room. It was time to make a home. It was time to give up on everything he'd left behind.

How many years had he pursued Alicia Layle? She'd been his perfect female for so very long. Ever since the day he'd met her. He'd been eight years old, but his fascination with her had lasted. Feminine and soft, with gentle manners and a warm persona. She was gracious and kind. Everyone in their small town adored her.

And she'd been the one to turn them all against him. Her sweet light had been an illusion.

Perhaps that's why his dreams of Alicia had been replaced in the last few months with a mouthy, boozy, slightly insane brat of a blonde with gorgeous tits and a perfectly round ass. Tiffany Hayes worked as a server and was always slightly, fascinatingly unkempt. Oh, she would try for perfection, but there would always be one thing off about her. He'd made it a habit to study her each and every time they worked together so he could find it. Sometimes it was nothing more than a spot on her shirt she'd forgotten to iron. And then there were the times she would show up and still have flecks of paint on her hands and he would wonder what she'd spent her day painting.

"Grace made me buy the apartment because she didn't want me driving home late at night," Chef was saying. "I tried to explain to her that we should find a place in the suburbs between Dallas and Fort Worth to cut down on the commute between restaurants, but she put her foot down. We moved last year when we found out she was pregnant

15

again and she swears we'll be buried in that house."

"How is she doing?" He'd heard the pregnancy and birth had been hard on Grace Taggart.

Chef took a deep breath and nodded, as though relieved at the answer he was going to give. "She's good. Much better than I had hoped for, but I still don't want to leave her or the kids for any real amount of time. It's why I'm going to ask you to sacrifice for the good of the team."

"I don't think that's a good idea, Chef, and I'm going to tell you why." What was he doing? His mouth was working without the aid of his inner self. That inner self was crying out for him to have a little fucking dignity, but the words kept coming out. "No one knows your menus like I do. No one knows Eric's cooking like I do. I understand the network is likely going to want to bring in a sommelier with more flair, but they aren't going to be as good a fit as I am."

Chef sat back, his eyes widening as though he was as surprised as Sebastian. "Really? And why is that?"

He should stand up and accept his layoff with grace. He should shake the chef's hand and hope for a good referral. He did stand, meaning to do just that. He was careful because the last thing he wanted was to end up on the floor. He went to put his hand out and he really meant to do all those dignified things he'd settled on.

"You know why, Chef? Because I am Top. I am everything you want in this place. I'm Southern. Born and raised on the kinds of food you serve. They're not a theory to me. They're not something quaint and rustic to serve on an off night. This food is my soul as much as the wine I pair with it. I speak your language in a way no other som is going to. I'll be honest. I don't like the idea of going on the television show. I'm a private person. I do, however, understand what you're doing and why you're doing it. You don't need a more experienced som. You need one with the right experience."

"There are only four master sommeliers in the state," Chef pointed out. "My list of applicants would be very limited."

"And I'm the only one of them who speaks your language. I know

I'm the youngest in that group, but I'm also the best. How many of them served? Not a one. You hire vets. I speak that language, too. I might not shout it the way some do, but I understand what men like Eric and Macon and Linc did for this country and how they need to be treated now." He set his hands on the desk, unwilling to even risk the possibility that he could lose his balance. This was too important. He didn't realize how much he wanted to stay. A vision of Tiffany floated across his brain. He couldn't forget that night when he'd taken her home and she'd pressed her body to his, her mouth roaming across his. And she'd been drunk so he'd tucked her into bed despite her protests. "You know those sommeliers likely won't want to work the bar when Linc has an episode. They take their skills seriously."

"I take your skills seriously," Chef said, a mysterious smile on his face.

"Then you should think twice about replacing me." He was well aware that his boss was probably shocked at how he was behaving. He was the always-in-control-and-never-flustered employee. He attempted to never show a moment's weakness, but he was fighting for his life. Well, not his life, but definitely his job and his passion. "I don't want to move anywhere. I don't need to work for a distributor or at some restaurant conglomerate. I believe in the idea behind Top. I believe in employing and training veterans. This isn't a job. This is a calling."

Chef sat back, his hands going behind his head. "This is a side of you I've never seen."

It was a side very few people saw. He'd learned at a young age to maintain control in all things. He took a step back and straightened out his suit. It wouldn't do to continue on. He'd said what he had to say. "I don't like to make a scene, but I believe in what I'm saying."

"Why, exactly, do you think I'm firing you?" It sounded like an academic question and not the be-all, end-all of Sebastian's life.

He thought about lying, but decided not to. He did owe Taggart, even if this was the end. "I know you had a meeting with Dan Jenkins. I know the network filmed it. I probably shouldn't have said anything, but I think it's a mistake."

Taggart had recently agreed to allow the Food Network to do a limited-run show about Top and its unique hiring practices. The chef had also agreed to do several personal appearances across the network.

Dan Jenkins was a few years older and miles more attractive. He also had all his limbs. He didn't have a problem with looking good on television. He would be slick on camera.

Chef sat back up. "I did meet with him. I've been asked to cook for a charity dinner benefitting the children's hospital and Dan is representing the distributor for the wine pairings. I'm not planning on changing soms. I have one who fits in quite nicely and it's good to know he has no plans to leave any time soon."

He felt his skin flush. "You're not firing me."

"Not even close, buddy. It wasn't a thought in my brain. You're perfect for Top and I hope you stay around for a very long time."

He wasn't being fired. Thank god. "I thought you might want someone with more on-screen experience."

There was a knock on the door and Chef sighed. "Come on in." He shot Sebastian a pointed stare. "I have my master som and don't think for a second that I don't understand how cheap I got you in the beginning. You took a chance on this place. I value that. I'm not of any mind to hire someone like Dan. Oh, I know he's considered the brightest star by the Court of Master Sommeliers, but here and with my partner, there's another meaning entirely to the word Master."

"Did you talk to him?" A massive slab of muscle strode in looking like he was ready to murder someone. Ian Taggart, Chef's older brother and not so silent partner in Top. He was wearing a dark blue swath of fabric across his chest that very likely contained his infant son. As far as Sebastian had heard, Charlotte Taggart had given birth to their son a few weeks before and that apparently meant the big guy became a marsupial with a child in his pouch at most functions. "Because I got real problems. I don't need to worry about the damn training program. It's not like I'm getting any right now. Have you ever tried to top a woman who recently had a baby you put up in her? Charlie's not having any of it. And Seth and I here are still outnumbered because someone neutered Bud and now the dog doesn't have a dick either. Or balls. Yeah. I think he's got a dick, but no balls. Isn't that right, Sean? It's the same thing. You kept your dick, but they cut off your balls. Dude, I don't know how you survived. It made the dog cranky so he ate one of my shoes. That made me cranky. God, I'm tired."

Chef's eyes had rolled to the back of his head. "I didn't have my damn balls cut off. I had a vasectomy, you moron."

"Same difference." Big Tag sank to the chair Sebastian had occupied. "Bud's left us for the female majority. He just follows the girls around. I think it's because the twins are so good at dropping food everywhere. But it's left me and the little man here on our own testosterone-wise." He put a hand on the bundle on his chest before looking over at Sebastian. "So you in or out?"

"Why would I be out?" He didn't understand the complex relationship the Taggart brothers seemed to have. There were four of them including younger twins Case and Theo, and they were ruthlessly sarcastic with each other. It seemed to be how they communicated. It was a completely different language than the one he spoke.

Chef held up a hand. "We haven't gotten there yet."

A tiny fist made its way outside the bundle. Big Tag reached out, letting the fingers curl around his forefinger. "What? Why haven't you gotten there? It's a simple question. Dude, will you take over the baby Doms for me? There's a new crop coming in and they need to be sown. Otherwise they'll all be like 'brah, let's go spank some bottoms and drink craft beer' and then I'll have to murder them. Seriously. I've been told not to murder them. Millennial Doms. Has it really come to this?"

And he was lost. "Millennial Doms?"

Chef put out a hand as though trying to slow things down. "It's a favor he's doing for Adam."

"I lost a bet," Big Tag said.

Chef shook his head. "Or you're being a genuinely nice guy helping out a man who worked for you for years."

"Lost a bet," Big Tag insisted.

Chef sighed. "Adam and Jake have worked for McKay-Taggart for years, but they've got a new company they want to start that will specialize in missing persons. They have a new software program that aids in facial recognition, but there's a little issue of another company competing for a similar patent. We all know Adam's process is better, but this company has a shit ton of money and could hold him up for years in court. The company is a tech firm based here in Dallas and owned by a man named Milo Jaye."

"Ah, the social media magnate." Jaye was young but seemingly very serious. He wasn't a Steve Jobs type who enjoyed media attention. "So you've worked some kind of deal with him? What could Adam give him that he can't buy for…" The answer hit him. "Ah, he wants a Sanctum membership."

Sanctum was the club Ian Taggart ran. A very exclusive BDSM club that had been started by the original members of the security firm McKay-Taggart. It had morphed into a play place for the rich and powerful. And the poor and playful who worked for or aided the Taggart brothers. He'd discovered that it was about half and half on the ridiculously powerful versus people Ian flat out liked.

Taggart had also been known to use the club to his own ends, making friends who could help out the company from time to time. Having the Dallas chief of police as a member guaranteed that McKay-Taggart's infrequent brushes with the law got handled quietly. In exchange, the company aided in any investigation the police asked of them. DPD often consulted with Eve McKay on profiles of potential criminals.

Big Tag patted the bundle on his chest. "Root around all you like, buddy. Nothing coming out of there." He looked back at Sebastian. "Yes, Milo Jaye wants a membership and he's bringing some women with him. I think he's trying to set up a harem or something. Dude's a freak, but hey, no one cares when you're a billionaire."

"He'll drop the lawsuit if he gets the required training to gain Master rights at Sanctum," Chef explained. "I personally think this was his play all along and we could have avoided this entirely if Ian had simply let the man in a training class."

"You know how I feel about douchebag names." Big Tag shook his head.

A groan came from Chef's mouth. "He has a list."

"Arlo, Milo, Kylo," Big Tag began. "Basically all the o's. Except dildo. If someone is named Dildo, I'll totally let them in. Ephram, Jeremiah. Basically anyone who sounds like they do civil war reenactments on weekends. Then you've got the moneybags. Chet, Thad, Brock. Oh, and anyone named Chazz. If you sound like you belong on a reality dating show, you're out."

"Because Seth doesn't rank on any of those lists," Chef shot back.

Big Tag shrugged. "Not my call. Charlie shot down John Wayne Taggart. Apparently when you shove a ten-pound baby out your hoo haw, you get naming rights. Also, I have zero intention of ever letting this one or the girls anywhere near my club. They can start their own. So will you do it?"

"Do what?" His head was kind of spinning. He wasn't sure if he was being asked to do something at the club or change his name to something more manly than Sebastian.

He was probably going to turn them down on the latter.

"Will you take on a private training class with a billionaire and decide whether or not he gets access to the club?" Big Tag huffed a little like Sebastian needed to get with his highly reasonable program.

Chef held out a hand. "Don't fall into his trap. He's not telling you the whole story."

He got the feeling he was going to need to sit down again. Unfortunately, Big Tag and his ten-pound addition were occupying the chair he'd sat in previously. He eased into the one to Big Tag's right. "What's the catch?"

"He wants a sub to train his females. Another female. Preferably one who can relate to them," Chef explained. "And he would prefer a couple. He wants a long-term D/s couple to train him and his subs."

"There are several couples who would fit the bill." Why were they asking him? He didn't even have a submissive he played with on a regular basis. "Deena and Eric would be excellent."

Eric and Deena Vail were a lovely couple who happened to be regulars at Sanctum. Sebastian admired the hell out of Eric, who was taking on the role of executive chef at the new Fort Worth Top.

"Yeah, Eric's kind of busy with the opening," Chef replied. "If I ask him to do anything else, he might explode. I know you're busy, too, but it's not your name on the door. And Deena's got her hands full."

He got why the two Taggarts in the room couldn't handle it. Their wives had recently had babies. "You have two other brothers. They both have subs."

Big Tag shook his head. "Nah. Case and Mia would work well, but Mia's on a story and I can't count on her to be around. It's the private jet. Give a woman a personal jet and she takes off. As for Theo and Erin, well, Theo's still kind of a bag of cats when it comes to memory and Erin would likely shoot the subs if they annoyed her. She's cool that way. So really it's just you. It makes sense when you think about it. Outside of Wade, you spend the most time in the club working. Wade's working with the bodyguard unit at McKay-Taggart right now so he can't do the extensive training needed to make it look good with a sub."

Yes, and there was still a problem with the scenario. Wade Rycroft was the Dom in residence at Sanctum, but apparently his day job was getting in the way. Sebastian had problems of his own. "I don't have a sub."

There was a knock on the door and it opened suddenly. Tiffany Hayes stood there wearing jean shorts, flip-flops, and a shirt that explained how she spoke fluent sarcasm. Her blonde hair was in a messy bun on top of her head and apparently she'd been called away from her art. Not only were there flecks of paint on her hands, there was a nice streak of blue by her chin.

Deep blue. Like her eyes.

"I'm so sorry, Chef." She started to back out. "I didn't realize you were having a meeting. Anyway, I'm here. I came as soon as I got your message. I'll wait out in the front."

Chef shook his head. "Don't bother. Come inside. You're a part of this meeting, too. I need you to be Sebastian's submissive for a few weeks."

What the hell was happening? At least he had a partner now. Going up against the Taggarts on his own might have been tough, but now Tiffany would shake her head and explain there was zero chance of that happening.

He turned, ready to back up her absolutely reasonable indignation.

She smiled brightly. "Sure. Sounds like a blast. Oh, my god, is that the new baby? Can I hold him?"

She squealed a little as Big Tag started to lift the kid out of his pouch, and when she bounced up and down, her breasts did the same.

And just like that he was totally uncomfortable.

And completely trapped.

CHAPTER TWO

Tiffany tried to concentrate on the baby in her arms. It shouldn't be hard. She adored babies and this one was a cutie. Seth Taggart was doing that baby grin that was probably more about gas than smiling. It was the kind of thing that made her heart clench and forced her to relax and forget about everything but the sweet kid she was holding.

But Sebastian was in the room. Big, gorgeous, stick-up-his-muscular-backside Sebastian.

Sebastian, whom she painted every night. Sebastian, whom she should run away from. Sebastian, whom she schemed over and plotted to get close to.

"Do you understand what he's asking?" Sebastian stood up with less grace than usual.

She'd noticed that Sebastian did everything with precision and grace. From pouring wine to opening doors for ladies to simply walking across the dining room floor, there was nothing he didn't do without his trademark care.

She had to wonder if he would make love with the same careful attention to details.

It kept her up at night, made her sweat thinking about it.

She bounced as she held the baby in her arms. She was pretty sure the biggest of the Taggarts had fallen asleep in the two point five seconds it had taken him to pass the baby off to her. Not that it was surprising. She could guess that a man who had three children under the age of four was likely sleep deprived. "I think he asked if I would bottom for you."

She had to play this one carefully. If she sounded too eager, he might run away on his bionic legs, and that wasn't what she wanted at all.

Sebastian stared at her for a moment and she gave him what she hoped was her most harmless of smiles. Of course, anyone who took the time to know her would have feared that smile, but luckily Sebastian tended to dismiss her. Like he did everyone. She didn't take it seriously.

He reminded her of the old story about Androcles and the lion. In this case she was an artsy version of the Roman runaway slave who found a lion in his cave. Sebastian was the growling, wine-loving lion who had a massive thorn in his paw. She simply had to get close enough to remove said thorn and claim her super-hot lion.

He was making it difficult.

He waved a hand as though dismissing her and turned back to Chef. "I don't think that's a good idea."

Big Tag yawned and settled a pair of aviators over his eyes. "They never do. Look, wine dude, I'm going to make this easy for you. First you're going to play the we-work-together card."

Sebastian nodded, pointing at Big Tag as though everyone should listen to him.

Tiffany watched. It was a trap. It always was with Big Tag.

"Everyone works together." Only Big Tag's mouth moved. The rest of his body was perfectly still. "You're in an industry where you don't take days off, so unless you're planning on being celibate or buying a fun blowup friend from the Internet, you should probably lower your standards and fuck where you eat." He chuckled. "That's funny because he really does eat here. Two, you're going to say things like 'but I couldn't possibly attempt to deceive this poor billionaire. I'm too upstanding to ever do that.' Screw upstanding. Have you heard what that fucker charges for an ad? Deceive him. Do it hard and charge him for it at the end."

Sebastian sighed. "I do understand what you're saying, but…"

"Here comes excuse number three," Big Tag proclaimed. "But we don't have time to work together. We'll never look like a real live couple. Problem solved since the two of you are going to be living together."

She understood why his wife yelled his name so often. She wasn't Charlotte Taggart, so Tiffany very calmly made her plea as Seth kicked his little legs free of his blanket. "Don't give him a heart attack, please, Sir." She frowned at Chef. "I thought you were going to tell him what happened."

"I didn't get the chance because I was too busy trying to fire him," Chef explained.

It was a good thing she was such a competent babysitter because she didn't miss a beat even as righteous anger flowed through her system. She put the baby in a nice but stable football hold and stared down her boss. She'd heard the rumors that he'd been meeting with that big old wine kiss-ass som. "You can't fire Sebastian."

Sebastian put up a hand. "Hold on."

"Oh, no, I would love to hear why I can't fire you," Chef said, a gleam in his eyes.

Something about that gleam almost made her wary, but she was too angry. When Eric had mentioned that Chef Taggart had met with another som, she'd shrugged it off because no one was better than Sebastian. "Sebastian gives everything to this restaurant. Everything. Did you know he's often here before the line chefs even show up and that sometimes he goes to market with Eric to help him pick produce for the evening? Apparently his sense of smell is incredible. He's like the bloodhound of grapes or something."

"I wouldn't say that," Sebastian began.

Because he was also incredibly humble. "He trains all of us on wine and pairings and even tests us from time to time. I personally think he should offer up some kind of reward program for getting it right because dear god, all that stuff is boring as hell, but he is on top of

26

it. All the women love him. Have you ever watched him sell wine to the book club women?"

"That's Charlie's group," Big Tag said. "Book club is a secret code name for 'drink a shit ton of wine,' so that's a little like shooting fish in a barrel. Try again."

"Well, he's still excellent at it. Chef would be a fool to fire him. That other guy looks like a moron and he hit on me the last time he was here. Ally, too. So he's going to be a terrible addition," she continued. "Also, he was a crappy tipper."

"He hit on you?" Sebastian asked, his voice dropping to a chilly tone.

"Only if you consider him asking me for a tour and then offering to spend some time in Javier's broom closet with him to be hitting on me," she shot back. The broom closet was famous as a place where couples would sometimes sneak away for some making out. Or in Javier's case, some near paternity suits had happened in there.

"Yes," Sebastian replied. "I do consider that hitting on you, and not in a proper fashion."

God, when his voice went all Southern, magnolia-dripping, deep as night and twice as dark it really did something for her. Like go all gooey soft and submissive kind of something.

"I didn't fire Sebastian." Chef was looking between them like an observer at a tennis match. "My meeting with Jenkins was about something else entirely, so everyone can stop berating me for something I never intended to do. Also, Sebastian, stop frothing at your very proper Southern mouth at the thought of someone hitting on Tiff. Seth is doing it right now."

Sure enough, the baby was currently trying to get his little mouth in the vicinity of her boob.

"Nah, he's just hungry all the time." Big Tag yawned. "He tries to suckle everything. The kid's an optimist. Thinks there's milk everywhere. Charlie sent him with a bottle. I'll get it."

The man looked beyond tired and she could plainly see the bag his wife had sent along. "It's fine. I'll feed him. Why don't you take a nap or something?"

He flipped up his sunglasses and for once there was zero sarcasm in his tone. "Are you sure?"

"Of course. You know I love babies." She also liked helping out. She especially enjoyed helping out people from work or the club. They were always appreciative and they tended to be quick to help others. It was one of the things she adored about the club. When she'd moved from one crappy apartment complex to another because she'd found way better light at the second, the Doms of Sanctum had been there to make everything simple.

They were a family and helping was what families did. Big Tag didn't have to allow her into his club. She hadn't paid a membership and neither had her friends, but he let them in and only required that someone work the childcare center every night. She had an in to a club she loved and all it cost her was a few hours of doing something she'd do for free.

Big Tag stood up and reached for the bag, handing it to her. "Thank you. You have no idea how much even twenty minutes will help. I appreciate your kindness very much, Tiffany. Sean?"

"There's a cot in the back room. Eric used it when he would watch the barbecue overnight. Feel free, brother." Chef turned his gaze back to Sebastian. "What I was going to explain to you was that I need you to share the apartment with Tiffany. There are two bedrooms so you'll each have some private space. She's training the waitstaff for Eric's restaurant so she'll be working the same hours as you. I was going to put her up at Eric and Deena's, but their guest bathroom sprung a leak and it's going to be weeks before it's back to being usable. Apparently it flooded the guest bedroom as well. Sharing the apartment with Tiffany would allow the two of you to get on the same page so you could look like a D/s couple for the purposes of training Milo Jaye, and it would spare me the expense of not only having to rent something for her, but also of getting her a bodyguard."

She felt her cheeks heat even as she pulled the bottle from the cooled bag it had nested in. What had her father done? They'd had a very restrained and loving argument about this and she'd thought she'd won. It looked like her dad was good at going around her. "I don't need a bodyguard."

"Why does she need a bodyguard?" Sebastian wasn't looking at her at all.

"I don't." This wasn't an issue.

Big Tag had stopped at the door. "Because there's the possibility that her ex-boyfriend could get out of prison and she's the one who put him away. His name is Bobby Len McMurtry and he's spent four years locked away because Tiffany testified against him. He's up for parole and the last thing he said before they took him away was that he would kill her for ratting on him. If you won't watch out for her, I'll put a trained guard on her ass twenty-four seven. She won't be able to work and I'll need to find someone else to bottom for you because I really need Milo to let Adam off the hook. It's all up to you. If you say no, she goes into protective custody until I can figure out how serious this asshole is and Adam likely loses years of his work. But really, give it some thought. We wouldn't want to put you out because you didn't want to spank a pretty girl and help a guy find himself the way we helped you."

He walked out and Tiffany had to admit that the man knew how to make an exit.

Sebastian sighed heavily. "I'll take responsibility for her. How long a time period are we talking about? And we're going to need a contract."

Chef nodded. "I've got one right here. Tiffany, why don't you feed Seth while Sebastian and I get down to business? Unless you have someone else you want to negotiate for you?"

"I'm twenty-eight years old." And Seth was turning a nice shade of red. He squirmed in her arms, a sure sign that he was getting ready to tune up. She couldn't shove the cold bottle at him. He needed it warmed up. Still, the idea of not being in on the negotiations rankled.

Almost as much as the resigned way Sebastian had given in. He could be a little more enthusiastic.

Chef started to reach for the phone. "All right, then. I'll call your father. After all, he's the one who called me so I could keep a watch out for McMurtry."

"Yes, you can negotiate for me." He really knew how to kick a girl in the puss. She tried to imagine her intellectual father coming to grips with a D/s contract. Why did the Taggart brothers have to live in the Dark Ages? She supposed this was one of those trade-off things her father always talked about. No light without dark. No joy without pain. No unpaid workers helping to move her without dudes who acted like she needed a guardian.

Sebastian looked grim as he sat down in front of Chef. "We'll go over the contract this evening after we've settled in. Are you packed?"

"Oh, I wasn't going out to Fort Worth until tomorrow." It would give her a little time to get everything ready. She hadn't expected things to move so quickly, and she definitely hadn't expected the whole D/s couple thing.

She'd totally expected the sharing the apartment thing since she'd been the one to flood the second floor of Deena and Eric's house. Not really, of course. However, she'd been the one to convince Deena to tell that particular story to everyone so she could have a shot at Sebastian.

That was all she needed. A shot. She needed to push them together in a situation where they were forced to stay close and then he would see how sparkly and awesome she could be and he would fall madly in love with her.

Except she hadn't counted on the D/s stuff.

She would take tonight to reexamine her plans. Tomorrow she would go in with a smile and fresh ideas about how to win over her very grumpy hottie.

"I'll be leaving at two. I want to avoid the traffic," he stated solemnly.

"That's a good idea."

"Excuse me, darlin'," he said, his eyes steady on her. "Let me make myself plain. We will be leaving at two so we can avoid the traffic."

"Is now a good time to explain that I have my own car?" She bounced the baby as both men stared at her. Yeah, those were not chef and som stares. Those were Dom stares. She knew when to retreat. It looked like she would start her campaign earlier than she'd planned. "Okay, then. I'll be ready."

"See that you are," Sebastian said. "And pack a bag of your fet wear. I'll look through it and if it's not acceptable, I'll purchase more for you. I have exacting standards, Tiffany, and I'll expect you to live up to them for the next eight weeks."

Somehow the idea of Sebastian's big hands brushing over her silky underthings and touching her corsets did something for her even if that stick up his ass was showing itself. "Of course, Sir."

She strode out as Seth started to cry. "I'm with you, baby boy. Sometimes it hurts to not get what you need."

But starting tonight, she would damn straight try.

CHAPTER THREE

Three hours later, Tiffany looked around her place with a sigh. It was mostly clean. She was pretty sure she'd picked up all the coffee mugs and granola wrappers. Fairly certain.

The place wouldn't implode while she was gone, but damn she was going to miss her easel and canvases.

Her cell phone trilled and she glanced down briefly before clicking to answer. "Hey, D. How's it going in Cowtown?"

Her best friend chuckled over the line. "Well, it would be way more fun if you were here."

She moved around her tiny, sunny apartment, closing up the blinds. "I'll be there in a couple of hours."

"But you won't be here," Deena replied. "Are you sure you can't run this scheme of yours from my place?"

"Your place recently flooded," she pointed out. It was best when scheming to always stick to the generalities of the scheme. "It's very sad."

"Okay, okay." She could practically see Deena throwing up her hands in mock surrender. "Your girl parts are in complete control. Does that man even understand what's coming for him?"

"I think he's got a pretty good idea since I signed a contract with him about an hour ago." That had been a surreal moment. Of all the ways she'd thought this thing could go early on, signing a contract with

32

Sebastian that stated she was his submissive for the next eight weeks wasn't one she would have bet on.

Of course, she wasn't certain how seriously Sebastian was planning on taking that contract.

"Excuse me?" Deena sounded as shocked as Tiffany had felt.

She closed the final curtain and turned off the light in her bathroom. "I know. The wheel of fate is turning in my direction. Apparently Big Tag needs a favor from Sebastian. We have to train some billionaire guy and his women so they can come play at Sanctum, but he's insistent on having an actual D/s couple do the job."

"There's one problem with that. You're not a D/s couple," Deena pointed out.

"Oh, according to the contract I signed we are."

She was his sub and that meant she was to obey his directives when it came to play. Because they were fast-tracking the get-to-know-you period, she had also agreed to work with him both at home and at Top so that they could look as close to a long-term couple as possible.

But he'd also been explicit about the fact that he wouldn't expect her to have sex with him, nor would he require her to sleep in the same bed as him.

Baby steps.

"Tiffany, are you really thinking about this? I'm pretty sure Sebastian is more hard core than any of the Doms you've played with before."

She wasn't worried about that. She'd enjoyed all the BDSM play she'd been involved with before. Spanking was a total turn-on for her, but she was months in and she hadn't had sex with anyone. Not even her hot-as-hell recent play partners. Over the months, she'd enjoyed playing at Sanctum and had found a regular group of Doms to bottom for. Bear was a gorgeous piece of manflesh who worked for McKay-Taggart as a bodyguard, and Michael Malone was equally hot. Both had been willing and she'd totally meant to sleep with them, and then it turned out neither one was Sebastian and her female parts had gone into lock-down.

If she didn't land Sebastian soon, her Hitachi was going to burn out, and she didn't have the cash for another one. She couldn't even go to Dad for a loan. She'd made a deal with herself when she'd decided on the starving-artist path. No loans from her father unless it was for education or an absolute necessity, like fixing her car so she could get to work.

Masturbatory aids did not fall into those categories so she needed that expensive piece of equipment to keep on vibrating.

"I'll be fine," she replied. "I'm actually a little worried that Sebastian won't take things seriously at all. Oh, don't get me wrong. I think he'll scene with me when we go to the club, and he'll likely want to go over protocol endlessly, but he didn't exactly seem eager to get his hands on me. Am I wrong about this? Am I being a total idiot to think we've got this amazing chemistry? He treats me more like an annoyance than a woman he wants to spend serious time with."

Deena sighed over the line. "Tell me why you're so into him again."

She was quiet for a moment, thinking back to that one night that had been such a turning point for her. "He's kind."

"That's not his reputation. He's known for being more chilly than kind," Deena pointed out.

"Only because you've never found yourself driven home by him. You've never had him hold your hand because you bawled your eyes out over how lonely you felt, how much you'd screwed everything up."

"Are you talking about the night of Chef's party?"

It had happened months ago. She knew it had been a meaningful night for Deena, but what no one with the exception of Sebastian knew was that it had been a rough day for her. She'd found out her father had a tumor.

She should have stayed home, but she'd found herself at the party trying to pretend like he wasn't going to potentially die and leave her an orphan. She'd been a twenty-eight-year-old terrified of losing her father since losing her mother was still a knife through her soul even ten years later.

"Yes, I am."

"You were worried about your dad that night, weren't you? That's why you drank so much," Deena said. "I didn't know at the time because you didn't bother to mention it until after he'd had his surgery and was given a clean bill of health."

They'd managed to get every bit of the tumor and it had turned out to be benign, but that evening all she could think of was how much she would miss her dad.

"He showed up," she said quietly. "Dad's surgery was two days later and Sebastian showed up and sat beside me in the waiting room. Dad had asked me not to tell my sisters because Berry had a job in New York and it's hard for V to come home from France. She doesn't like to fly."

Her younger sister, Versace, didn't like to do anything that could harm the earth, and most forms of transportation did the trick. If V couldn't get somewhere in her biodiesel, ancient-as-hell VW bug, she usually didn't go at all. So Tiffany had been there all alone in a cold hospital waiting room worried as hell that she was going to have to call her sisters and tell them Daddy was gone.

And then Sebastian had sat down beside her, offering her a Styrofoam cup of coffee with a little cream and two sugars, exactly as she liked it. He'd sat down and told her about his own father and the time had passed.

She hadn't been alone on what could have been the worst day of her life because Sebastian Lowe had taken his day off to ensure she had someone to talk to.

If she'd been attracted to him before, she wasn't sure what to call how she felt about him after. Infatuated. Bewitched. Slightly in love.

What the hell was she going to do if this didn't work?

"You never told me that," Deena said quietly. "Of course, that was right about the time I was all caught up in my drama with Eric, so I bet you didn't want to burden me. You know, you do that far too often."

She didn't like to be a burden. It was more fun to be helpful. "I was okay. Sebastian saw to that."

And then he'd promptly taken to avoiding her. He was polite enough, but there was a chill that she wanted to thaw. Needed to thaw.

She wanted to get back to that moment when his hand had slid over hers. To the night where he'd put his arms around her and promised her everything would be all right, when his mouth had hovered over hers and she'd been so sure he was going to kiss her.

If she thought for a second that he didn't want her, that this wasn't all about his damn legs or lack thereof, she would have hesitated. It wasn't that she thought she was the be-all, end-all of attraction. But she'd felt his longing. And then she'd watched him withdraw the minute she'd seen him without his legs.

Damn it, the man didn't need legs to be amazing and gorgeous. He didn't need anything at all. He was the sexiest man ever without them.

There was a brisk knock on her door and she realized it was exactly two o'clock.

"I have to go, D. Are you going to be anywhere near the restaurant tomorrow? I'm starting training with Eric's chosen front of house." She moved toward the door.

"I'll stop in. Love you."

"Back at you." She was so thankful to have Deena in her life. "He's here. See you tomorrow."

She hung up the phone and opened the door. There he was. He was stunningly masculine in slacks and a button down he'd totally buttoned up and a suit coat. No tie for him, which made the look casual for the always dressed up sommelier. The trouble was she knew exactly how hot the man was under his polished exterior. "Hey. Come on in and I'll get ready to go."

He looked so incongruous stepping inside her bohemian apartment. He was perfectly done up from his hair down to his wing-tip shoes. "I thought we agreed you would be ready at two."

And she was. Mostly. She gave him a smile as she moved toward her bedroom. She wasn't going to sit in a car with him for forty minutes without making sure her makeup wasn't smudged. "I won't be but a second. And I packed light. Just the two suitcases and an overnight bag."

"I'll bring you back here if you need more. We're going to be gone for at least eight weeks. I'll make sure we have the same days off so I can drive you." He took off his sunglasses and looked around the place.

It was easy to see he wasn't impressed, but then she wasn't much of a housekeeper. She was too busy with her art. She would drop everything when inspired. Although when she wasn't inspired, it wasn't like she found a mad love for cleaning.

"As long as we have a washing machine, I should be fine. I'll get my purse and we can go." She went into the bathroom and took a deep breath.

What was she doing? Was this the stupidest thing she'd ever done? No, that had probably been her very short and ill-advised punk-rock band phase. This was totally different. She was pursuing her dreams. This was what she'd been taught to do. When she wanted something, she went after it. She loved painting so she was pursuing it in the only way she knew how. She wanted independence so she'd turned her back on the family money.

She wanted Sebastian and that meant she had to get close to him.

Damn, she needed some lip gloss. Her skin was a tad on the pale side, a fact she attributed to spending too much time worried about the light for her paintings and getting no sunlight for her own self. She happened to know that she and Sebastian had a balcony at Chef's apartment that would be perfect for catching a few rays, and she'd bought a bikini she hoped would make Sebastian's mouth water.

How were the girls? She readjusted. Sometimes her nipples went a little crazy when they got in the bra and one would point north and the other southeasterly. If those headlights were coming on, she wanted them pointed directly at her target.

Target made him sound like she was going to do something bad to him. She wasn't. She was doing this for him, too. Sebastian was lonely. He'd told her that night when she was fairly certain he thought she'd been too drunk to remember what he'd said.

Do you have any idea how long it's been since I got to hold a woman? Damn, but you feel good in my arms, darlin'.

And then she'd thrown up because Chef wasn't chintzy with the tequila.

Nipples aligned. Lip gloss on. She could do this. A little hair poof up and she was ready to go.

Did she smell good? Yes. She seemed to be okay. She wasn't sure Sebastian would like perfume. It could ruin his nose. He talked about his nose a lot.

Maybe she should have learned more about wine. It was his obsession. All she knew was she liked it and she was fairly good at remembering his pairings. Chef's pork chops Marsala went particularly well with a Pinot Noir. Sebastian liked to pair Top's Oysters Rockerfeller with a Sauvignon Blanc.

But the menu at Top was about all she knew. And he was apparently crazy about champagne, but only certain champagnes because she'd overheard him telling Eric that Prosecco wasn't champagne.

But it was bubbly so she didn't get the difference.

She was overthinking this. All right. Back to basics. Nipples forward, mascara on, lips glossed. It was time.

She grabbed her bag and stepped out into her apartment where she found Sebastian and none of her luggage. "Uhm, where are the bags?"

He was frowning, his handsome face set in grim lines. "You were gone for twenty minutes. I had the time to load the car all by myself."

He'd carried her heavy-ass bags down three flights of steps? No wonder he looked so pissed. She tried a bright smile on him. "Well, at least I'm leaving the easel and paints behind. Thank you so much for that. Sorry I'm late."

"I think I explained that we needed to leave at two o'clock."

The deep Dom voice was back. Damn it. She'd lost track of time and irritated him again. "I'm sorry, Sebastian. I promise I won't keep us waiting any longer. I'll lock up and we can head out of here."

He eased his suit coat off, carefully folding it and laying it over her tiny breakfast bar. "I'm afraid you are going to delay us further. I like to begin as I mean to proceed. I was very specific with what time we would leave and I even went so far as to explain why we needed to leave at this time. You chose to disregard my order."

"Your order?" What the hell was happening? He was rolling up his dress shirt sleeves, revealing ridiculously muscled forearms.

"Yes, Tiffany," he continued in that dark but infinitely patient tone of his. "Perhaps I was too polite. I prefer to be polite, so let me explain a few things to you. We're involved in a D/s relationship now. There might not be any sex, but I take it seriously all the same. I am the dominant partner. You are the submissive one. That means that I will carry your bags and ensure your peace and comfort. It means I'll do my utmost to make sure you're safe and cared for. And you'll obey me. Now I'm not an unreasonable man. I certainly won't dictate your life, though we will have a few rules pertaining to our cohabitation. Those will be in place to keep our relationship healthy and free of the drama that happens with so many others. I'll listen to your concerns about the rules and attempt to make accommodations."

He was pacing around, his eyes moving as though he was trying to find something.

"Accommodations? Rules? Uhm, I thought we were going to a couple of play parties and maybe we would scene a little."

"Ah, so you weren't really listening," he said with a sigh that told her he was disappointed. He stopped at her kitchen table and pulled out one of her chairs. "How do you think we convince a highly intelligent man that we're an experienced D/s couple if we don't live as a D/s couple? Twenty-four seven."

"No one's twenty-four seven," she said quickly, a little tingle of fear running through her. Well, perhaps not fear exactly. Or maybe she liked being the tiniest bit afraid. It was like she was reaching the crest of that first deep dive on a roller coaster. She knew it would be okay, but damn she also knew it would be a wild ride.

"Perhaps your friends aren't, but I have some who are," Sebastian corrected her. He turned the chair around so its seat faced her. "Some people live quite happily that way. Twenty-four seven doesn't necessarily mean that the Dom is standing over the submissive all day. It simply means that he takes an interest in every part of her daily life. Chef and I decided this was the best way for the two of us to pull this off. You agreed to obey me."

"I thought that was for the club."

"We're not going to the club more than once or twice before we have to start the training sessions with Milo Jaye," he explained. A sense of calm seemed to have fallen over him, as though he'd made his decision and was perfectly at peace with it. "We'll need to play privately. We'll need to talk as well. I think daily sessions of some sort will likely meet the needs of the task Master Ian set before us. This will be very demanding, Tiffany. I'm not sure you thought this through as well as you should have. There's still time. I can try to find someone else, but I do understand how convenient it will be for the two of us to be living together and working together. I like to think of it as a total immersion class. But if you want to change your mind, now is the time to do it. I can have a talk with Kelly from work. She's planning on starting the training program soon, but perhaps one-on-one training will bring her up to speed."

Kelly? New girl Kelly? Kelly, with the dark hair and a butt you could bounce a quarter off of? Yoga Kelly, who could put her foot behind her ear? No fucking way. "I'm fine with it, Sebastian. I mean, Sir. And I really am sorry I took so long. I'm ready now."

He nodded. "I'm glad to hear that. We can get going after we settle the issue. Please pull your shorts down and place your palms flat on the seat. I'll show you how wide I expect your legs to be. And from now on, I would prefer you greet me properly when I pick you up. I'll expect you to let me in and then to sink to your knees and find a submissive position when we've been apart for more than a few hours. I'll expect you to prepare dinner if we're not going out. If I am the one greeting you at the end of a day, you can expect only a slightly different ritual. If you've worked and I have not, I will prepare a meal for you. I'll have a glass of wine waiting and you may choose what we do that evening. I'm tough, but I'm not unfair."

He wanted her to do what? "Why am I leaning over the chair? Okay, that sounds silly. I get that we're talking about a spanking, right? I'm getting spanked because I made us late?"

"Yes. Unless you had a very good reason for spending twenty minutes in the bathroom." He watched her carefully. "I'm willing to listen."

Well, I was trying to make sure my nips were all aligned for you, Sir. And guess what? I was right to do it since they are hard as rocks right now and straining against my bra. And perfectly straight.

Yeah, she wasn't going to tell him that. "I suspect that doing my hair and making sure my makeup looked good won't get me out of anything."

"Not at all. Now do as I asked and we can move on with our day."

It wasn't her first rodeo. She'd been spanked before, though it was always during play and not in a disciplinary fashion. Her training Dom had a rough hand and it never bothered her. She enjoyed the sensation. How much worse could it be?

She wasn't going to show fear. She gave him a jaunty smile and leaned over. "Do your worst, Sir."

"I will as soon as you do as I asked. We're going to have to work on how you listen. I'm rather surprised because you're very good at doing it when you work. I did mention that your shorts are in the way. Also, if you're wearing underwear, I'll need them. I do not allow my submissive to wear panties unless she's working. I understand that can be difficult. But when you're not working you will not be allowed them. You will also give up your bras when we're home alone or when we're not in the vanilla world. Again, I understand it's more proper to wear one at work or outside doing normal daily activities, but there will be none when we're alone."

She stood back up, slightly shocked that he'd changed his mind so fast. "You said we weren't having sex."

He moved into her space, those brilliant blue eyes of his steady on her. "Does your lack of a bra indicate that sex is forthcoming? Will the fact that you have no underwear on force my penis to fall inside your body? Do not mistake me, Tiffany. This is not me demanding sexual favors from you. This is me training you how to be my sub. I've taken a few with whom I had no sexual contact with at all."

"Seriously?" Who signed a contract with that man and didn't want him to fall inside her vagina?

"I acted as a professional during my time in London. It might shock you to know I also topped male subs and I managed to not have sex with them as well."

"So you don't ever have sex with your subs?" That killed so many of her fantasies.

"I didn't say that, but my sexual history is a conversation for another day. Come along, now. Every second you wait is another hundred or so cars we have to fight our way through on 183. Bare bottom, please, and you will thank me for the discipline afterward."

Wow. She was here and the hill the roller coaster was about to go over looked so much bigger from this vantage point. She couldn't see over the other side, but wasn't that the fun of taking the ride?

She pushed her shorts off her hips and handed them over. She didn't need to give him her undies. She didn't wear them. His eyes had widened and it was so good to know she could shock him. Maybe her backside wasn't as perfect as his, but it was nice. She'd been told by several Doms that she had a lovely ass. "I don't wear underwear unless I'm working, and even then it's nothing more than a teeny tiny thong. You can have this, too. I only wore it because you seem so proper, Sir."

She reached back and unhooked her bra, freeing her breasts. She pulled it through the arm of her T-shirt. Now she didn't have to worry about her nipples. They would sit right where they needed to be.

Sebastian took the shorts and there was the faintest trace of pink in his cheeks. "Excellent. It's a count of twenty for being late, ten more for questioning me, and another ten for failing to listen to instructions. I do not require a count."

She leaned over and placed her hands flat on the seat, tilting her backside up like her training Dom had preferred. "I'm ready, Sir."

"I'm glad one of us is," he muttered before his hand came down on her backside.

The sound cracked through the air and Tiffany gasped. He hadn't been playing around with that smack. His hand came down again and again. At least ten times before he stopped and stepped back.

"How are you, Tiffany?"

Her ass was on fire and tears had started up, but she wasn't about to stop. She was experienced enough to know that there was a point to the pain. He wasn't doing anything to mitigate it though. He wasn't caressing her ass to hold the heat against her skin. He wasn't soothing her.

And she was still getting hot. She could still feel her pussy getting warm and wet even as her eyes dripped with tears. "I'm fine, Sir."

"How many disciplinary spankings have you received?"

"None, Sir."

"I don't want to hurt you, not in a way that doesn't feed something inside you. A disciplinary spanking is different from an erotic one."

"I can handle it." It hurt, but she found something freeing about being able to take it. And she couldn't help how her heart rate tripled at the thought of his hand on her again. The pain flared into something more. It wasn't like she got off on twisting her ankle or whacking her elbow. That just hurt, but something about a spanking did it for her, and now she knew it wasn't simply when playing. Something about the methodical way Sebastian went about his discipline made her ache for more.

"Then I'll continue." His left hand steadied on her lower back. "You have a lovely backside, Tiffany. It's quite beautiful and your skin is beautiful as well."

There was the Dom. Her sister had flipped her shit when she found out Tiffany had joined a BDSM club. She'd asked why she wanted to be abused.

The smack came down hard again. He was exploring her skin with the flat of his hand, but there was such care taken. He peppered her but never struck the same place too many times. Every place he smacked flared with pain and then sent a shiver through her as the pain morphed into something more.

This wasn't abuse. She couldn't seem to explain that to V. This was something that called to her, something that other people might not get. It was something that connected her to Sebastian. Even as she wept at the pain, let the emotion flow over her, she could feel the connection to her Dom.

Her Dom. For now.

Fire licked along her flesh and she cried out. He hadn't told her to be silent, so that very likely meant he enjoyed the sounds of his submissive. She cried out as he pushed her harder. The last five were damn near unbearable, but she took a deep breath, allowing each smack to sink in. Even the tears felt good when she thought about it. Emotion was never wasted. Crying now would relax her, express her anxiety.

And maybe teach her to not be late. It was rude when she'd known damn well he wanted to leave.

Sebastian needed his control. She had to think of him, too. She couldn't simply think of her own needs. That might work if all she wanted was to hop into bed with him, but she needed more. She wanted to try with him and that meant she had to be good for him, too. If he needed to be on time, she needed to make an effort.

She would find out if he would give back to her, too.

Sebastian stepped away and she could hear him take a long breath. "That's all. You did very well. Now stand up and let's finish. You will thank me for my discipline and we can continue with our day."

Our day. She liked the sound of that. She forced herself to stand, feeling the ache in both her backside and deep in her pussy. She took the shorts he offered her and stepped into them. The connection she'd felt seemed to have washed away and now he was chilly again as he rolled down his shirt sleeves and refastened the buttons on his wrists.

But it was only the first day and she hadn't performed the way she would have liked. Time. They needed time and patience. She buttoned the fly on her shorts and tried to wipe away her tears before she looked up at him. "Thank you, Sir. Thank you for the discipline. I will try not to make us late again."

She wanted more, but she had to be patient. She wanted him to put his arms around her and soothe her, but they weren't there yet.

From what she could tell, Sebastian hadn't had a real relationship since he'd lost his legs. He was sensitive about them. She had to gently extract that thorn before her lion would start purring for her.

He slipped the suit coat on. "You're welcome. Shall we?"

She nodded but looked back at her easel as she gathered her purse. That was the hard thing to leave behind, but it wasn't practical and she likely wouldn't have time to paint anyway. "I'm ready."

Sebastian followed her gaze. "And your art? You're leaving it?"

She sniffled. "I probably won't have time to work on it. It's all right. It's big and difficult to move around. I'll sketch some but I'll survive. Besides, I don't have any canvases right now anyway. I finished one up yesterday."

She'd finished a canvas of a man in greens and blues. A man who stood tall, even without his legs. She'd moved it into her tiny office to let it finish drying, but mostly because it was a damn window into her soul and Sebastian wasn't ready to see how she viewed him yet.

"Do you want the easel?" he asked quietly.

It eased her anxiety. It brought her peace and calm. "Yes, but it would be a bother to bring."

"I'll carry it down. There's plenty of room. Gather your supplies. I'm sure we can find what you lack in Fort Worth," he said decisively. "We'll find a place for you to work as well. Hurry along."

He struggled for a moment, but found the mechanism that allowed the easel to fold up.

And she knew she was making the right decision.

CHAPTER FOUR

Sebastian pulled the cork out of the 2014 Riesling. He poured it in his glass, noting the fine, clear color of the wine. It wasn't an expensive vintage, but it had a high rating. 91 points on the critics' scale. Of course that was subjective, but for the most part the big publications like *Wine Spectator* and *Wine Advocate* knew quality.

And it should pair well with the pork tenderloin Eric had been kind enough to drop off. Eric had smiled a knowing smile as he'd dropped off dinner for two and told him how nice it was going to be to have neighbors around. He and Deena were only a mile away, but when Sebastian had invited them to come over and share the dinner, Eric had declined.

Leaving Sebastian alone with the only woman he'd really desired in years. The one woman he was certain he shouldn't want because she was as far from his idea of perfection as a woman could be.

He was stuck with her for eight weeks. Or rather she was stuck with him. Beautiful, vivacious Tiffany was going to be stuck with his dour, wounded self.

I can't even look at you anymore, Sebastian. Do you think I want this? Do you think I want to stand in front of the town and pretend I can love you? Pretend I can want you?

He took a deep breath and tried to banish that particular voice. He could still feel the cool of the air conditioner as he'd made his plea to the woman he'd loved for so long. The woman who couldn't stand the sight of him.

Not that she was the only one. His own mother had died while he was working in London and his sister hadn't bothered to call and invite him to the funeral.

That was what happened when a man chose poorly. He lost everything.

"The tenderloin should be ready in about twenty minutes," Tiffany said as she bounced in. "Eric wants me to reheat slowly so it doesn't get dry."

And she really bounced. She'd been serious about the no bra thing. Those beautiful breasts were moving freely, making his palms itch to get on her again. How sensitive were they? Could he make her squeal and squirm by tugging on her nipples?

Would she recoil in horror if he actually made love to her? Or would she retreat into that saucy, flirty exterior she put on and try not to show how much the sight of him disturbed her? She'd seen him once without his legs—a miscalculation on his part—and that was how she'd chosen to handle it. She'd turned a nice shade of red and tried to tell him it was all right and that she found him appealing.

Of course she did. Everyone loved nasty scars and misshapen limbs.

So why when he'd started to dream about sex again had it been with Tiffany and not Alicia? When had he started to let go of that dream?

He was worried it had been the minute Tiffany had come into his life, and that scared the hell out of him.

"Excellent. It gives us a chance to go over the house rules." He poured a second glass. He needed to take control. It was the only way to proceed. Tiffany could be reckless when it came to her personal life. She could also be far too kind and he wasn't going to ruin this time for her.

"How do you do that?" She was shaking her head as she hopped up

47

on the barstool in front of him. "I'm always in awe of how you manage to pour the exact same amount into each glass."

Ah, this was something he could talk about. "Precision. Care. Years and years of training. It's something the Court of Master Sommeliers scores a som on. There's three parts to the master test. Blind tasting, service, and theory. I was always best at the service part. Only had to take that once. My family ran a small restaurant in the town I came from. By the time I was a teenager, I was working behind a bar. Oh, I wasn't legally supposed to, but no one really cared. My father loved wine and how it played with food."

"Your father was a chef?"

"Not by the industry standards. He was taught by his father. Lowe's was a south Georgia institution. It had been around for fifty years."

"I would love to go there sometime."

"It's gone now." Because of him. "After my father died, they had to close up shop, I'm afraid. Here you go. I think you'll find this goes well with the pork. Rieslings tend to do well with fish and pork."

She took the glass from him and dove right in, swallowing a mouthful. "It's pretty tasty."

Philistine. He shook his head. "How on earth did you grow up in the household you did and not learn to savor something as fine as wine?"

He'd learned a lot about her that day in the hospital. He'd learned even more when he'd snuck back up and visited her father. Harlon Hayes had headed an empire of his own. He'd come from old money and for years had run his family's department store empire before selling out at the ripe old age of forty-five and founding a charitable organization. Still, Tiffany had been raised around too much money to behave like a teen downing her first tequila shot.

"My mom loved Manhattans and margaritas. Daddy still drinks his bourbon." She shrugged and took another drink. "Sorry. It's all alcohol to me."

That was one thing he could help her with. "Stop. You have to consider the wine before you drink it. Look at the color."

She groaned a little but if there was one thing he was going to do while they were forced together, it was to teach her a greater appreciation of wine. "It's yellow."

He held the glass up to the light. "It's a clear, bright wine. The color and clarity of the wine tells me it's been filtered, as are all American wines. I would call this a star bright wine because of how much light is filtered through it."

She held up her own glass. "I hadn't thought about it that way. It's pretty. I like the term star bright."

"Take a deep whiff and tell me what you smell."

Her nose wrinkled. "Sebastian, I smell wine."

"But there's so much underneath it." He held it up and let the scents wash over him. What he loved was the complexity, the warring scents that blended somehow to make the vintage. "Lime. Crisp green apple with the hint of wet rocks."

She smiled, the sight somehow going straight to his dick. "Wet rocks? I'm not sure that sounds appetizing."

Because she didn't understand the exercise. "Wine is about the land it comes from. This Riesling is from the Columbia Valley in Washington State."

"I thought you only liked European wines."

Everyone thought he was a snob. "Not at all. I appreciate many different types of wine. I love an Argentine Malbec and a French Bordeaux. One of my favorite wines to drink is a shitass strawberry wine sold in boxes in convenience stores around Southern Georgia. It costs seven dollars a box, and that's a big box."

"Seriously? I would not have taken you for a lover of cheap hooch. I've never even seen you drink a beer."

"I wasn't surrounded by beer in my youth. My father loved wine. He sampled it and appreciated it, and when I was a teenager and couldn't get my hands on anything good, my best friend and I found a man who would buy us strawberry wine as long as we paid for a pack of cigarettes. We would take it out to the beach and we were the heroes of the high school. When I drink that wine, I'm young again. I'm sitting on the beach looking out over the ocean with my feet in the sand and a whole life ahead of me."

"I would like to try that wine sometime," she said wistfully.

He couldn't help but wince. "It tastes like hell, but it's important to me. My point is that wine isn't something to be snobbish about. It's something to love. It's something that brings people together and it's been doing it for thousands of years. What I love about Riesling is it's a transparent wine."

She held the glass up again. "Not entirely."

She'd likely slept through the entire wine for beginners course he'd given for all the servers. She'd probably memorized the pairings list he'd given her and picked up no theory at all. "I wasn't talking about how it looks. I'm talking about the grapes and how Riesling grapes tend to embody the region they were grown in. It's why Rieslings vary pretty wildly. An Alsace Riesling is higher in alcohol. It's got more mineral notes and it's full bodied while German Rieslings can be quite sweet and fruity. There's a vineyard in Australia that produces Rieslings that zip with lime and citrus tones. Every Riesling is different and the wine's taste comes from the earth it was grown in, from the air it breathed and the rainfall that nourished the vines. It's a little like people. It's all about where it came from. That is why I love Riesling."

"Okay." Tiffany held the glass up to the light. "I like the color. It's like when sunlight filters in and turns a room bright. I don't think my sense of smell is anywhere near as good as yours though. I mostly smell wine."

"It's all right," he replied. "I just wanted you to think about it before you drank it."

"Because it's meaningful to you." She took a slow swallow this time, as though truly considering the taste. "It isn't as sweet as some of the Rieslings I've tried. I like it."

"Good." He took a sip himself, letting the notes flow. Broad. Dry. Citrus and green apple. "It's quite a nice wine for the price. It's why I put it on the menu. It's going to pair with the pork dishes and some of the fish."

"I'll make note of that." She sat back.

Damn but she was a beautiful woman. She was also something he needed to keep his hands off of. No matter what Big Tag said, he did not date women he worked with.

He didn't really date anyone. He played with subs. When the need got too great, he found a partner for a brief time. He didn't sleep with anyone. He fucked, and that was starting to get very old. Empty.

"So you said something about house rules?" Tiffany leaned forward, her elbows on the bar. "Are these housekeeping rules or like big bad Dom rules?"

"I don't suppose I differentiate." He couldn't let those big eyes of hers soften him up. It had almost happened at her apartment. When she'd stood up after he'd spanked her and there had been tears running down her face, his impulse had been to reach for her. He'd wanted to draw her in the way he had that night when she was drunk and she'd cried on his shoulder. He'd wanted to smooth back her hair and promise her everything was going to be all right, that he could fix things for her. It was a path that was sure to lead to discomfort for her and humiliation for him. "I prefer a clean living space. I don't like for things to be messy. I expect that you will keep your things in their proper place."

Because no matter how hard he tried, he could still trip. The legs he now walked on were only a year old. He'd spent the first two years in a wheelchair.

The Garden's Wheelchair Dom.

He still wasn't completely comfortable in the prosthetics.

"I can try," she said with a frown. "I'll be honest, I'm not the world's biggest neat freak."

He'd been able to tell that from the state of her apartment. It had been cluttered, a bit dusty. With the exception of her easel. That had been perfectly taken care of. He rather wished he'd taken the time to ask to see her art.

He'd seen one painting that night he'd taken her home. It had been a painting of three laughing girls, the swirling colors so vibrant he could hear them giggling as they splashed in a puddle on a rainy day. The figures had been more impressions than photographic reality, but he'd known what she was trying to convey.

"If you cook I'll clean, and the other way around." He'd started a list in his head on the long drive. The drive that would have been considerably shorter had they left at the proper time. As she'd sung along to sugary pop songs after she'd changed his radio, he'd sat and considered how to proceed.

With caution. Lots and lots of caution.

"I'm not the best cook in the world," he continued, "but I can manage. Most nights, of course, we'll be eating at Top as our training sessions for the new restaurant will last long hours, but I would prefer to eat breakfast here rather than skipping the meal or picking up fast food. Eric made sure the fridge was stocked with a few items I requested."

"Breakfast." She gave him a little salute with her free hand. "I can manage that."

"In addition to our duties at Top, we will now be taking on the additional task of appearing to be a long-term D/s couple, and we need to talk about what that should look like." Another thing he'd been thinking about ever since that moment the trap had closed around him. "You know you probably could have gotten us out of this assignment. It's much more difficult for the Dom to say no. The sub always holds the power. Is there a reason you didn't use yours today?"

"I didn't want to," she replied simply. "I don't have a full-time Dom and I thought it would be interesting to see what that's like."

Was she thinking at all? "You know nothing about how I function as a dominant partner."

"And now I do," she replied. "You like rules and schedules and you tend to be very fair."

"I can be quite exacting in my standards."

"I can be quite flexible," she shot back as the sexiest smile crossed her face. "I'm serious about that. I can still do the splits and everything."

"You're far too reckless, Tiffany." He didn't appreciate recklessness so why was she like a siren calling to him? If he listened, he would end up wrecked.

"You're far too uptight, Sebastian."

"Well, I've found being reckless and following an emotional path tends to lead a man into trouble."

"Sometimes trouble can be fun," she teased.

"And sometimes it can lead to tragedy."

She sobered a bit, leaning toward him. Her voice softened. "Yes, but anything can lead to tragedy. You can do absolutely nothing wrong, make all the right moves, and still have things end in tragedy. But real happiness and joy, those don't tend to come along without some risk. Those things are worth it."

She was so very young and sheltered. "Did you take a risk with your former boyfriend?"

Her nose wrinkled as if in distaste. "Which one?"

He probably wouldn't like to know how many there had been. "The one who's in jail."

Her eyes strayed away.

Dear god. "The one who's about to get out. Is there really more than one of them?"

"I've had a colorful life," she replied. "And no, not really. I didn't take much of a risk on Bobby. I've done some crazy things in my life, but some would say that dating Bobby was the most normal. I know Big Tag made him sound like a serial killer, but he was an investment banker. I met him through my sister. Berry met him at a fashion show, which should have told me to run for the hills, but he was funny and seemed nice. Unfortunately, he also had a problem with cocaine, and that led him to getting involved in a pyramid scheme that defrauded a bunch of investors."

So even when she attempted to be normal it all turned into chaos. "You turned him in?"

"Of course," she replied. "I couldn't let him hurt people the way he was."

One thing he had learned about her was how kind she could be. A bit naïve, but kind. It was one of the things about her that called to him. In the real world, she had likely been taken advantage of many times. It made him wonder. He knew he should let it all go, but he was curious. "Was it hard to turn him in?"

She shook her head. "In some ways. I did care about him. I went to him first and asked him to stop and make reparations. He told me if I went to the cops he would hurt me. He tried to convince me that he could make the cops believe I was in on it."

"And you weren't afraid?"

"I'm an artist, not an idiot. He couldn't prove anything, but I would have gone to the cops anyway," she explained simply. "He was hurting people and I could stop it. I couldn't live with myself if I didn't."

And she was incredibly moral. He admired that about her. "So he's getting out now and he's sworn revenge?"

She rolled her bratty, beautiful eyes. "He said a bunch of shit. That doesn't mean he's really coming after me. The last time he wrote me a letter I wrote him one right back and explained that I worked in a place where all the dudes knew how to kill people, and he would be stupid to come after me. And I've heard nothing else. You know what I remember most about him? Besides all the crime stuff? He made really excellent sandwiches. He bought his bread from some gourmet place uptown and I've never found anything quite like it. I should buy a loaf and get Macon to deconstruct it for me because it's seriously expensive. I can't pay ten dollars for a damn loaf of bread."

He shook his head because sometimes she talked really fast. She also seemed very good about burying the lead. "He writes you? From prison?"

"Yeah, though he doesn't send the letters directly to me. From what I can tell, he sends them to a friend of his and then the friend sends them to me. But that was only a few times. Apparently someone has the job of reading all the prison mail, but there's a ton of it so they really only read the first couple of pages and those are like full of bullshit and then he gets to the 'I'm going to kill you, bitch' stuff." She held up a hand. "But that was all a few years back. The last letter he managed to get out was very apologetic. I have to wonder, though. If I wanted to brutally murder someone, I would probably apologize to them, too. You know, make 'em comfortable so they didn't shoot me on sight."

"You are not allowed out of this apartment without an escort." When the hell had she been planning on mentioning that her ex-boyfriend was still trying to communicate with her? Did her father know? Did anyone at all? "If at any time he attempts to contact you, you will immediately find me and inform me. If you feel threatened, you may call the police first, but I damn straight better be the second person you call, though you shouldn't have to call me because I don't know that you'll be allowed out of my sight. Do you understand how serious this is?"

"Bas, it's not a big deal. He was a smart man. He's doing white-collar time and he definitely won't want to go back. I was joking about him actually killing me. His sister reached out to tell me he really is remorseful. Apparently he's gone through rehab in prison and he wants to make amends."

"Or he wants to murder you and this is a good way to get close. And I swear if you call me Bas again, that will be a very long spanking that will not conclude until your ass is so red you won't sit for a week. Am I clear?"

She hopped off her barstool and walked around the bar, picking up the bottle of wine and refilling his glass. "Yes, Sebastian. I think you might need some more. You find me annoying, don't you?"

He found her disturbing. "I think your life is a bit more chaotic than what I would prefer."

She put a hand on his arm, smiling up at him. "It isn't as bad as you think. I'm mostly boring."

She was so close and he couldn't help but think about that contract they'd signed only hours before. It gave him the right to protect her, to comfort her. He'd explained that they could ignore the part that gave him the right to fuck her, to spread her legs and put his mouth on her. To taste her and wrap her scent around himself.

He had the right to lean over and kiss her. Naturally she had the right to say no, but that contract had opened a door he'd meant to keep fully closed and locked with a chair shoved under the handle.

"Sebastian, I think we should talk about how this is going to go. I promise I'll do what you ask of me. I'm starting to understand how much you need this and I want to give you what you need," she began.

He found himself starting to lean into her. She had no idea what he really needed. Would she run if she knew? Or could he use that naïve, eager curiosity to his advantage?

How much would it hurt when she eventually realized how unworthy he was?

It didn't seem to matter to his cock. His cock was starting to strain against his slacks. "You can't begin to understand what I need."

Her lips curled up. "So tell me. I think you'll find I'm very open-minded."

He took a step back, trying to find his equilibrium. His back hit against the island and he felt his right leg buckle. God, he hated falling and he didn't want to do it in front of her. He managed to catch himself but only just.

Tiffany reached out to get a hand on him and he saw the nauseating look of sympathy in her eyes.

He pulled back. Yes, this was why he should stay away. The very last thing he wanted from her was sympathy. "I'm fine."

He hated that look. It always took him back to that moment when he'd realized he'd lost everything.

I can't stand to look at you.

"Sebastian, it's okay. You lost your balance," she said. "You got it back. You didn't even spill your wine."

But he could have. He could have spilled everything all over the floor and she would have been the one to clean it all up. God, if he couldn't handle a serene, reasonable woman like Alicia, what the hell did he have for someone like Tiffany? "I don't need any help. You can stand back. Here's another rule. Don't touch me unless you have permission. That's a hard and fast rule. I don't know how your other Doms behaved, but I prefer that we keep things proper between us."

She took a step back, her eyes widening. "I'm sorry. I was only trying to help."

There were the wounded doe eyes he'd been sure he'd see at some point. Tiffany was a pretty, happy butterfly flitting around the flowers.

He was the gaping, hulking beast who clumsily smashed butterflies and hurt their tender feelings.

It was better she knew that now.

"May I touch you, Sir?" Her eyes had lost their wounded look.

"I don't think that's necessary right now." He wasn't sure what she was doing, but he knew he couldn't handle it.

She nodded. "All right, then. Roar away, lion. I can handle it."

"What?" He wasn't sure he'd heard her right.

She smiled brightly. "Nothing at all, Sir. I think dinner is ready. I'll set the table."

She started to turn and he couldn't let it go. "Why do you want to touch me?"

"Because I thought you could use a hug, Sir. You don't seem to understand a few truths about the world."

And she was going to tell him? Tiffany was a sweet girl, but she'd also always had a safety net. She'd grown up wealthy and surrounded by a family who loved her and supported everything she did. She was going to tell him about life? "What truth in life have I missed?"

She opened the stove and reached inside. "That we all stumble and we all fall and we all need a hug every now and then. I know I do. It's been a very long and rough day. I'm an affectionate person and that tends to mean I need affection in my life. I think this whole thing will be very difficult for me if I'm not allowed to touch you. But I understand that this isn't about my pleasure. It's about a favor for the Taggarts, whom I owe very much to. I'll survive."

She almost made it sound like she wanted to touch him. Damn it.

What was her game? What did she want from him?

When was the last time someone hugged him out of pure and genuine need?

His life had become rigid and he needed that. He needed the control and he certainly needed to have discipline. Distance. He'd found keeping a good emotional distance from people helped him concentrate on his goals.

It wasn't that he didn't like the people around him. He liked them very much, including Tiffany. He'd simply learned that he functioned better with distance.

But wasn't it his duty as her dominant partner to give her what she needed? He didn't like being touched anymore, but he was responsible for her comfort while she was under his care. He'd been careful in selecting his partners. He always sought out submissives who required no emotion from him.

Tiffany hadn't been his choice, but for the next several weeks, she was his.

Perhaps if he explained it to her, she would understand. "The no-touching rule isn't meant to hurt your feelings. It's simply my way as a Dom."

She set the dish on the stove. "I understand."

But it was easy to see she was still hurt. He could tell her to find her affection elsewhere, but what would that mean? They didn't have to keep up the ruse at work. Except Big Tag had tasked him with her protection and not simply the training issue.

Any way he looked at it, they were stuck together. He could give her what she needed or explain that she was free to find her affection elsewhere.

That idea rankled far more than he wanted to admit.

"I think for the remainder of our contract that I don't want you to flirt with other men," he said slowly, the idea ruminating in his head. She was his sub no matter how she'd come under his protection. He could look at this as nothing more than an exercise in flexibility. It didn't have to mean a thing. It was all about giving her what she needed. When he really thought about it, this could make him a better Dom. More disciplined.

She turned. "So I'm not allowed to touch you and I'm not allowed to flirt. What exactly constitutes flirting? Should I not hug anyone at all? I didn't expect that of you, Sebastian. I have to say, I'm disappointed."

"Do you have the slightest bit of patience?"

She frowned. "It's not something I'm known for."

He would have to fix that. Yes, now he could see that he could help her with any number of issues, but he would have to be flexible. This could work and the next few weeks would be easy and peaceful if only he accepted her needs. "I understand that you require physical affection. I have my own needs. I require that you show me some loyalty while you're under contract to me. Despite the fact that this is all for show, our coworkers will know about the change in our status and I would prefer that there was no gossip surrounding us. If you require a hug, you should get it from me. I'll remove my rule about touching, but you should understand it's been in place for a long time and I'll have to get used to it."

Her lips curled up in a brilliant smile. Damn, when that girl smiled the whole room lit up. She moved toward him cautiously and stepped into his space.

She was small compared to him, delicate to his hulking beast. He could try to hide it in slick suits and polished manners, but he knew who he was inside.

She tilted her head up, making eye contact with him. "I could use a hug right now, Sir. I missed my aftercare from the spanking and it's bothered me ever since."

"It was a disciplinary spanking." He'd praised her for doing well. Still, he remembered how vulnerable she'd looked afterward. Had the absence of physical affection been harder on her than the spanking? He hadn't meant to hurt her in that fashion. God, he felt awkward. He wasn't sure exactly how to press on. Should he start the hug? Around her shoulders or should he take her waist?

"I know it was, but I can be quite insecure, and words don't work the way a hug would. If you want to show me I've done something well, I would like for you to touch me in some way. I know you're the Dom, but I hope you'll think about it. I think it could make us a better team." She eased her arms around him, moving slowly, as though she understood how weird this was for him.

Her body nestled against his, her head resting on his chest.

Her hair was the color of Chardonnay against the light. It was wheat and sunlight and with the shine of fine crystal. He let his arms move around her, trying to forget the awkward feel of her.

It wasn't that awkward. She seemed perfectly comfortable. Perhaps he was doing all right. He took a deep breath, determined to give her this time. She'd performed admirably before, taking her discipline with grace. She should have this if she needed it. Her hair smelled like strawberries and cream. He breathed her in, focusing on the delicate scents that made up Tiffany Hayes. Under the fruit notes of her hair there was a clean, soapy scent. She smelled good. He let his arms circle her until he could feel the skin at the nape of her neck. Soft and smooth and warm like a blanket against his hand.

It wasn't so bad. He could handle this.

It was quite nice.

Her head turned up and she seemed calmer than she'd been before. "Thank you, Sir. You give good hugs. You're so big, you make me feel safe."

He stepped back and took a deep breath, unwilling to admit how much her words meant to him. "Some people would say a woman as delicate as yourself should be careful around men as large as I am."

She was right back to being happy, perky Tiffany. She turned on her heels and moved back to the oven where she was heating the vegetable dish Eric had brought to accompany the pork loin. "Some people are morons."

He was about to chastise her for using a rude word when she held up her large spoon and turned back to him.

"Could you pour me another glass, please, Sir? It was delicious.

I'm so looking forward to dinner. I've worked up an appetite." She winked his way and turned back around, giving him a very good view of her round ass.

He steadied his hand and poured her another glass.

He was getting pretty hungry himself.

CHAPTER FIVE

As first days went, it had gone pretty damn well. Tiffany placed the final dish away and sighed with satisfaction. Sebastian was educable. She'd worried a little that he might prove too damaged to get through to after the spanking that had led to no touching of any kind, but now she realized her Master was merely ignorant, and ignorance could totally be cured.

He didn't know it yet, but that man needed more than mere hugs.

He needed the brilliant attention of a submissive who saw through his bullshit. She heard the sound of a newscast from the living room. She'd sent him off after dinner, accepting the simple job of cleaning for the both of them before prepping veg for breakfast omelets. He'd been a perfectly pleasant dinner companion, talking about plans for the new restaurant and politely answering the questions she asked him.

He'd put some distance between them again and that obviously made him comfortable. The trouble was she'd felt the way he sighed when he finally relaxed against her body. She'd heard him breathe in her scent and felt the way his fingers had played with the skin at the nape of her neck. She also noted the way he'd flushed at the end of their hug.

How long had it been since he'd had a woman offer him simple affection? Something had happened in his past, something that had nothing to do with losing his legs. Sebastian's thorn was emotional, but that didn't mean she wouldn't still pull it out.

Not that he wasn't still all touchy about his legs. It was eight o'clock at night and he was still in slacks.

It was time to start getting him more comfortable with their situation. The Taggarts had dropped this miracle into her lap and she wasn't about to waste it.

"Are you through with your wine, Sir?" There was still maybe half a glass in the bottle.

Sebastian looked down as though surprised to see his glass empty. He shook his head. "I'm finished. I don't normally have more than a glass at night."

Because he was twelve kinds of control freaky. They had to work on that.

"I'll clean the glasses in a little while." Normally she would leave them in the sink until she needed them again, but she was going to bend to his needs. He'd already started bending to hers. Having a clean kitchen might be nice for a change. She sank down beside him. "Should we talk about the morning schedule? There's only one bathroom. Unless you take your shower at night."

"No, I take it in the morning, but I'll get up early so we have time."

"How do you do it?" The question was a calculated risk, but one she felt like she had to take. They had to start talking about the elephant in the room. His legs. Or lack thereof. They would be living together. She didn't want him hiding in his room like a shrinking virgin afraid she might see his shame.

It wasn't freaking shame and she was going to make sure he damn well understood that.

"How do I shower? I turn on the water and use soap."

It was the first time she'd heard him be really sarcastic. She rolled her eyes. "Yeah, not what I'm talking about. Are the old legs there waterproof? Can you surf in them?"

"I handle it." His face had gone a polite blank. It was his usual expression, the one that told her he was on his guard. He was almost

63

always on guard.

She wasn't going to let that grumpy tone get her down. "I'm curious."

"Be curious about something else." He reached over and turned off the television. "We do have to talk however. I think we need a solid front when it comes to Milo Jaye. He's coming by tonight to pick up the training contract and I don't want to meet him without the two of us being on the same page."

The chilly tone of his voice let her know she might not like his page. Touchy lion. "I think we can handle it. I'm quite good at going with the flow."

He nodded, lips turned down in a grumpy frown. Somehow he managed to make it sexy. "Yes, that's exactly what I want to avoid. I've thought this over a bit and realized that it's important how we present ourselves to Jaye. Big Tag told us he was expecting a long-term D/s couple, but he didn't state what kind of couple we should be."

Oh, she knew exactly what was coming. He was going to try to maneuver them into a no-sex position, and that was not a part of her plan. If they were pretending to be a D/s couple, they would need to be a super-hot D/s couple. "He's only coming by to pick up a contract, nothing more. We don't have to decide on anything yet. We simply smile and be friendly."

"I think that would be a mistake. Like I told you earlier, I prefer to begin as I mean to continue. I'll explain our situation to him and he'll understand."

She was scrambling. Sometimes playing dumb was a good way to stall. "Our situation? I think that would defeat the point, right? Big Tag wants him to think we've been together for a long time."

He sighed. "We can be together for a long time in several different ways. We need to talk about our backstory."

Good. She could make a backstory talk last a long time. Anything to keep him from ordering her to pretend like they were some sterile, never-touch-for-anything-but-discipline couple. She couldn't play dumb if she actually heard the words. "I was thinking we met in high school. You were the chess nerd and I was the super-cool head of the student council."

He put a hand out. "I was not a nerd."

"But you were in the chess club." She'd noted that he hadn't argued with that portion of her story.

"Chess is an intellectual pursuit," he huffed. "It does not make one a nerd. And there are several problems with your story. First of all, I'm trying to imagine you running a student council. Exactly what kind of school was this?"

He was so right about that. She hadn't been into student government. "I thought student government was better than explaining that I spent all my time skateboarding and working for the yearbook. I went through a photography phase, but mostly I made out with my boyfriend in the dark room. Besides, I was thinking we could have met when I needed a tutor for geometry. I bet you were good at geometry. That's where you found your thirst for topping a pretty sub. You would spank me when I didn't get a problem right and totally reward me when I did. I'm very reward based. It actually works better on me than punishment."

He shook his head and the look on his face told her the diversion plan was working. "Okay, first of all, how are we going to explain the difference in our accents and ages? I'm older than you. I can't be both a nerd tutor and have been obviously held back for several grades. Also, we will give ourselves away if anyone asks me about geometry. I was horrible at math. Tiffany, darlin', let's keep this simple."

She loved his accent so much. She loved it when he was being all dommy, but she also loved the slightly amused sound he got when she'd done something silly. "Okay. We met at Top. You were the handsome, dashing sommelier and I was the waitress with a heart of gold and a hard bottom."

His lips curled up. "You're not a hard bottom."

Now he was besmirching her honor as a submissive. "Am, too."

Every second she kept him from saying the words was one more for Milo Jaye to show his ass up and save her whole hastily thought out plan. She didn't have time to think of another one.

One brow arched over his eyes and he sat back, his big, muscular arms going over his chest. "Oh, really? Do you think I won't test that?"

If her poor backside had to ache, then she could handle it. The soreness from the earlier spanking was gone and she missed it. "I expect that you will. You know what I love? A good long spanking over a comfy lap. Why don't I lay myself right down over yours and we'll see who gives out first?"

His skin flushed slightly and she glanced down discreetly. Sure enough, his slacks were a little more tented than they had been before.

Proof positive she was doing the right thing. She stood up, ready to completely bare her ass. It was a sacrifice she actually wouldn't mind making in the slightest, so it didn't necessarily count as a sacrifice. Actually, her nipples were a little hard at the thought of his hand slamming down on her ass. She would find a way to end up completely naked and cuddled in his arms.

A smart girl got what she wanted. A good girl made sure her Dom got what he needed, too.

She was going to make sure she was a very good girl.

"You want to push the boundaries?" His mouth had taken on a hard line, those sensual lips flattening.

Hell, yeah. He thought he was talking about her boundaries, but she intended to push his own. By the time her ass was red, he wouldn't be able to keep that careful distance. The trouble was he always selected women who didn't press against those carefully placed walls of his. She wasn't going to push them. She was going to break them all down and get her guy.

Tiffany hooked her fingers into the belt loops of her shorts and got ready to bare all.

That was when the doorbell rang.

She wasn't sure if she should curse the heavens or thank god she'd been saved. That was Milo Jaye and she hadn't once heard Sebastian's cowardly, protect-his-wounded-ass-heart plan. It left her free for what came next. "I'll get it, Sir."

"Tiffany," he began.

She could hear the admonishment in his voice, but she pressed on. She threw open the door with a smile. A young man stood in the doorway, two women to his right. They were at least four inches taller than him and neither one was wearing heels. Milo Jaye had curly dark hair and wore a pair of mirrored aviators despite the fact that it was dark outside. He looked like someone had picked up a men's fashion magazine and found a short-and-needed-some-muscle-sized version of cutting edge clothing.

His chin was up, but his shoulders were slumped. An odd combo for a Dom, but then he hadn't been through training. Training would give him the confidence to not need the flashy clothes, the sunglasses when it was dark. At least he'd come to the right place. She gave him a bright smile. "Hello."

Jaye sniffed and looked her over. "Hello, you must be Tiffany."

"I am."

One shoulder shrugged up and down. "Shouldn't you…you know…greet me properly or something?"

Oh, he was going to be so much fun. "Hello, Mr. Jaye. How are you this evening?"

"I meant, aren't you supposed to get to your knees and greet me?" His shoulders suddenly went back as if he remembered he was in charge. "Or are you not a submissive?"

"She is and she's mine, so she certainly won't be getting on her damn knees for someone who hasn't earned his Master rights," a dark voice said behind her. She felt Sebastian's hands slide over her shoulders and felt a deep gratitude to the very delusional Milo Jaye. "Though you should understand that she's never going to kneel for you. She's mine and if you want to learn a damn thing from me, you'll remember that."

Sweet, sweet jealousy. It fed her. It nourished her. She would totally get rid of it at some point because he would understand she was only into him, but for now, she loved it.

Jaye's eyes slid away. "Sorry. You're twelve kinds of possessive.

67

Got it. I kind of thought submissives were supposed to honor Doms. Guess I have a lot to learn."

"How did she not honor you?" Sebastian asked. "Tiffany was perfectly polite. She greeted you. I'm sure she smiled because Tiffany always smiles. She struggles not to. That was all she owed you at this point."

"But at some point, she'll greet me naked, right?" Jaye asked.

She heard Sebastian growl behind her and his hand started toward the door. If she didn't stop him, he would slam the door in the billionaire's face and they would fail. She leaned back against him. "I think what he's trying to say is at some point I'll teach his very lovely submissives the proper and super-sexy way to greet their Master, right? Hi, girls. I'm Tiff. Why don't you come in?"

Sebastian huffed, but he moved back, allowing her to invite the group into their temporary home.

"Gina, Honey, come along." Milo Jaye sort of strutted inside the apartment, his skinny legs in tight jeans that ended in motorcycle boots. "You Master S?"

Dear god. She was going to have to ensure that her Dom didn't murder anyone tonight. "His name is Sebastian. I'm Tiffany. We're not in a club or at an event, so you should feel free to call him Sebastian. The Master title is only necessary when we're playing or in a training session."

Honey and Gina moved into the apartment, looking around curiously.

Gina gave her a big smile. "Thanks for having us. I'm very interested in the lifestyle."

Honey sniffed as though she'd smelled something bad. "Yes, she's read far too many romance novels. Is this really where you live?"

Ah, there was always one in a group. "Not at all. It's a façade. We actually live in an alternate dimension where people are polite to each other. Can I offer you a drink?"

Jaye waved a hand as Gina started to speak. "No. We won't be here long. We have to be home soon."

Gina's mouth closed but her skin had flushed. Honey showed not a single sign that she'd heard anything at all. She was busy flicking at her fingernails like the world bored her to tears.

Something was off with the group. They weren't at all connected. None of them. Interesting.

"I'll get the contract," Sebastian said. "It's in my bedroom, if you'll excuse me for a moment."

He turned and walked back toward the bedroom. She had maybe a minute or two to set her plan in motion. It was time to spring the trap and ensure her lion stayed in the cage. She should probably feel guilty. She was totally topping from the bottom, and at some point that would get her in trouble, but she accepted that fact. Besides, it was a good cage she was trapping him in. It was a sex cage, and she was going to be in there with him.

"Sebastian and I are so looking forward to our training sessions," she said with a gracious smile.

Milo stood in the hallway, glancing around. He still hadn't taken off his sunglasses. "Yeah, I think it's going to be good to finally find my place. Gina here's been talking about these books for a while. She makes them sound very hot."

She couldn't blurt out that she and her Master were very in love and had lots of sex, so you should expect our relationship to be super hot at all times. She had to be a bit more subtle, but time was running out. "A D/s relationship can be very hot. It's definitely helped our sex life."

Yes. She mentally high-fived herself.

"How, exactly?" Gina asked.

Honey had her phone out, completely ignoring the world around her.

"Yes, I would love to hear how D/s has helped our sex life," Sebastian said, his eyes on her.

Yep, she was going to pay for this later. He was standing there with the contract in hand, and it was obvious to her what he wanted. He wanted her to get them out of this situation.

She probably could. She could explain that D/s had helped them be better friends and led them to finding good sex with the lovers they took to their separate beds. That would be boring. "I always loved how Sebastian made love to me, but after I really embraced my submissive side, I go crazy for him. It helped us find our best selves and to serve our love in a way we hadn't before."

"That is a very interesting way to put it, Tiffany." His jaw had tightened as he stepped into the room.

She was in for it. There was nothing to do now but commit. She stepped over to Sebastian and wound her arm around his. "You know I want everyone to be as happy as we are. If this trio thinks that learning BDSM roles and exploring types of play will make them happy, then I'm thrilled to help them out."

"I do think it will help us," Gina said, stepping closer to Milo.

Milo reached out awkwardly, his hand finding her arm and kind of pulling her in. She stumbled a bit but found her footing. "I'm looking forward to the training. I can see that you two are very happy, and that's what I want for the three of us, too. I work most of the time and have a very stressful life. Gina thinks this might be just the way to unwind after a rough day."

Sebastian handed him the contract. "Read over it and we'll meet in a few days to discuss how to proceed. If you choose to proceed. There's a list of books I would like for you to read before we begin your formal training, and I would like for you to attend an evening at Sanctum next week. I want you to actually see what you're getting into before you commit."

"Yeah, I have a lot to learn. I'm sorry if I came off like a douchebag in the beginning," he said, looking down at the contract.

Gina's eyes were up and steady on Sebastian. "He'll be excellent at this. He's excellent at everything. He merely needs some time to get used to the role."

Interesting. She wasn't sure why Honey was here, but Gina was definitely into Milo.

"The first thing he can do is respect other Doms by taking off those sunglasses." Somehow Sebastian managed to sound both polite and biting at the same time.

Milo started and the sunglasses were suddenly in his hands, clear green eyes looking up at Sebastian. "Sorry, sir. Do I call you sir? Is there some protocol I need to follow until I can get Master rights?"

"Sebastian is fine," he replied. "You can call me Master Sebastian when we're in the kink world."

Milo grinned like a five-year-old with an ice cream. "Kink world. I like the sound of that. It might make up for losing potentially millions of dollars. Might."

"I was under the impression you wouldn't have actually won that case," Sebastian said. "I rather thought this was all a way to force Ian Taggart to allow you into Sanctum. I have to ask. With all your money and power, why not start your own club? If you really could have won the patent, why lose millions?"

He suddenly seemed more confident, a bit taller. When Milo Jaye talked about his business, she believed him. "Maybe I could have. Maybe not. Maybe I had been working on it or maybe I found a weakness and exploited it to get what I wanted."

Gina held out a hand. "Hey, he did try to get into the club the normal way. That Ian person is a jerk."

"I would suggest you call him Master Ian the next time you see him." There was Sebastian's Dom voice.

It was interesting that it didn't seem to work on Gina. Her chin was still tilted up even as she replied. "Of course."

She had her work cut out with that one. "Don't worry about it. We'll go over how to behave when playing. It's all simple. The rules of the club are all plainly stated and everyone will help you. Despite Master Ian's persona, he's quite nice. You'll like it at Sanctum and I don't think Mr. Jaye will miss a few million dollars."

"We'll see," he said. He nodded to Sebastian. "All right, then. I'll leave you two to the rest of your evening. It's good to know Taggart took my request seriously. I don't want some couple that's never worked together trying to teach us how to be a good threesome. I was actually hoping Miles and his family would be the ones to teach us."

Adam, Jake, and Serena would have been the best bet, but apparently Adam wasn't about to train the man who'd threatened him. Still, she wasn't going to say it out loud.

"Unfortunately, the nature of Serena's business makes it difficult for her to be involved, and submissive training is as important as Dom training." Tiffany was pleased with how reasonable she managed to sound.

"Yes, it is," Sebastian said. "It really helps to train the sub to listen to her Dom and not go rogue. Going rogue tends to end poorly for everyone involved, but especially for the submissive. Learning to allow your Dom to lead can be a hard lesson, but a valuable one."

She was in so much trouble. It sent a shiver down her spine that wasn't at all about fear.

Gina's hand slid down to find Milo's. "I look forward to it and it was lovely to meet you, Tiffany. Honey, please come and say good-bye."

Honey hopped up immediately, her hair bouncing. "Thank god. This was so boring."

"Honey…" Gina's voice had gone low. "Don't be rude."

Honey gave them a smile Tiffany was sure no one in their right mind would believe. "Sorry. I've had a lovely time."

Tiffany ushered them out the door, her heart starting to flutter in her chest. What was he going to do to her? She turned back around and decided to pretend like absolutely nothing was wrong. Fake it until you make it. That was her mantra of the day. "Well, that was weird."

Sebastian was somehow frowning at her with his whole body. "That did not go the way I would have liked."

"I know. I don't think he's a Dom. You've got your work cut out for you." She went about cleaning up the living room, grabbing the wine glasses and taking them to the kitchen.

"You knew I wanted to talk about it before we gave them a backstory."

Yep. She knew. "I'm sorry. It happened so fast and I didn't

actually give them any history. I just talked about how happy we are. We're supposed to be happy, right?"

He was still for a moment. "Tiffany, why do I get the feeling you're manipulating me?"

Shit. She needed to avoid this particular conversation at all costs. "I was only trying to keep up appearances. If you think I did something wrong, I'm willing to take whatever punishment you choose."

"But you don't, do you?" He stared at her as though contemplating what to do next. "If I send you to your room and tell you not to come out except for work and put you under high protocol at all times, I suspect you'll give me trouble."

High protocol? She did not intend to spend this time with him asking for permission to speak. "It would be really hard for us to work together if I can't even communicate with you. Sebastian, I get it. I should have held back, but I was impulsive and I started talking. It's something I do and it's probably going to make you crazy. I know your instinct is to punish me by pushing me away, but I think that would be a mistake."

"And I think you are very good at playing me. I reserve the right to punish you for tonight. I have to think about it. Good night, Tiffany. We leave for work in the morning at nine a.m. Do not be late." He turned and walked away.

"Good night, Sir."

He didn't turn around and she hoped she hadn't hurt her cause.

CHAPTER SIX

"**S**o you should read the material provided and I'll test you on it at the end of the week," Sebastian said, looking at the waitstaff Eric and Deena had hired. Four women and two men. A few of them had real experience, but several were straight out of the military.

He had to teach them wine. Tiffany had to teach them service. He was fairly certain she had the harder job.

But Tiffany's service was surprisingly close to perfect. He wasn't thinking about her restaurant service. He knew damn well that was near perfect. Her service as a sub was what had his head slightly spinning. And his dick in knots.

They'd been living together for five days and it had been smooth and peaceful. Not once had she given him trouble. No. She'd given him the warmth of her smile and the quickness of her mind. He'd spent days getting to know her and now he sort of missed her when she walked out of a room.

"Test? Like a multiple choice kind of thing?" one of the men asked. He thought the man was named Austin. He still wore his hair high and tight.

"No." That Marine needed to understand the way of their world. It could be a difficult transition. "I need you to memorize these facts, not guess at them. I don't expect that any of you will become experts, but you do need to understand the fundamentals of how food pairs with wine and you must be able to remember the list of featured wines. I'll always pair the wines myself, but you have to effectively communicate with customers and that means having a rudimentary knowledge."

"So that means study," a deep voice said from the back of the room. "I need you to sound like you know what you're doing. Pair up and help each other. I expect you to know both our menu and our wine list. No one wants to order food from a server who can't remember what he's serving. Good night, guys."

The class stood and started to shuffle out of the dining room and back toward the staff rooms. He could hear them. Some were interested in the subject and others talked about how stuffy the teacher was.

One very creative server mentioned that he might have a wine bottle stuffed up his butt.

Like he'd never heard that before. Eric strode across the floor. He was wearing jeans and a T-shirt, a smile on his face. Eric Vail was obviously a happy man. He smiled even as he yelled at his new staff of chefs. Like his mentor, Eric tended to treat the kitchen like an Army unit he was heading. It worked for him since all his line chefs had come from the military.

"All right, Sebastian," he began, "you've had five days with these guys. What do you think?"

Five days. He'd been training these people for five days, but most of what he remembered about the last five days was how Tiffany managed to occupy his every damn thought. How she smiled as she sat down across from him at breakfast. How she sat a little too close every night when they watched the news and tried to unwind a bit before going to bed.

He'd told himself to go straight to his room when they got home after a long day, to give himself some distance from her sunny smile, her ingratiating manner.

But that wasn't what Eric was asking about. "I think they'll be fine once they've had some experience. Two of the women are quite good. Emma and Abigail don't need much wine training."

"They've both worked in five-star restaurants before. It's the boys and Sally who are going to give you trouble, but I think they can work out if we give them some time and patience."

He was the very definition of patience. Normally. He was surprisingly antsy about dealing with his submissive. "Don't worry, Eric. They'll be ready for opening. It's all going to go great. You worry about the menu. Tiffany and I will handle front of house."

Eric leaned against the bar. "Speaking of Tiffany, how is that going? I was surprised to hear you let yourself get wrangled into that clusterfuck. I had dinner with Sean last night. He said you and Tiff were going to train some billionaire tech guru in D/s. Is that why you've been topping her all week?"

He'd hoped that had gone unnoticed. He'd tried to be subtle, and Tiffany had been quite good about obeying his dictates since that night she'd gone rogue and doomed them both to pretending to be some kind of lovey-dovey, hearts-and-flowers couple in front of Jaye and his subs. She'd been damn near perfect, and there was a part of him that was waiting for her to break and for the brat to show back up.

Not that he didn't owe her some punishment. He simply hadn't felt comfortable enough to give it to her yet. "I got put in a corner. I then got put in another corner by Tiffany's out of control romanticism."

Eric's arms crossed over his chest. "Romanticism?"

"We were only supposed to train Jaye and convince him we were a long-term D/s couple."

Eric nodded. "Sure. That actually shouldn't be too hard. You're both experienced. Try a couple of scenes together and get a feel for what she needs and then explain to Jaye that you top her for disciplinary purposes only. So much easier than pretending to have some form of real romantic…ah, she got to him first."

At least he wasn't alone in his logic. "She told him how much we loved each other. How D/s had made our sex lives so much more intimate."

"Ah, so she totally flanked you," Eric said with a grin.

"I don't think we're at war." If they were then she was certainly not an aggressive combatant. She'd been lovely for days, making his life easier, being a pleasant companion. The night before, after they'd gotten home from a long day, he'd watched a late edition of the news and she'd sank to her knees beside him and put her head in his lap. She'd explained that she was merely trying to get used to the position since they would be going to Sanctum soon. He'd found himself petting her hair and relaxing, the weight of her head against his thigh soothing. "She panicked. It's my fault. I should have had the discussion with her earlier so she would have known my plans for us."

"That's not like you. You don't tend to put things off."

He'd gotten lost in the conversation. "We were discussing other things and it got away from me. By the time I got back around to the topic at hand, she had some crazy scheme where we met in high school and she was the student body president and then I was supposed to spank her when she got a math problem wrong. Or something like that."

He still wasn't exactly sure.

Eric laughed, slapping a hand against the bar. "You got the full treatment, my man. You know you're in trouble, right?"

"With Milo Jaye? Yes, I suspect I am." He'd thought about it long and hard for days. "He doesn't seem very dominant to me. His girlfriend seems to have taken control and they're quite awkward together. I have no idea why the third girl is there. She's useless."

Eric shook his head. "I wasn't talking about the training situation. I was talking about Tiffany."

"We've settled into a nice routine." Comfortable. Easy. Much more peaceful than he would have suspected. She was different than she seemed. He'd stayed away from her for numerous reasons, but one of them had been her chaotic nature and her inability to keep her nose in her own business. Yet for days she'd been calm, settling into their daily routine with a grace he'd never suspected. They were working together quite nicely and she'd ceased asking embarrassing questions. "She has her space and I have mine. We've gone over a few of the training methods we'll use on our charges and everything else has been work or sleep."

"Ah, the calm before the storm. You know how everything gets real calm and still right before a tornado hits? It's kind of like all the wind has been sucked up and the world seems peaceful. Then you realize all that air is nothing but fuel for the storm and it's heading right for you."

"What are you talking about?"

Eric shrugged like this should all be evident to him. "Tiffany. She's up to something. I know when a woman is plotting. She's been whispering with Deena."

"They're friends. Maybe Deena's plotting. Maybe you're the one who's getting flanked." He didn't like the thought of Tiffany planning something behind his back. And what exactly would she plan? "You know it's far more likely that Deena would be planning something. Tiffany would know that we should simply talk about what she needs. We have a contract in place and a schedule that she follows to the letter."

"Damn, she's following a schedule?" Eric sounded like he couldn't quite believe it. "Now I know she's up to something. Look, I get it. This relationship of yours is new and it's all D/s based, so you're feeling totally superior to my sad-sack marriage, but mark my words, brother. That woman wants you and not in a strictly D/s fashion."

"Wants me?"

"Yeah, she's seducing you with submission," Eric said smoothly. "She's lulling you into a false sense of control, and you're going to wake up six weeks from now in her bed and you'll have moved in, and when did you put that collar around her neck? That's when she turns into a real live woman, and those are difficult to deal with."

What the hell was Eric talking about? "We don't have that kind of relationship. I'm not looking for a romantic connection with her."

Eric sighed and was silent for a moment. "Then I'm going to ask you to go to Big Tag and stop this thing. Deena and I will take over. I've already talked to her about it and we can handle both. I'll deal with Jaye and we'll move Tiffany out of the apartment. I'll find something for her."

And leave him alone? He'd gotten used to having companionship, used to talking to her over meals. He liked the fact that she sought him out even when they were working and made sure he stopped for lunch. "Things are working out fine. I'm not sure why you think we should stop."

"Because you don't want a romantic relationship with her and I suspect very strongly that she does," Eric pointed out.

That made him stop. It wasn't a good idea. She would need far more from him than he was willing to give her. And she wasn't attracted to him. They were simply thrown in together because of circumstances. "I think you're wrong, but I'll discuss it with her."

"She's a wonderful woman," Eric said quietly. "She's beautiful and bright. Are you sure you don't want her? I think she might be ready for something more serious than mere play."

He had to steady himself, the pain in his leg shooting through him. He needed more padding. There was a scratch on his right stump that should have been dealt with days before. He wasn't taking care of himself. He was more concerned with Tiffany seeing him without his prosthetic than he was with taking care of his legs. Hell, he didn't want her to see his prosthetic at all. And he damn sure didn't want her to see his wheelchair. He normally used it for a portion of the day to give his legs time to breathe, but he was reluctant to do it around her.

Did he want her? Yes. Did he think it could work? No. Not long term. Maybe. Maybe if she really was attracted to him. Or perhaps she was attracted to his lifestyle. Opposites could attract. Perhaps what he offered her was peace and safety. Her life was chaotic. She seemed to enjoy the order he brought to their home.

He enjoyed calling that apartment their home. It was reason enough to walk away, but couldn't seem to bring himself to do it.

"Sebastian, it's all right to want her." Eric's voice had gone low, almost sympathetic. "She's a great woman. She's fun and kind. I think she's going to make someone an excellent partner, but she's also reckless. When she wants something, she tends to throw her whole soul into going for it. You know she walked away from a very comfortable upbringing because she wants to be an artist. She doesn't want to use her father's money or influence."

"She's not afraid of hard work." It was one of the things he admired about her.

"So you like her. That's a good sign."

"I do," he replied. "I like her more than I thought I would. If your next question is about whether or not I want her physically, then yes. Like you said. She's a beautiful woman, but she's going to want more than I'll be willing to give."

"Have you asked her?" Eric asked. "Have you offered what you're willing to give? I think you might be surprised."

Frustration welled through him. "I don't honestly know that this is your business. If you're warning me off her, then I have to think about how to respond. I understand that you're watching out for your wife's friend. I'll consider it."

Something about the way Eric's face fell made Sebastian feel like he'd disappointed the man. "That wasn't what I was trying to do at all. I was trying to be your friend. Maybe we have two different versions of friendship."

He turned to walk away and Sebastian realized it was one of those moments. He'd had a few of them. Moments when everything changed. If he allowed Eric to walk away, they would be friendly but not friends.

Wasn't that what he wanted? Hadn't friendship gotten him in enough trouble? He'd managed to spend the last three years of his life with almost no real entanglements. He'd performed his duties, done his job, and studied for his Master Som test. He'd passed that and now what? Was he really going to spend the rest of his life without any intimacies?

Tiffany was making him soft, making him want something he shouldn't.

"What makes you think she's interested in more than getting through the next few weeks with me?"

Eric turned, a smile creasing his face. "Are we going to do this? Like, really?"

Sometimes he didn't understand people. "Uhm, I don't know. If you mean are we going to talk, then yes. If you mean anything else, I'm quite worried."

"Sebastian, you have to chill, my man. We're talking. We're talking about our women. I never thought we would talk about our women." Eric slid his big body onto the barstool in front of Sebastian. "To be honest, I thought we might be talking about your man."

"You know it's sad that in this day and age the mere act of presenting oneself in a slightly more formal fashion brings one's sexuality into question." Just because he didn't wear jeans and grubby T-shirts didn't mean a thing, and yet this wasn't his first conversation about his sexuality. "I happen to know several homosexual men who are completely untidy in both appearance and their domesticity. Am I to assume that Tiffany's predilection for sniffing her clothing to ensure they've seen the inside of a washing machine is an indicator of her preference for masculine sexual companions?"

A grin crossed Eric's face. "God, I love it when you get pissed. I think that was your version of throwing me the finger. Why don't we taste a little of that Scotch I'm planning on charging fifty dollars a glass for? Pour us some and then tell me why you're so scared of Tiff."

He started to reply, to tell Eric that he certainly wasn't afraid of her. Except he was and if Eric was going to be his friend, he should probably be honest with him. After all, he had helped Eric see Deena in a different light before they'd gotten married. He'd understood Deena's need to distance. Eric was a bit more like Tiffany. Despite the scar on his face and his time as a Navy SEAL, Eric tended to view the world as a fundamentally good place populated with good people. Basically his opposite. "She's so different from me."

He turned and pulled down the Scotch. It looked like he might need it. He uncorked it and let the scent wash over him.

"Yes, and that's a good thing," Eric continued. "Though I think you would be surprised at how you're more alike than different. Like we talked about, she's a hard worker. She's loyal to her friends. She's kind."

"Well, I will admit that I'm a hard worker." He poured Eric two fingers worth. Yes, this little therapy session would cost him if he wasn't sitting here and having it with the owner of the place. He poured his own. "I don't actually have many friends so I can't say I'm all that loyal. And I certainly wouldn't call myself kind."

"Really? Why'd you send that money to Linc's mom when her power got cut off? Don't think I don't know who did it. Linc was trying to hustle to get a loan so he could get her power back on, but I heard you paying it over the phone and making damn sure they turned it back on that day."

There was no privacy in the world. "That wasn't kindness. I had a wine dinner that night and I couldn't lose my bartender. That was all."

Eric stared at him.

Eric had likely been excellent with the men under his command when he'd been a SEAL. That steely-eyed stare cut right through him. "All right. I couldn't stand how upset he was. Also, his mother is elderly and they struggle. It was hot that day. No one should die because they don't have money. I had it. She needed it. That was all."

"I'm sure you staying late to clean so other people can get back to their wives or families isn't a big deal either."

It was a mere matter of logic. "I don't have a family. It's easy for me to stay behind."

"Tiffany does it, too. Have you ever noticed that she stays behind when you do?" Eric asked. "She's got a car but she always seems to walk to work and you give her a ride home. Javier's closer, but she asks you. Have you ever wondered why?"

He had, actually. "I thought it was because I'm easier to deal with than Javi. She knows I wouldn't hit on her."

"I think she's been trying to get you to hit on her. I think she's a little desperate to get you to hit on her. That's why you should let her down easy if you're not interested. She's ready to get serious about someone, but it doesn't have to be you. I've got a couple of friends I've been thinking of introducing her to."

"Don't you fucking introduce my sub to other men." The words came out of his mouth before he could even think about them.

Eric's eyes widened. "Well, there's my answer."

He'd sounded like a damn caveman. The idea of Eric setting Tiffany up with someone else had set him off and that wasn't a good thing. Still, he couldn't help the fact that he was a little angry that Eric thought to set up a submissive under contract to another Dom. To him. She was under contract to him. "She's not dating while we have a contract between us."

"All that matters is the contract?"

This was why he didn't have friends. They challenged a man. They forced him to face the truth. "No. I have to admit that living with her the last week has made me more protective of her. It's made me more than interested in her, but she doesn't know what she's in for. I have needs she might find unsavory."

"I don't know," Eric said. "She's pretty hard core. She was the one in our training class who tried pretty much everything. I would definitely say she's open to any and all experiences when it comes to the lifestyle. She was the best puppy in our puppy play class."

If only that was all he was talking about. "I meant my physical needs. Not my sexual ones. I don't want her to see me in the wheelchair. I'm already pushing it to not use the damn thing."

Eric shook his head. "Wait. Are you telling me you're staying away from Tiffany because of your legs?"

He couldn't possibly understand. "I have to deal with some physical things that she would find unpleasant."

"Or she would find them all right because she was helping someone she cares about," Eric pointed out.

He didn't want her to sacrifice for him. "She's beautiful. She shouldn't be stuck with someone who's not. You're right. She's kind, and I worry she's confusing kindness for attraction."

Eric's eyes rolled. "For a smart man, you play dumb well. Come on, man. She's not a martyr. She's a grown woman and she knows what she wants. If you want her, test her. Show her those needs you think will make her run away. If you don't, you're going to keep the two of you in limbo because Tiffany won't give up. She'll spend the next several months of her life trying to catch you."

How long had it been since a woman tried to catch him? Had any woman ever wanted him so much she chased him? Worked to get him? There had only been Alicia for most of his life and he'd been the one to chase her. He had to wonder if she'd ever really wanted him or if he'd been nothing more than a habit. Or worse, a way to shelter herself. He'd been the friend for so long and then a boy she'd cared about had hurt her. Had he been a way for her to hide from that pain?

He had nothing now. He had nothing to offer Tiffany but a decent paying job, and she didn't need the money. She'd turned her back on it, but from what he understood, her father would give it to her any time she asked. So why would she try to get close to him except out of kindness? Unless she truly wanted him. But he had to face the fact that she was also acting the way she was because they'd been forced together and she was making the best of a situation. "I don't want to push her if she's only trying to help out Ian and Sean. If I do, I could make things awkward for both of us. I might ask her about it after all this is over."

"You think this is all about helping out the Taggarts? Sebastian, we need to talk about manipulative women. Now I know the word manipulation gets a bad rap, but sometimes it's needed. Sometimes it's merely a way to get a stubborn person to admit to what they want."

"I haven't seen any sign of her manipulating me. She got a little flustered the other night and screwed up some of my plans, but I suppose I can understand that. She's a sweet girl who happens to be submissive."

"Sebastian, my house is perfect," Eric said with a sigh. "My guest room is perfect. And if you think she didn't stall you and put you in a position where you had to play lovers in front of Milo Jaye, you're high and don't deserve this intensely excellent Scotch."

He stopped. "What?"

Eric's lips curved up as he took another sip and then put the glass down. "I was told if you asked to explain that our guest room is unavailable due to water damage. At the time we weren't close friends, but we're close friends now, right?"

She'd plotted this? She'd planned to put him in a position where they were living together?

She had plotted this.

"Yeah, we're best friends, Eric." He needed to make something clear because suddenly it seemed so very right that he do this. That he find his first real friend in years. That he open himself up the tiniest bit. "We are friends. I'm sorry if I don't always behave that way. Know that from now on I will."

"You behave better than you think you do," Eric admitted. "We all consider you a part of our family. And I definitely count you as a friend. You gave me some excellent advice once so I'm going to do the same for you. Push her. Test her. She wants it. I think she intends to pass every test you set. I think she's the right woman, and the right woman won't falter or even blink at these needs you talk about. You know Ally never had a problem with Macon's leg. In fact, she kind of developed a kink around it. Would that bother you?"

"Did Allyson date other men who'd lost a limb?"

"Nope. Neither has Tiff."

There was kink and then there was kink. He wasn't sure how he would feel if it was the missing limbs alone that attracted her, but the idea that she could adapt intrigued him. So often with women it was all about love. A woman in love could look past what she would normally find distasteful. A woman in love could find beauty in the oddest places.

He'd never had a woman be in love with him. Not that way. Oh, he'd had a woman manipulate and deceive him, but he hadn't had one plot and plan how to get him into bed with her. All in all, he greatly found he preferred the latter. "She's topping me from the bottom."

"Yes, she is, my brother. What are you going to do about it?"

He took a long drink, not bothering to concentrate on the color of the liquor or to appreciate the oaky flavor. He needed the reinforcement. "I think we should have a nice long chat."

"I think that might help clarify things." Eric held up his glass. "Welcome to the club, the led around by some sweet, gorgeous, soft woman club. Consider me your sponsor and understand that while you might get annoyed, this is a club you don't want to leave."

He wasn't sure he belonged in the club, but he was damn straight going to find out. He knew exactly how to start. "Can I use your office?"

CHAPTER SEVEN

Tiffany walked into Eric's office and noted that Deena had done a really lovely job with the small space she'd been given to work with. The Fort Worth version of Top had a slightly larger dining room but the office was about half of what Sean Taggart occupied. It made for an intimate space. Sebastian was standing beside Eric's desk, a scowl on his handsome face.

Maybe this was too intimate. What had she done to put that look on his face? "Sebastian? Are you all right?"

"I would like for you to tell me something and I think you should give your answer careful consideration." There was that deep voice that made her knees weak.

"All right." Something had definitely gone wrong. She scrambled to try to figure out what it could possibly be. Their first week together had been as nice as she'd thought it could be. She'd been on her best behavior. He'd seemed happy. He'd started to pet her hair at night when she put her head on his lap. He'd seemed awkward at first, but now he barely looked down at her, merely moved his hand to her head when she joined him. They'd enjoyed a nice morning together and then she'd been working with Deena doing a mock dinner service with the waitstaff. She hadn't seen him enough to piss him off today. "What's your question?"

"How is Deena's guest bedroom? Did they get the water damage cleaned up?"

Oh, shit. She was going to have such a long talk with Deena about her rat-fink husband. And to think she'd been a damn bridesmaid. She'd celebrated with them and what did Eric do? He turned her in the first chance he got. Damn it.

Sebastian was staring at her like a cop who had found his murder suspect with a gun in her hand and standing over a dead body. There was nowhere to run.

"I lied about the guest room." Tears started to pool in her eyes as the bitter truth washed over her. She'd made her play and now it was done. He would shove her out.

She'd needed more time. So much more time. He was stubborn and he needed time and proximity to make him relax.

"Why did you lie?" His question came out on a harsh grind as Sebastian's arms crossed over his chest.

A thousand and one answers leapt to her mind. She could save some face. She could lie through her teeth and then regroup. Or she could put it all on the line and see what he would do.

"Because I wanted to stay with you. I wanted to get close to you."

The expression on his face didn't change at all. "Turn around and walk to the door."

"Sebastian," she began. That had been a mistake. He wasn't ready.

"I said turn around and walk to that door. Do not disobey me in this, Tiffany. You've made me look like a fool enough for the day. Do as I say."

Well, that answered all her questions. She couldn't help the tears that blurred her vision as she turned away from him. She'd made her play and failed. It wasn't the first time she'd failed at something. Wouldn't be the last. So why did it feel like the damn world was ending? Why was this man so important?

It didn't matter because it was over. Once she walked out that door, he would likely be polite and he would be a gentleman, but he would never be her Dom again.

"Now lock it."

She stopped, her hand on the door. "What?"

"You're struggling to listen today so let me make myself clear one last time. You will lock the door. You will remove your clothes, fold them, and put them to the side. You will accept your punishment with grace and then you will go about the rest of your day, but you will also understand that things are going to change now. I won't be manipulated. If I find out you've been anything less than honest with me again, there will be no more contract. I'll go to Big Tag and explain that this isn't going to work out. When you want something from me, you'll ask me. You won't go behind my back and twist and turn the truth in order to get what you want. You'll be brave enough to ask for what you want and I'll do the same. Tiffany, I would like very much to move our relationship to a sexual level. I believe we'll both enjoy the experience."

"Yes." What the hell had happened? Maybe she wasn't going to harangue Eric. "I think we would be good together."

"See. That wasn't hard. Now do as I asked and we can get your punishment over. Don't think for a second those tears are going to sway me."

She brushed them aside. It looked like she wouldn't need to cry. "I wasn't crying because I was afraid of the discipline. I was crying because I thought you were sending me away."

For the first time his face softened and he stepped close to her. He towered over her and his big hand came out, his thumb brushing across her cheek to wipe away her tears. "I don't know where this is going, but I think I would be foolish to not try with you. I need you to understand, though, that I'm not sure how much I have to offer you. I won't fool myself by saying this is all about sex. I do have feelings for you. I don't know how much that will mean. I haven't had a relationship with a woman in a very long time. I lost someone I cared about quite deeply and it wounded me to the core. I don't know that I can love you the way you deserve to be loved."

But two weeks ago he would never have even said the word love around her. He might not see it, but he could change. He could grow. "I'll take that risk."

He stepped back and she knew the Dom was in the house again. "Then do as I asked."

Take off her clothes and take her punishment. She could do that. It would be the first time he'd touched her with more than easy affection since that first day. Despite the fact that he'd told her he would punish her for what happened with Milo Jaye, he hadn't mentioned discipline again. They'd been quiet and simple, and while it had been nice to spend that kind of time with him, she wanted this part, too. Needed it. She might need it more from Sebastian than she'd ever needed it at all. D/s had been fun. It had been a game and she'd enjoyed it, but she craved Sebastian's dominance.

She worked quickly, folding her clothes as instructed. When she'd dreamed about this, she'd thought about wild and crazy passion, but that wasn't Sebastian. He was thoughtful, careful, and he wanted her to be that way, too. He watched her as she exposed her body to him, his eyes hot, but he remained perfectly still.

He was savoring her. He was looking at her like she was a glass of wine he wanted to be able to describe with precision.

"Am I star bright, Sebastian?" She was down to her bra and skirt. She reached back and released the clip that held her hair up.

"No, Tiffany. That's not the term I would use to describe your light." His voice was even deeper than normal. "The proper term would be brilliant."

She had to smile at that. She released the clasp of her bra and laid it on top of the pile. "I don't think that's a word you would typically use to describe me."

"Only because you don't understand what it means to me. Take off the skirt. We haven't had a formal presentation. Had we begun this properly, I would have had you present yourself to me, your body displayed for my pleasure so I could enjoy you and praise how beautiful you are. So you could show me everything you're offering me."

He wasn't ready for everything she was offering to him. Right now, he was ready for her body, but she damn straight intended to give him her heart and soul. One step at a time. It would be a dangerous game with a man who wasn't as honorable as Sebastian. If they didn't end up together, it wouldn't be because he'd used her for sex and discarded her. He wasn't a man who would do that. Other things might come between them, but he wouldn't use her. He was giving them a chance and it was time to take it.

Tiffany slid the skirt down her hips. "I've never presented myself outside of a training class before."

"Never?"

"I've never once been serious about a Dom. Not the way I am about you." It was actually nice to not hide her affection. She'd walked such a slim tightrope. She would still be careful not to push him too hard, but she could relax a little.

"Thread your fingers together, arms behind your back. Present your breasts to me."

This was really happening. She was certain her Sebastian was going to make this hard as hell on her. He would get her twenty kinds of hot and bothered and then spank her and send her on her way, but they were on the road to actual, real sex. She would have to put up with it because she got the feeling her Hitachi was going to be a no-no for a while. She drew her hands behind her back and found the position he wanted, letting her breasts thrust out in offering to her desired Master.

Cool air hit her skin, but she was hot on the inside. Sebastian was staring at her, considering her in that deliberate way of his, and it did something for her. Her nipples tightened under his gaze and she was aware of every inch of her skin.

"Spread your legs," he commanded as he finally moved. He took a step toward her as he began to roll up his shirt sleeves. She'd seen the man in leathers, but he was never more masterful than when he was in one of those perfectly tailored suits of his.

She moved her legs apart, grateful she'd kept up a grooming routine. Positive thinking had saved her from having a bush only a Sasquatch could love. She was bare and sensitive.

"You're very comfortable with your nudity." He walked behind her and his fingertips brushed her hair to one side. "Do you enjoy being naked, Tiffany?"

"I might have spent some time living in a nudist colony," she admitted. "It was a nice place on a mountain."

"Why does that not surprise me?" His fingers whispered across her shoulder blades. "Did you live there with a boyfriend?"

She fought hard not to lean back against his touch. He was teasing her and it was going to make her crazy, but she was determined to prove to him that she could play his games. "No boyfriend that time. Just a crazy friend from high school who thought it would be fun to travel across the country in her Mustang. We got to this crazy town, she met a guy who'd been visiting from Seattle, and suddenly I had no friend, no car, and about twenty-nine dollars in my pocket."

His hand wound into her hair and she found herself looking up into seriously blue eyes. "Tell me you called your father."

Oh, he thought she was far smarter than she was. "I couldn't. It was my declaration of independence. I found a job at the nudist colony, which was really more of a resort. I worked the laundry at first. You would think there wouldn't be much of a call for it, but those people go through towels like crazy. After a while, I kind of joined them. There wasn't anything sexual about it. Not really. There was nothing more than a very lovely freedom to be me. I found myself there."

"You could have been killed," he said on a low growl. "You should have called your father."

"But then I wouldn't have had the experience. Sebastian, if we never throw ourselves in the water, we don't learn to swim."

"And you never have to worry about drowning. Tell me you understand how dangerous it was to be an eighteen-year-old girl out in the world on her own without anyone to watch out for her."

"But I found several people who did help me. I also figured out how strong I was, that I could do anything I wanted to."

He shook his head. "You need a keeper."

"I kind of thought I had one." At least that was what the contract stated.

"You do now and you should understand I won't tolerate you placing yourself in danger. I worry that we'll have two very different definitions of danger, but I'm too far along to stop. I don't know that I like this feeling. I prefer to be in control and I'm not right now."

She needed him to understand she was willing to bend. "You are. Sebastian, I'm not eighteen anymore. I don't need some crazy adventure to find myself. I need this. I need you. I need what only you can give me."

He tilted her head back, fingers twisting lightly in her hair. Not enough to hurt, but enough to light up her scalp, to make her shiver. "I think you could be very good at manipulating me."

"I'm not trying to do that." His mouth was so close. All she would have to do was go up on her toes and she could feel those lips against hers. She remained perfectly still because that would prove to him that she couldn't follow orders here where he needed it the most. "I'm trying to be honest with you."

"I'm not going to change, Tiffany. What you see is what you get."

But he'd already started to change. He'd bent for her in ways that surprised her. He could be so rigid, but he'd made allowances and she expected after they started sleeping together they would both find themselves bending. They would figure out who they were as a couple. It was natural. "I don't need you to change."

Not fundamentally. She loved the core of strength deep inside him.

"I hope you mean what you say. Remember that I warned you." His mouth came down on hers, warmth spreading to every part of her body. He didn't rush the kiss, didn't slam his mouth to hers and take off running. No. He was deliberate, thoughtful in the way he kissed. He brought their lips together, brushing across her mouth before deepening the kiss. Over and over he kissed her, drugging her before his tongue ran over her bottom lip.

She was already hot and wet and ready and he'd barely touched her.

Her breasts brushed against the fabric of his dress shirt as he finally dominated her mouth, his tongue moving inside to tangle with

93

hers. She wanted her arms around him, but she was fairly certain he wasn't ready for that yet. This would be D/s sex in the beginning, something she'd waited for. Now she was so happy she'd waited for the right man. She'd held off all other Doms because somehow deep down she'd known Sebastian was the right Dom for her.

His hand came out of her hair, running down her neck and over her chest. "Tell me how much you've learned. You've taken the training class and you've played around a bit, but I've never watched you scene so I'm not sure what you like."

She liked him. She loved the way his big palm covered her breast. She wasn't a tiny girl by any means, but she felt petite against him. "I took the training class because I was curious. Deena wanted to take it and she didn't want to go alone. I knew when I read the materials Big Tag requires subs to read that I would enjoy playing around the edges of D/s."

He rolled her nipple between his thumb and forefinger, tweaking her on the right side of pain. "I don't play around the edges. I swim in the deep water, darlin'. You need to think about this."

He really should let her finish. "The longer I go, the harder I want it. I started out enjoying an erotic spanking. I'm afraid I'm the freak who gets seriously turned on by the disciplinary ones. I'm willing to try almost everything. I can handle anything with the exception of what we've talked about before. Withdrawing affection makes me feel small. I don't like it."

His breath heated her neck and she could feel his lips there. "I'm feeling very affectionate. But you'll have to be patient with me. I haven't dealt with a woman like you in a long time. I've offered my services to people who required discipline, not affection. I might be bad at it."

It didn't feel like it. And as long as he was willing to learn, they could work together. He felt perfectly affectionate at night. He seemed to enjoy making physical contact with her. She was almost certain that Sebastian had forgotten how nice it was to cuddle, to hug, to be truly close to another human being. For some reason, he didn't remember what it meant to be connected to a woman. She was going to make damn sure that woman was her and only her. "I can be patient, Sir. Master. I want to call you Master. I think it would be better for our cover."

He ran his tongue over the sensitive flesh of her neck right before sinking his teeth in. Gently. It was just enough to make her squirm. "I think you know exactly how to make me want you. I think you're excellent at manipulating me."

She had to get him off that word. "Or I'm perfect for you."

Both hands cupped her breasts, pulling her back against him. "I'm a little suspicious of perfection, but damn, I can't help but try with you."

She could feel the linen of his shirt at her back, the buttons brushing against her spine. Sebastian molded his hands around her breasts, shaping and cupping them as though he was trying to memorize their weight and feel.

"You have a beautiful body. Your skin is soft. I love the way your nipples respond. I'm going to enjoy playing with them. Do you understand that as we move this relationship to a sexual place, I'm going to become a little more demanding?"

She could feel some of his demand at the small of her back, but she wouldn't use the word *little* when describing it. "What are you going to require of me?"

"I'll toss aside any thought of being professional at work." His teeth grazed her ear while he pulled gently on her nipples, rolling them and tugging until she could imagine his mouth there. "Oh, I'll be perfectly staid when we're in the company of customers, but the minute they're gone or we find ourselves alone, I'll remind you that you're mine. I'll take you into the backroom and put my hands on you so I can remember how silky your skin is. I'll kiss you for long moments because I'll need it to calm down after some idiot asks me to put ice in a twenty-year-old Cabernet."

That would drive him crazy. She could suddenly see whole new ways they could help each other. "Will you find a way to calm me when the customers get obnoxious?"

"Oh, I'll think of a hundred ways. Sometimes I'll simply ask you to open your shirt so I can see your breasts. Sometimes I'll find a place so you can spread out and I can feast on your pussy until you want to scream. You won't be able to because we'll be here and there will be people listening in. I'll have to gag you so you won't give us away. I'll have to tie you up so you can't cause trouble."

Her whole body was thrumming with arousal at his words. "Break times are going to be very interesting."

One hand started to make its way down her body, inching toward her pussy. "I'll make all the times very interesting and after work, you should understand that I won't attempt to hide our relationship. Perhaps I should, but I know myself. If I'm going to try this, I'll need the other men to know that you're mine. I'll be a possessive bastard and I won't put up with flirting or cheating of any kind."

"Good, because I won't either. You should understand that while I might submit to you in the bedroom, I'm not going to put up with other women." She couldn't stand the thought, and that should scare her a little, too. She'd never been possessive before, but she wanted Sebastian in a way she'd never wanted another man.

His hand was almost there, so close to her clitoris. She was almost worried that if he slid the pad of his thumb over her, she would go off like a rocket, and she wanted this to last.

"I won't ever cheat on you. You should understand that. It's a touchy subject for me."

There were lots of touchy subjects for him. He was a mass of touchiness at times, but now all she was thinking about was how nice it was to be touched by him. "You don't have to worry about me, Master. I only want you. I've wanted you for a very long time. I won't screw it up now."

"You almost make me forget," he whispered in her ear. His hand drifted lower, close, so close.

And then he released her.

Tiffany groaned in dismay.

"Don't make that sound at me. You knew there was punishment coming. I'm not withdrawing affection, brat. I'm getting this out of the way and then we can talk about how we'll move forward."

She would be a mass of arousal by then and he expected her to talk rationally? He was a mean Master, but then she'd known he would be a tough nut to crack. And she had lied to him. It had been for the greater good, but it had been lying. She placed her hands on the desk, spreading her legs wide and leaning over so her backside was in the air. That was how he'd wanted her the first time. She wanted to learn his habits and needs and teach him her own.

It started with kink, but she would let the kink lead them so much deeper.

She felt him move away, heard his shoes across the hardwood floors. Then she heard something she hadn't expected, the slap of something against skin. She looked up because that hadn't been her flesh taking the smack. He was staring down at her, a paddle in his hand.

Oh, shit. Her heart rate pulsed up and she could feel adrenaline flooding her system. There it was, that primal voice that told her to flee. The one she would ignore because running away when she was so close to the finish line seemed like a cowardly thing to do.

Besides, the torture was part of the game.

"You don't have to be quiet during this session," he said, his voice grim.

"I'm going to try," she replied with an anxious laugh. "Because there are a bunch of people walking around out there."

"I told you I won't hide the fact that you're my submissive from the staff. Not if this is more than a cover for Milo Jaye. If this is real, there will be no hiding from the people who know us."

"Some of them aren't in the lifestyle. They might not understand." Though the Taggarts tended to be careful about who they hired, she didn't want anyone to think Sebastian was abusing her.

"I don't care," he replied. "I only care about living our particular truth. And that begins with not lying to me again."

She heard the slap before she felt the fire. Pain lashed against her skin and he proved he'd gone easy on her the first time. This was the real Dom, the one who wouldn't accept her deception, the one who would push her to be the best she could be, the one she was falling in love with.

He brought the paddle down again and again, utterly merciless in his discipline, but then she knew how to stop him if she wanted. They'd agreed on a safe word—one word she could utter that would stop all play—but she wasn't going to use it. The pain was harsh, but she could feel something building under it.

The first time she'd taken a spanking from a Dom had been playful, the second a bit more intense, the third, she'd forced herself through and found the joy at the end. It had all built to this. This was the fun of the exchange, the give and take, the driving will to see the scene through because she knew what was on the other side of every smack he gave her. Her body would flush with pain and then her skin would come alive and she would shiver with the thrill.

For now, she endured. He'd been right. She couldn't stay completely quiet. She was already crying and as he laid that paddle all over, she found herself gasping and groaning.

Finally, he laid the paddle down on the desk and put a hand on her poor backside. "How are you? Was I too rough with you?"

"You were a horrible brute, Sebastian." She could feel the tears dripping from her cheeks and the glow was settling in, that glow she felt after a long session. Like she was lit from within, like she could fly if she really wanted to.

Subspace. It was a lovely place to be. It had been something she'd held herself back from before because in this space she wanted to serve. She wanted to be vulnerable and submissive and she'd never found a man she'd trusted enough to allow herself to give in. Subspace had been deferred in exchange for protecting herself.

She wasn't going to do that with Sebastian. Despite what some of her friends thought, she really did protect herself most of the time, but when she found something she truly wanted she threw herself all in.

She was going to the deep end of the pool with this man.

He ran a hand over her. "I didn't cause welts. You should be all right tomorrow. Sore and perhaps a tiny bit bruised."

"I'll like it. I'll enjoy that feeling and I'll remember how it felt to be naked in front of you." He took her far too seriously so she let him off the hook. "I do know how you could make me feel better."

She didn't want to talk. Not at all.

"Stand up and turn around."

He was going to do it. She was going to get a lecture and that would be torture. The spanking had gotten her all hot and wet, and now her real punishment began. She forced herself to turn. She wasn't going to whine or beg even though she wanted to. She wanted to be in his arms, wanted him to cuddle her.

Instead, he unrolled a towel and covered the desktop with it. He smoothed it out carefully and placed the few items that had been there to the side. She watched with curiosity because she certainly hadn't assumed she would be sitting on the desk for this particular talk. She'd expected to get on her knees or perhaps to sit in his lap, maybe after she'd gotten dressed again.

Sebastian was way kinkier than she'd given him credit for.

"Settle yourself on the towel," he stated implacably. He'd turned around and it was good to see she wasn't the only one who was aroused. Sebastian's slacks had a nice tent to them.

She wanted to see him naked. The glimpse she'd gotten of him all those months before wasn't enough. He'd had his boxers on and all she'd gotten was a peek at his cut chest and muscular arms before he'd yelled at her and covered up.

He held out a hand to help her hop up on the desk. Such a gentleman. "Lean back and spread your legs."

And such a pervert. It seemed like Sebastian liked to inspect his subs. Luckily, she enjoyed being viewed as a work of art. It might be different if he was into criticism, but she got the feeling Sebastian would never find her less than gorgeous. It made it easy for her to do his bidding. She let her legs open, offering him a view of her pussy.

"That is what I wanted to see." His voice had gone husky, his Southern accent even deeper and slower than usual. Like honey dripping. Sweet and sultry. "You weren't lying to me about how you respond to discipline. This pussy is soaked with arousal. You enjoyed the paddle."

"I've never had a paddle before. It was more intense, but yes, I enjoyed it. Did you enjoy spanking me?" The way he was frowning made her a bit worried that he was more of a sadist than she'd dreamed. "Does it bother you that I enjoyed punishment?"

He moved between her legs, his hand brushing against her core. He touched her gently, skimming her sensitive flesh. "Not at all. You talked about the fact that you experimented with D/s. Well, all of my experience up until now has been transactional. I offered discipline and they gave me purpose. You're different. I want something different from you, Tiffany."

"What's that?" *Please let it be sex.*

"When you get on your knees for me, I want you to mean it. I want you to submit to me not because I'm some Dom."

"I'll do it because you're Sebastian. Because you're my Dom." How long had he felt so alone? It was there on his face. Somewhere under his desire, beneath the sex, he longed, too. This was what she wanted. This was how she could connect to him. "Talk to me. Tell me how we proceed with this because I want to. I want to see if we can work. I think I might need you far more than those other subs."

His jaw tightened. "All they needed me for was dominance. I don't know anything else. But by god, I can give you this."

His hand moved over her and she bit back a gasp. He knew exactly how and where to touch her. One big finger slid over her clitoris while his mouth came down on hers. Harder this time, as though he wasn't quite as in control as he'd been the first time he'd kissed her. His tongue immediately slid inside, gliding against hers in a way that had her melting beneath his kiss.

"I want you to come for me," he whispered against her lips. "I want to watch you come, feel your pussy clench around my hand, and then I'm going to shove my cock deep inside you. I want you to come because there's no way I can last. I need to see to you before I can take what you're offering me. Tell me you want my cock."

How could he even question it? Could he not feel how close to the edge she already was? "Yes. Please, Sebastian. Please give me your cock."

"Come for me first. Show me how well you can obey. I want to feel you. I want to taste you. I want to know you." His thumb moved over her clitoris, pushing down firmly as he pressed two fingers high into her pussy.

He fucked her with his fingers, his mouth claiming hers again. There was something so sexy about being naked and open to him while he was still fully dressed. He pulled back from the kiss, his fingers still moving against her, and she let her head fall back.

The orgasm came on like a wave she couldn't stop. It started deep inside her body and pulsed out. She couldn't stop the cry that came out of her throat as the pleasure overtook her.

Sebastian kept up the pressure, watching her as she rode out the orgasm. When he seemed satisfied, when her whole body was limp and it took real effort to keep herself upright, he pulled his hand away.

He brought his soaked fingers to his lips and sucked her arousal into his mouth.

She was exhausted. She was so ready to feel that man move inside her. She watched, waiting for the moment when he tossed off his own clothes and she was skin to skin with him. Finally.

He reached into his pocket and came back with a condom. Before she knew it, he was unzipping those perfectly pressed slacks of his. "Touch me."

She could do that. It felt like she'd been waiting years to touch him. She forced herself to sit up and reached out for his cock. It was a thing of beauty, long and thick with a plump purple head. She gripped him, stroking him up and down, satisfied when he groaned.

He leaned over, lowering his head to hers. "Damn, you feel good. No more. I can't take it. I need to be inside you."

He pulled her hand away and tugged the condom over his erection. She reached up, wanting to get his shirt off, but he moved quickly. He spread her legs and pulled on her hips, forcing her to lean back in order to stay balanced. She could feel the hard press of his cock, but she was so wet he eased inside her.

He gripped her hips, but she could do nothing but cling to him. He thrust in and out, gaining ground by the inch. He filled her and she found her legs wrapping around his waist as she watched him. His face had tightened, his whole body taut and ready. He pumped deep inside her, angling her hips up so he could thrust in as far as she would hold him.

For the second time, she couldn't hold back. He ground his pelvis against her, hitting her clitoris again and again as his cock found her sweet spot. He thrust over it and she went blissfully over the edge once more.

Sebastian's thrusts lost their rhythm as he fucked her hard. His whole body tightened and he pressed inside one last time.

She couldn't hold herself up a second longer. She let her body sag down, reveling in the pure pleasure that was still pounding through her. It had given way from the primal rhythm to a languid peace.

Sebastian stared down at her, his hand coming out to touch her chest. "It's time to get cleaned up. I have to accept an order from a winery in thirty minutes. Do you have a class?"

He turned away, pulling the condom from his cock and neatly tying it up.

She wished he'd held her, but she had to take a deep breath. Baby steps. She hadn't expected him to be so passionate. "No. I'm free the rest of the day, but I was going to stay and find a place to help."

"You can help me." He cleared his throat as though trying to find his decorum again. "If you don't have something to do, I would prefer you spend your time with me. Though we're going to have to get you dressed again. I know I said I wouldn't hide our relationship from our coworkers, but I likely will hide your body unless we're in a club."

His words were oh so reasonable, but she could hear the

possessiveness behind them. It was a good first step.

He helped her up and his head came down, lightly kissing her on the forehead. After the passion from before, it felt like the sweetest gesture. "Get dressed, sweetheart. I'll clean up here. Don't forget we have to meet Jaye and his submissives at the club tonight. We'll finish up here early, have dinner, and then get ready to go into Dallas."

Where they would no longer have to pretend to be lovers. They were and they'd done it in a very Sebastian fashion. He'd made the decision and there would be no wondering about her status with him. He wouldn't ghost on her and she wouldn't sit around wondering if that one time was all she would get. He'd made a commitment to her to give this thing a try.

She started to do her Master's bidding, but she was already planning.

It was a nice start, but next time she was getting his pants off.

CHAPTER EIGHT

Sebastian shifted, his right leg aching in a way that let him know things were about to get bad.

He ignored it. Tiffany was going to spend the day out with Deena tomorrow and he could try to properly look after himself once she was out of the apartment.

"So that guy has two subs? Like me?" Jaye stared out over the dungeon floor, his eyes wide with curiosity.

Jaye looked oddly uncomfortable in his leathers, as though they were slightly too big even though they'd been custom fitted for him.

It was obvious that while Jaye might not have studied the materials Sebastian had given him as well as he should have, he'd gotten up to speed on club gossip. Mostly. "Not exactly. That's Jake Dean. He's got one sub whom he shares with his partner. You know his partner. He's the one you're shaking down in order to gain access here."

Jaye frowned. "It's not a shakedown. It's business and you know it actually wasn't my idea. It was Gina's, so you should really stop making me out to be the villain here. Do you think he's going to punch me?"

Sebastian studied Milo Jaye for a moment. He was an odd duck, as his father would have said. Jaye was perfectly competent when they talked about his business. Sebastian had gone to Jaye's office for a session and found the man to be comfortably alpha when it came to talking about his work. The minute he talked about anything else, he got that swaggering confidence that told Sebastian he was overcompensating. And it was very intriguing to discover that he hadn't been the one to come up with the plan that had Big Tag pissed off.

"As long as you hold up your end of the bargain, I wouldn't expect Jake to bother you," Sebastian replied, wondering how Tiffany was doing with the submissives.

They were still in the locker room. He wanted her out here with him. God, he was an idiot. She'd been away from him for thirty minutes and he was annoyed that she wasn't at his side. He really was on thin ice with this woman.

One week into their relationship, a few hours into their sexual relationship, and he was already worried about losing her.

That brought him right back to the pain in his damn leg. He'd lost his balance in the shower two days before and his right stump had a good-sized scratch on it. Nothing that would need stitches, but enough to irritate him. Enough that he should have asked for help with cleaning and bandaging.

He wasn't going to force her to be his nursemaid. He was going to be her Dom and she wouldn't ever have to see him in a lesser light.

He wasn't going to make the same mistakes with her that he'd made with Alicia.

"When Tiffany brings your subs out, we'll take a tour of the dungeon and then watch a few scenes."

Jaye nodded. "That sounds good. But it's only Gina tonight. Honey had other plans."

"You know I can't clear her for the dungeon unless she's been trained." He was a bit worried that the whole thing would fall apart because Honey wasn't as invested in the lifestyle as Gina was. Gina, who seemed to be running the entire show. Honestly, Sebastian wasn't certain Milo was invested in the same way Gina was, and that could be a problem.

"To tell you the truth, I'm kind of hoping she decides she doesn't want to play," Milo confided. "It's funny, but Gina and I brought in

Honey because we thought we needed something to spark our sex lives, you know. G and I have been together since we were kids."

"But you're not married." Wasn't that what kids did? They fell in love and thought they could make it through anything together. It's what he'd done. Oh, he'd been proven so very wrong, but he'd believed in that ring he'd given Alicia.

Seeing Tiffany wearing a collar she'd picked out for herself hadn't sat well with him.

He'd allowed her to select her own collar in the beginning because it hadn't meant anything. Now he wanted her wearing something he'd bought for her, selected for her. Something that really meant she was his.

"We never got around to it," Milo was saying. "We started up the business and then things went crazy. We woke up one day and we'd been together for years, but something was missing. We met Honey and Gina suggested we try something new. You know the sex was pretty nice for a while but now I…well, let's say maybe that dude has the right idea. Maybe having a partner is better than trying to please two women."

"Especially when you obviously don't love one of them."

"She's all right, but sometimes I wish it was just me and G again." He stared out over the dungeon. "I worry that if this doesn't work, she's going to leave me. God, I hope she takes Honey with her. Maybe I could deal with it if I was alone, but if she leaves Honey and takes the dogs, I'll be really upset."

It was sad to know that even a billion dollars didn't guarantee happiness.

"Is this really what you want to do?" Sebastian felt something he hadn't in a very long time. Sympathy. It welled up inside him, reminding him that he used to be the guy everyone turned to. "I don't know how this works if you don't truly feel the need to dominate her."

Milo was silent for a moment. "I want to try. I won't know if I never try, right? I don't have a problem with it. Whatever floats your boat, you know." He stood up a little taller. "I will make this work.

She's worth it. She's…hell, I can't imagine life without her so I will make this work."

He had to give it to the man. At least he knew what he wanted. "Good. I think making the decision is an important part of the process."

He'd made the decision to try with Tiffany. Why her? That was what he hadn't quite figured out yet. Yes, he wanted her. After having her, he wanted her even more. Lust was something he thought he'd outgrown, but she had proven him wrong.

She was sweet and kind and chaotic. She was a brat who challenged him. She'd been saucy and mouthed off this afternoon while they'd been working on the restaurant's new wine cellar. And it had given him the perfect opportunity to prove that he meant what he'd said. He'd put her pretty nipples in clamps right then and there. He hadn't actually had clamps, but he'd made do with clothespins he'd found. She'd done the rest of her work wincing and squirming.

And when her punishment had been done, he'd gotten his mouth on her, easing the clamps off and soothing her tortured nipples with his mouth.

Where was she? The lust he could handle. This yearning was something he wasn't entirely comfortable with.

"How did you meet your sub?" Milo asked.

"We work together at a restaurant the Taggart brothers own." At least he didn't have to lie about that.

"And when did you realize you were interested in the lifestyle? Tell me it wasn't when you read that book. Gina got all hot and bothered when she read that *Fifty Shades* book," he said with a shake of his head.

"No, that isn't how I got involved." He stared out over the floor and wished Big Tag had found someone else to be the baby Dom mentor. He didn't mind dungeon duty, didn't mind dealing with ensuring Doms knew how to use the equipment or teaching classes on proper technique. This was something different. This was more personal and it made him anxious. "After I left my military service and decided to become a sommelier, I worked at a club in London while I studied for my certification. I got involved there."

"You had a mentor? Did you ever feel like a complete dope around him?"

Damon Knight had been his mentor. Damon Knight might have saved his life.

You can stay in that wheelchair feeling sorry for yourself or you can stand on your own. You can be meaningful to someone who needs you. It's your choice, Sebastian, but don't think for a second that you're the first or the last of us who had to make this choice. I might not have lost my legs, but I lost my unit. Every one of them. I know where you are and I know how hard this is going to be, but you are not alone unless you choose to be.

"Yes, I did have a mentor, and yes, he made me feel like I was clumsy and awkward," Sebastian said. "He was a very elegant British man. He didn't mean to make me feel small. I did that to myself."

"So you felt small and that made you want to dominate a woman?" Jaye asked.

How to make him understand? When he'd taken this damn assignment, he'd thought he would show the man the ropes and then release him into the wild. Milo Jaye was more complex than a man who wanted to spank his girl. He was confused and searching for something. He needed knowledge. "It's not about physical domination. Not from my viewpoint. It's about need, I suppose. I needed to find a place in the world. I had been so very out of control and I found a way to take it again."

"By spanking chicks."

It made him chuckle. It kind of felt good to laugh. "No, although I admit, I do enjoy that. What I meant was I retook control of my life by helping other people. Domination doesn't have to be sexual. The power exchange is about two people serving each other's needs. I topped in a professional capacity while I was in England. I had clients who required what I like to call extreme accountability. They were people who were looking for discipline in their lives, but needed oversight."

Jaye leaned over, obviously interested in the conversation. He'd dropped all his swagger. "Explain how that would work."

"Say I have a client who's a writer. She's smart and very good at her job, but loses focus because she's a social media junkie. We would write a contract and she would prove to me she got her word count done before she jumped on the Internet. If she did not, there would be strict punishments. Very often just the fact that a client is accountable makes them more disciplined. There were other clients who simply needed a way to relax. Some people would exercise or meditate. My clients found their relaxation through submission."

Milo seemed to get very serious. "I thought it was all about sex. I did read some of what you gave me. It talked about how some people enjoy the sensation of pain."

"Properly administered pain, but it's different for everyone. For some people they accept the pain as a way to release their emotions." Tiffany had cried, but it hadn't been that horrible wail he'd heard when a submissive finally let loose after too much build up. Tiffany had cried because she hurt and then she'd grinned with almost pride. That was the moment he'd known what kind of sub she was. Nothing like what he'd dealt with before. She enjoyed the challenge, loved the pleasure she got, and yet she was still her happy, vibrant self even in the midst.

She was so bright, and he was a stupid moth to her flame.

"What am I supposed to get out of it? What do you get out of it?"

Pure pleasure. Emotion. Feeling for the first time in years. A vision of Tiffany smiling up at him slammed across his brain. "I get to feel like someone needs me for something more than helping them choose a glass of wine. I get to feel important for a few moments in the day."

He got to briefly feel whole again.

Milo shook his head. "I don't think that's my problem, man, but damn. I now totally get it. I should join this place for the scenery. G, you look gorgeous."

Gina was walking up the stairs wearing some fet wear. He was sure she looked lovely, but it wasn't like he could really see her. Tiffany was all he could see. This was why he'd stayed away from her. He'd avoided her when they were in the dungeon, telling himself that they worked together. Such a hypocrite and such a coward.

She was stunning in a strip of a skirt and a tiny crop top that showed off the fact that she wasn't wearing a bra. As he'd requested. She was wearing thigh-high fishnet stockings that showed off her long legs, made longer by the fuck-me heels that finished the outfit perfectly. Her hair was piled on top of her head, blonde ringlets framing her pretty face. The only real makeup he could tell she was wearing was ruby-red lipstick that made her mouth look like perfect sin.

And she was all his for now.

Tiffany winked Gina's way and both women fell to their knees. Tiffany was graceful, her body finding the position with ease. Gina kind of crashed down and cursed, shoving her hair out of her eyes.

"Typically, Doms prefer the greeting without the cuss words," Tiffany said with a smile that seemed to put the other woman at ease.

"I'll try to remember that," Gina replied.

"Head down. Palms up," Tiffany instructed. "Though you should talk to your Dom about what sort of greeting he would prefer. Nothing is hard and fast. You should practice in the way that suits you both the best."

"I thought this was all about suiting me. I'm the Dom, right?" Milo had that swagger back.

His boss was so going to owe him for not smacking the moron. "I thought you said you read the material. If you had, you would have seen that the brand of D/s I teach is as much about what the submissive needs as the Dominant. In some ways more, since the sub is truly in control."

Tiffany's head came up, her eyes sparkling with humor.

"Wait a minute. What's the point in being the damn Dom if I'm not in control?" Milo asked.

Sebastian held a hand out to his sub. "I think we're going to have to start with some conversation."

Tiffany gracefully rose and took her place at his side. "I think that might be a very good plan, Master. Should I get us all something to drink?"

"I'll take a beer," Milo said.

Gina frowned as he helped her stand. "No, you won't. Did you not read any of the rules? We can't play if you have a beer…"

They began to argue and Sebastian sighed. How had crazy, chaotic, gorgeous Tiffany become the calm in the storm of his life? Yet there she was and all he wished was that they were back in their apartment, getting ready to settle in for the evening. She would put her head in his lap and read and the world would seem peaceful.

He was either getting old or far too attached.

"Some tea would be nice," he told her because they needed no liquor to confuse his charge's brain. Jaye was confused enough as it was. Sebastian was beginning to believe the man might not be right for this kind of lifestyle.

"I'll have the lounge prepare a table for us," she said, going up on her toes to kiss his cheek. "And perhaps a talk with Master Kai could straighten out things for our guest. I saw him a little earlier. You know how he loves to talk philosophy. Perhaps I'll find him and we could let him counsel Milo and Gina while we watch some of the scenes."

She was smart, too. So fucking smart. That did something for him. Kai could talk for hours. And honestly, it would be good to get his take on the couple. Kai Ferguson was the resident psychologist. Normally the couple wouldn't even be here without Kai's approval. They were circumventing the normal process or they already would have gotten to know the doc.

"I think that is a brilliant idea." And then he could have some time with her. Time in the world they both enjoyed.

He watched as she walked away. Milo and Gina were still arguing, but he had to wonder if things weren't finally turning around for him.

He winced as he started for the table. It fit that just as he found a woman he was crazy about, his damn legs would go bad. He had to suck it up. It would clear up in a day or two and it wasn't like he couldn't take a little pain.

She was worth it.

* * * *

Tiffany sipped her tea and silently cursed her too-good-to-be-true ideas.

She'd hoped to be able to slip away with Sebastian while Kai worked his magic. Instead, Kai had decided it was a good time to hold a Dom conference or something. Kai's wife, Kori, had decided to show Gina around while Tiffany waited close by in case Sebastian needed to demonstrate any of the techniques they were talking about.

"They look so peaceful."

At least she wasn't alone. Deena had shown up and Eric had joined the big bad Doms at their table across the lounge. Milo looked out of place surrounded by massive men in leather. She turned to figure out what Deena was talking about because those Doms didn't look peaceful. If she had to put a word to it, she would say they looked perplexed.

Oh, but those two did look peaceful.

Ian and Charlotte Taggart were all dressed up for play. Big Tag was in his leathers, worn motorcycle boots on his feet, while Charlotte was in a micro-mini and a corset that tucked in her waist. Yep, those two would have been a force on the dungeon floor if they hadn't fallen asleep on the couch. They hadn't even pretended apparently. They were spooning, Big Tag curled around his wife's body.

"I'm never having kids," Deena swore.

Somehow she didn't think they were seeing the same thing. Deena was seeing two people who had three kids under the age of four and how tired they were. Tiffany was seeing a team. Big Tag and Charlotte were building a future and they were in it together. Awake. Asleep. Even when they were too tired, they'd gotten out and tried to play, and when that hadn't worked, they held onto each other and found some peace.

"Have you and Eric talked about it at all? Kids, I mean."

"We're too busy with the restaurant right now." Deena glanced over to the Dom table, smiling as she took in her husband. "But seriously, someday we'll start a family. But a small one. I don't want a baseball team or anything. One or two might be cool. But for now we're all about our restaurant baby. Eric eats, breathes, and sleeps Top. I mean it about the sleep. He was talking in his sleep last night, arguing with himself about whether or not he should go with the Chilean sea bass or his blackened trout for the soft open. It's all he talks about. Menus and gossip. Everyone's so interested in whatever is happening between you and the bionic man."

Tiffany felt her eyes narrow. "You can't call him that. You know he's sensitive. Even Doms have their sensitivities."

"Hey, you're the one who came up with the nickname." Deena leaned in. "Did you really get busy in the office today? Eric said he played cupid for you this afternoon and you should thank him. A lot, if those screams were what I think they were."

She wasn't a woman who embarrassed easily. "I had a very nice time but Eric is a rat fink who told on us, and I got a really nasty spanking out of it. My backside still hurts."

"Oh, my god," a new voice said. Ally Miles lowered herself down to the pillow beside Tiffany. "You finally got it on with the som. He's the Som Dom. I came up with that."

"It's horrible," her husband, Macon, said. He was dressed for play, his big chest covered in an open leather vest he would likely shed at some point in time. Macon Miles was a stunning man. He was also Top's pastry chef. Ally was a server at the Dallas restaurant, Tiffany's closest friend there since Deena had left the front of house for Top's business offices.

Macon pulled up a chair and eased into it. Like Sebastian, he'd served his country and sacrificed a part of himself. Macon had a prosthetic leg, but unlike Sebastian, he didn't hide it. Tonight he was wearing long pants, but Macon seemed to prefer athletic shorts when he wasn't in his chef whites.

Deena frowned up at him. "You know the Dom table is over there."

Macon frowned. "I will have a long discussion with Eric about your tone later. And there's zero chance I'm getting stuck in that. I try to stay out of Big Tag's machinations. And Kai's got his lecture face on. Nope. I'll stay here and listen to you lovely ladies talk about Tiffany's newfound sex life."

"It's not newfound." Exactly.

Ally shook her head. "Oh, so you've had a bunch of lovers and not mentioned them at all? Face it, girl, it's been a long time for you and that man is the reason. So I'm very happy to know that he finally manned up and took responsibility."

"How is Sebastian responsible for Tiffany's dry spell?" Macon asked.

"She's been crazy about him since the night of Kyle Hawthorne's going-away party," Deena supplied helpfully. "She got super drunk and he took her home and she's been crazy about him ever since. She went all through training class without any nookie. A couple of the Doms have been hitting on her, but she's only got eyes for Sebastian."

She should have switched to wine the minute she realized she wouldn't be playing with Sebastian tonight. "You know I didn't gossip about you when you were dating Eric."

Ally's jaw dropped open. "Are you trying to bring lightning down on us?"

"That wasn't gossip. That was friends talking about other friends. Because we care." That needed to be made very clear.

Ally shrugged. "All right. Since you're all gossip-free now, you totally won't want to learn everything Macon knows about Sebastian."

What? That perked her right up. Sebastian was a tightwad when it came to talking about himself. He would talk about wine and food and art all night long. He would listen to her. But he rarely ever talked about himself. She'd learned about his past in tiny snippets he let slip from time to time. She knew he'd worked for a while in London. Knew he'd gone into the Army during his twenties and had been discharged after his accident. She knew so little else.

She was hungry to know more about him. It wasn't gossip. Not really.

Macon held his hands up. "Oh, that goes against a whole bunch of codes. Seriously, there's a Dom Code. That sleeping giant over there made me sign it."

"But you're the Pie Maker," Tiffany pointed out. Macon could do no wrong in Ian Taggart's world because he was the one who made the sweets Big Tag never seemed to get sick of. Everyone knew if Big Tag was in a bad mood, you handed him one of Macon's pies and the world changed.

"I'm also a guy who likes Sebastian." Macon frowned.

"It's okay," Ally replied with a ready smile. "He totally talked to me. I didn't sign Tag's code, so I can tell you everything."

"Allyson!" Macon bit out her name.

"Do you honestly think they'll be able to do this on their own?" Ally's eyes got big and wide as she looked up at her husband. "Where would we be if Chef and Grace hadn't meddled in our relationship?"

Deena looked up at Macon, too. Her lip actually trembled a bit. "I don't know where Eric and I would be without well-meaning meddling. Probably alone. Without love or friends. Sad. I know I thank the day my friends meddled in my relationship."

God, they were good.

Macon shook his head. "Fine. You can ask me a couple of questions, but don't expect me to give any advice. I'm bad at that. I take my cues from Big Tag and never get involved in other dudes' relationships."

That was not how she'd heard it. She'd heard Big Tag was a terrible gossip and often played fairy godmother, but she wasn't going to be the one to point that out. Besides, she did have questions. "Do you have any idea why he's so touchy about his legs? Don't get me wrong. I can imagine that it's hard to lose a piece of yourself, but he's so secretive about them. He's not like you. You don't hide it. You let yourself be comfortable."

"It's because I'm a sexy beast," Macon replied with a ready smile. "I'm joking, but I'm kind of not. In the beginning, I didn't want anyone to look at me. *I* didn't want to look at me. I wore pants that covered me for a long time. I didn't want to use crutches around people because I thought it made me look weak."

"What changed?" She kind of thought she knew the answer, but she wanted to hear it from him.

His hand came out, touching Ally's head. "She did want to look at me. She did want to touch me. And when I finally let her, I realized how much I was missing. It sounds like you and Sebastian are already moving in that direction. I'm glad to hear that. You should know he's a good man."

She already knew how good he was. "Do you know how he lost them? Weren't you in the hospital together?"

He nodded. "We were initially in a hospital in Germany. We weren't injured together. We were in two separate accidents, but we were in similar shape. He'd been there for a few days when I showed up. Ramstein was where we did the beginning stages of recovery before they shipped us home. We shared a room for a few weeks. He was in a chopper accident. He was lucky to live, but I know that at the time it doesn't feel that way. Like me, he lost some friends. I think he lost a very close friend from how he would talk when he was drugged up. He would call out for a man named Gary. I know he also talked about a woman named Alicia, but when I asked about her a few months back he would only tell me she was a woman from his hometown."

Alicia. "He says he doesn't speak to anyone there now. Is that why he went to London?"

"We both had a shit time when we got home. I came here to be around Adam, but right around that time, Sebastian called me and asked if he could stay. He came for a week, met with Ian, and they decided to send him to London. Back then he was in a wheelchair."

"He couldn't walk?" How hard would that have been for a man like Sebastian? To be stuck in a chair.

"His injury was more extensive than mine. Losing both limbs is exponentially harder. There was a doctor in London who specialized in getting double amputees back on their feet, so to speak. He looked so good when he got back to the States, but honestly, I'm still worried about him. Less over the last few weeks. It's good to see him warm up."

He was quite warm. He simply needed to remember that it was okay to care about people. "Do you have any idea why he stopped talking to his mother? I know they didn't talk for months before she died."

"There was some kind of big fight after he got home," Macon explained. "I'm not sure what it was about. His father passed while Sebastian was in the hospital. Maybe his mom was too emotional to deal with it all. I'm not sure. He won't talk about it, but I know he hasn't been home in years. He hasn't talked to his sister in forever. I don't think he plans to."

"He has a sister?" How much did she really know about Sebastian? How much would he tell her?

Macon nodded. "A younger one. Her name was Ramona. I know he was very excited to see her when she came to travel back with him. They looked like they were close. She held his hand and took care of him. I don't know what happened when they got back home."

She looked over at her Dom. Even among the group, his chair was pushed back slightly as though he constantly needed to put some distance between him and everyone around him. Even here he seemed a bit alone.

Had he pushed his family away? Had he been so worried about being a burden that he shoved them all away?

Would he even let her help him?

"I'm worried he's not going to let me in," she said quietly.

Macon shook his head. "You're already in more than I would have thought possible. He's living with you. He's letting you see a side of him no one else does. He might not be asking for help yet, but I think that might come naturally now that he's let down his guard."

"Let down his guard?"

"Well, we think the reason he so rarely invited anyone over to his place was that he didn't want anyone to see his legs or to see him using his chair," Ally explained. "Like Macon used to be all freaked out about using crutches, but obviously he has to. He's got to take a shower. Though mostly he lets me take care of him there now."

"That's because you know exactly how to make sure I'm thoroughly clean, baby." He winked down at his wife before looking back to Tiffany. "But seriously, he's got to give his legs time to breathe, give them a break. He's got to have a hard time in the shower. Honestly, I have no idea how he deals with all that on his own. I mean he's adapted and everything, but having a partner to help him has to make his life easier."

A hollow feeling opened in the center of her chest. "I don't help him with anything. Nothing like that."

Deena put a hand on her arm. "It's okay. The relationship is brand new. The fact that he let you see him at all is a big step in the right direction."

"Are you telling me he hasn't used his chair the entire time you two have been in that apartment?" Macon asked.

She wished she'd never started down this road. "I'm saying that he hasn't let me see anything at all and no, as far as I can tell he's not using his chair. I don't know that he has one in the apartment. Is he putting himself through pain so I won't see him like that?"

Had she done that to him?

"It sounds like he's being a stubborn bastard," Macon replied. "But as long as he's healthy I wouldn't try to argue with him. He's an adult and treating him like a child who needs tending will only alienate him further. I should know. Just let the relationship take a natural flow. He'll come around when he realizes you won't run at the sight of his legs. I think someone did and it's stuck with him."

Tiffany watched as Kori walked back over with Gina at her side.

Gina immediately frowned as she looked over at the Doms. "I should go join them. Milo doesn't like to be overwhelmed."

"Or you should join them because you belong there." Tiffany had watched the woman all night. Sometimes people tried to shove themselves into places they didn't fit, places and roles that didn't suit them. They did it for a lot of different reasons. Because society saw them in that place. Because it took bravery to change a relationship even for the better. Because it was easier to stay in one place.

"What does that mean?" Gina asked, her tone proving Tiffany's point.

Kori's lips turned up in a knowing smile. "Yeah, I was going to suggest that, too. I thought I'd go find Vince and Chris and maybe turn some of this over to them."

Thank god she wasn't the only one to figure it out. She turned to Gina, who needed to start making some of these decisions. "Do you think Milo would be more comfortable around male submissives?"

Gina's jaw dropped a bit and she took her time, the answer slowly dawning. "Holy shit. I'm the Domme. He's the sub."

Tiffany couldn't help but smile at her. "I'm sure he's the boss at work, but I would put money on the fact that you run everything personal. You're likely the one who keeps the relationship going. You're the one who forces him to relax. You're the one who makes the decisions about sex, aren't you?"

"I thought he was losing interest." She didn't take her eyes off Milo. "We've been together for so long."

Tiffany stood and walked to the woman who in a few weeks she would be showing deference to when they were in the dungeon. "I would bet you initiated sex with him the first time."

"Almost all the times," Gina admitted.

"Does that bother you?" Kori asked.

Gina waved it off. "Not until I watch some movie that points out how wrong it is. I'm not supposed to be the aggressive one."

Thank god for Sanctum. "They're wrong. You get to be whoever you are here. When you accept who you are here, you'll find it easier to be honest in real life. You've been looking for a way to fix something that feels broken, right?"

Gina's cheeks turned a nice shade of pink. "I love him, but lately I feel like I'm not giving him what he needs."

Spoken like a Domme. "Is that why you brought in Honey? You

119

thought you could spice things up by showing him how kinky you can be?"

Her eyes were on Milo as she spoke, softening with obvious affection. "Yes. Now that I think about it, I can see the real times he got hot were when I ordered Honey around. I'm so getting rid of her."

"I think you should do what's best for your relationship with Milo," Kori said. "And I would very much like to introduce you to a couple friends of mine. Mistresses Jackie and Althea would be excellent at helping you to find where you belong."

Kai had stood up, ushering Milo over. Sebastian walked beside them. There was a tightness to his jaw that made her worry, but the minute he saw her, he seemed to shove aside whatever was bothering him. His hand came out and she found herself rushing to get to his side.

"Darlin', I think we have a problem," he said, his voice low.

"Oh, we've figured it out." She tucked herself under his arm, hoping he would simply see it as a sign of affection. It was, but it was also an offer of strength. If he was tired, she would like to help him. But she had to be sneaky about it.

Kai put a hand on Milo's shoulder and grinned at his wife. "Want to switch, baby?"

"I think that's an excellent idea," Kori said.

Milo was frowning. "Now, wait a minute. I don't know how this works. I know I said some things back there, but I'm not one of the women. Not that there's anything wrong with it, but I'm a man."

Gina stepped up, putting her hands on her lover's face and instantly calming him. "Do you like it when I take control?"

His eyes dropped, but he managed to answer. "Yes."

"Does that make me less of a woman?" Gina asked.

Now his eyes came up, meeting hers. "Absolutely not. You're the best woman I know. You're mine. I don't want anyone else."

"Good, because Honey is gone when we get home, and I'm taking control when you're not at work. I'll be in charge and you'll look to me to see to your comfort and your pleasure. Can you do that for me, Milo?" Gina asked.

His lips tugged up and his shoulders seemed to relax. "I think I can, G. I mean, Mistress. I like that."

Tiffany's heart threatened to melt.

Sebastian looked down at her before his hand came up, brushing away a tear. "Softie."

She was. She cried at things like sentimental commercials and romance novels, and she definitely cried when true love found a way.

Kori held out a hand to Milo. "Come on. I'm going to introduce you to Vince and Chris. They're a few of the male submissives who play here at Sanctum. I think Harrison is running around somewhere, too. You'll find you have a lot in common with them. They're all high achievers who find relaxation in submitting to their Mistresses or Masters."

"And I'll introduce Gina to some of our Dommes," Kai said. "I think it would be best if we bring you both in for some light counseling. Not like therapy sessions, but just to help you adjust to the situation. I think you'll find when you consider it, you've actually been in these roles for a very long time."

"Well, if we'd come here first we would have avoided Honey," Milo said.

"I thought you were into her," Gina shot back.

Milo shook his head. "Only you. Only ever you, baby. Since we were dumbass kids playing around with code, it's only ever been you."

Gina leaned over, kissing her boyfriend/new submissive. "Only you."

God, she wanted that. Was she fooling herself into believing that she was the woman for Sebastian?

"Could you please tell Mr. Miles that his patent is safe from me?" Milo said, looking more comfortable than she'd ever seen. "I'll instruct my lawyers to withdraw our claim on Monday morning. And if Mr. Miles has any further trouble, let him know I'll help him in any way I can."

Sebastian nodded. "I will happily let him know. And Milo, Mistress Gina, welcome to Sanctum."

The group broke up, Kori and Kai taking over for them.

Gina and Milo no longer needed them.

They'd fulfilled their promise to Ian Taggart and there was zero reason for them to keep up the pretense.

"Did you figure out he was a sub?" a sleepy voice asked.

Ian Taggart yawned like a tired lion, his arm tightening around his wife as he made no move to get up off the couch.

"You might have mentioned that," Sebastian replied.

"And take all the fun out of it?" Big Tag let his eyes drift closed again.

"Well, it certainly could have shortened the job," Sebastian shot back.

"More than one job to be done, Lowe," he said cryptically. "I suppose you'll want to move out now, Tiffany. It's okay. Sean and I have a backup plan. Javier can move in with Lowe and Tiffany can have the single. It should be fun for you, Lowe. I hear Javi brings a new woman home with him every night."

Sebastian's arm tightened around her shoulders. "I think I'm fine with the living arrangements. Tiffany and I are doing quite well. What do you say, sweetheart?"

He looked down at her, his jaw tight again as though he was worried about her answer. She gave him what she hoped was a brilliant smile.

"I'm perfectly happy with the living arrangements, Master." She breathed an inward sigh of relief. They still had some time. They had weeks until the soft open.

She had weeks to figure out how to open him up, how to get him to see she could be a partner for him.

"Then my job here is done," Big Tag said.

Charlotte's hand came up, gently hitting her husband in the chest. "Don't call the police. I can handle it. Get me a nail gun."

Big Tag's lips curled up. "She talks in her sleep. She says the sweetest things. Here's your nail gun, baby. Take him out."

"Fucker thinks he can come into my house." Charlotte snuggled closer to her husband.

They had an interesting relationship.

"You want to play or are you ready to head home?" Sebastian asked.

She was suddenly more than ready to be alone with him. "Home." She so loved the sound of that.

CHAPTER NINE

Sebastian slid the key out and opened the door, surprised at how happy he was to be back here. This apartment had rapidly become more comfortable than his own home, perhaps because of Grace Taggart's feminine touch with decorating, or more likely because of the way Tiffany looked curled up on the couch.

He'd almost lost her. "Losing her" might be hyperbolic, but they were the first words that had gone through his mind when he'd realized there was no more reason for them to stay together.

Except that they wanted to.

"Would you like a glass of wine, Sebastian? I think we still have the Pinot Noir from last night," she said as she breezed through. "If you're hungry, I could make you a sandwich."

He was hungry. So fucking hungry. "I would prefer it if you would remove your clothing and lie on your bed and wait for me. I'll join you in a moment."

Her eyes widened. "You don't want to talk about what happened tonight?"

He wasn't sure why they would need to talk about it, but she did have needs he didn't quite understand. "If you want to discuss the fact that we didn't immediately recognize the problem with Milo and Gina, we certainly can do that, but you can't be upset with yourself. It wasn't until I sat down with the man and truly started talking to him that I realized it. Seeing him among my peers pointed out certain aspects of his personality that were incompatible with having a sexually Dominant nature."

"I wasn't talking about that," she admitted. "I was talking about the fact that Master Ian did know we weren't the right teachers for them and he still put us in an awkward position. Then he said something about having more than one problem to solve. I think he was talking about us."

Only because Master Ian was a horrible meddler when it came to the people around him. "Yes, I suspect he was attempting to play matchmaker. And it worked. Now go and get naked so I can enjoy the fruits of his plotting."

"You're not angry?"

"Well, I'm getting annoyed because I didn't get a chance to play with my sub tonight and now it seems like she wants to psychoanalyze me when all I really want to do is get my mouth on her pussy." That was about as baldly as he could put it, but sometimes she needed that ruthless honesty. It wasn't anything he ever would have said to her before they'd started a sexual relationship, but she should get used to him using dirty talk around her.

God knew he thought about her all the time. The dirty talk wasn't what bothered him. The other thoughts that ran through his head did.

The thought that he could keep her, that he might be able to love this woman. Those were the thoughts that disturbed him.

But he was shoving that all aside for the moment because he wasn't ready to let her go. He would in the end because it was the kindest thing to do. She deserved someone who could love her with his whole heart, who didn't see the world through the filter of betrayal and loss. She was a bright light. He wasn't going to be the one who took that from her. But maybe for a little while, he could bask in her warmth, saving it up for the cold nights to come.

"I thought you would be mad at Big Tag for manipulating you."

"Are you mad at him?" He hadn't thought of that. "Because it sort of played into your own manipulations."

"But my manipulations were all about getting you into bed and they worked. I also got spanked for them, might I point out."

He wept for her poor bottom. Little masochist. "I wasn't about to spank Big Tag. I don't think he would sit still for that. And I could do worse, Tiffany. I could tie you up and play with your little pussy until you're begging for me, and then I would untie you and go to bed."

That would actually be punishment for him, and he hadn't done anything wrong.

"I'll be good, Master." She stopped. "Should I go back to calling you Sir?"

He'd thought about it on the long car ride back from Sanctum. "Our contract states that you should call me Master. That contract is good through the opening of the restaurant. Let's honor that time period."

"And when it's done?"

He would very likely have to let her go. Or would he? It would be easier when they weren't living together. There was no reason at all they couldn't continue a D/s relationship. He would have to think about it. "We'll renegotiate if we want to, but for now you can either obey my instructions or use your safe word."

That answer seemed to satisfy her. She pulled her shirt over her head. Her breasts came into view. She hadn't put on a bra in the locker room. From what he could tell, she never wore one unless she was working the dining room. Like he'd asked.

She seemed ready to please him. He wasn't foolish enough to expect that would work long term if he didn't bend for her.

How much could he give her? How much could he take? He knew if he asked for too much, she would run and she would be right to. No one needed to take on a burden. No one.

"Did I mention how beautiful you were in fet wear?" He liked watching her undress. Damn but she was doing it for him, at his command. He would get his play in. He would take her every day between now and when their contract was up. He would revel in her.

"I'm glad you think so, Master."

Every time that word came out of her mouth, he could swear his cock responded. "You're even more beautiful naked. Are you going to do as I asked?"

She shimmied out of her skirt and sure enough, she was an obedient girl. She wasn't wearing any underwear. Her golden form was on display for him. "Are you asking me if I want you to eat my pussy? Because the answer is yes. The answer is I've been waiting forever for you to get that gorgeous mouth of yours on my pussy. And have I mentioned how sexy you were in your leathers? The only thing sexier than that hot bod in a set of leathers is your sensual, ridiculously hot mouth talking sex and sin my way."

She turned on her heels and started walking back toward her bedroom.

She was going to kill him.

The way he'd felt about Alicia had been a youthful thing. It had been about hope for the future, dreams for a family. A young man's love.

What he felt for Tiffany was completely different. It was primal and there was an edge of caveman to it.

He was a gentleman. He'd been raised to be a gentleman and to treat the women in his life in a certain way. He would never, ever have spoken to Alicia the way he talked to Tiffany. If he'd told Alicia he wanted to tie her up, she would have smacked the shit out of him and shuddered in lady-like horror.

Why did that make her a lady? He'd watched two people give over to their instincts tonight, watched them turn from societal norms to something that worked for them.

Why couldn't he have that, too?

Tiffany wasn't any less a lady than Alicia. She might be more because she didn't question her own needs or judge others. She tossed off her clothes, knowing damn well how lovely she was, and she offered all of her loveliness up to the world. She was kind to the people around her.

He shrugged out of his jacket. He'd still put it on, still needed the armor of a suit, but he'd started to wonder if he needed it around her.

Could she handle the real him?

He followed her into her bedroom, his cock already hard as a rock.

Damn. There she was. She'd done exactly as he'd asked. She'd placed herself on the bed, her ass toward the end, her legs spread.

It was the perfect position for a man who would be most comfortable getting to his knees.

He wasn't that man. "Back up. Put your head on the pillow."

How long had it been since he'd done this? He'd had some sex, though the encounters had been hurried affairs that had been more about servicing a submissive who needed it than filling his own wants.

He needed her. He needed to know he could still have this, but somehow it hadn't mattered until he'd gotten close to her. He wasn't going to lie to himself. This wasn't about any woman or simple sex. This was about Tiffany, about making love to her, dominating her. About giving to her, and damn straight about taking what he needed from her.

"I thought," she began.

He didn't want her thinking. He didn't want to discuss why he wouldn't get to his knees. He wasn't about to tell her that it would hurt to do it because he hadn't been taking care of himself. No sympathy. It wasn't what he wanted from her. He had a sudden, savage need for her obedience. He gripped her ankles and flipped her over, his hand coming down in a rapid arc as he laid ten smacks across her pretty ass. "Don't think. Do as I ask. Are you frightened? Have I asked you to do something that you find repulsive?"

"Of course not," she replied, but he could hear the frustration in her voice.

"Then do as I ask or tell me you don't want to play." He wasn't sure what he would do if she told him to go to hell. He wasn't asking so much. He simply didn't want to bring his legs into this. He wanted to play with her, not tell her his sob story.

She got to her knees, her pinkened ass on display. Her head turned and there was a stubborn stare in her eyes. "Yes, Master."

She wanted to ask him questions, wanted to push it, but she complied with his orders. She turned and gracefully lay back on the bed. So graceful. So delicate. He wasn't even close to her beauty, likely hadn't been even when he'd had two legs.

She slowly spread her legs for him, somehow making the gesture an elegant dance meant to seduce him. He didn't need it. He was thoroughly seduced by her.

In two easy moves, he twisted his tie off and pulled his shirt over his head. He'd missed the skin-to-skin contact with her earlier. His chest and back had some scarring, but he was careful about the gym. He was muscular and well defined, his upper-body strength needed to make up for his lack of legs.

"You're even more beautiful without clothes, too." Her lips had curled up like the cat who'd gotten all the cream.

When she looked at him like that, he forgot he wasn't whole.

He left his slacks on. They would never come off. He would play it like it was all a part of his kink, but for now he concentrated on her. If he gave her enough pleasure, she wouldn't notice how much he was holding back, how much he simply didn't have to give to her. He moved to the end of the bed and climbed on with her. He managed not to wince at the pain that flared through his right leg. It didn't matter. It would heal eventually.

But this…this mattered. She was so fucking gorgeous. He didn't have to hold back with this woman, didn't have to pretend or prevaricate. She knew he was a pervert and she was fine with it. He breathed in the scent of her arousal while he stared down at the prettiest pussy he'd ever seen.

Plump and ripe and perfectly smooth. He leaned over and laid a chaste kiss on her mound. "You're to remain perfectly still. Do you need me to tie you up?"

He didn't want to stop what he was doing, but he had to see what she wanted. This was a lover's game and he had to give her a chance.

"I'll be still." Her voice had gone breathless.

129

He looked up her body and she was staring down at him, her hands having gone to the headboard at the top of the bed. Her fingers had curled around the slats as though she were about to hold on for dear life. Or attempt to make her Master happy by following his rules.

He let his hands run along the silky skin of her inner thighs, spreading them wider until she was completely open to his mercy.

He was going to have none.

"Tell me this is mine." He wanted to hear it from her. He had her name on a contract, but he needed to hear it from her lips that she was his now that they had zero reason to continue except that they wanted to.

He wanted to.

"It's yours, Sebastian. All yours," she replied without hesitation. "I'm so glad we didn't end this tonight. I want to try this with you. Not because Big Tag said so or because Adam needed us. I want to try because I think we could be very good for each other. I want to try because the idea of going back to being polite to each other at work makes me insane."

It made him insane, too. Work would change. Eventually they would go back to Dallas and to their separate homes, but he would still be her Master at work. He could be if he wasn't a complete chickenshit. He could have her and she would never have to know how broken he was.

All she would ever have to know was how good he could make her feel.

"I don't want to be polite, Tiffany. And I don't want to be friends or coworkers. I want this." He lowered his head and let his tongue run lightly over her.

She shivered beneath him but held her place. A low moan came from her throat and it went straight to his dick. Yes, that was what he wanted to hear from her. He wanted her moaning his name, calling out for him.

He settled in, loving how wet she was. He'd done that. She was responding to him and he intended to make sure she never regretted it.

Here in bed and in play he would give her everything he had. Everything she could need.

He ran his tongue lightly over her swollen clitoris before spearing her. He covered her mound with his mouth and fucked her with his tongue. In and out and all around. Taking her in. Lapping her up. He wasn't going to treat her like a wine he was trying. She was a glass of water and he'd been in the desert for years.

He sucked at her labia, drawing one side gently in before giving the other side the same treatment. He licked and laved his affection all over her soaked and aroused flesh.

Tiffany whimpered and moaned, her legs tensing on either side of him.

He kissed his way to her clitoris. The little bud was swollen and ready. Which was good because he couldn't wait any longer. He needed to be inside her, and she was so slick and prepped for him. But he wasn't taking a thing from her until she'd come all over his tongue.

"Have I told you how good you taste?" He growled the words against her pussy.

"Please, Sebastian. Please."

Sweet words, but he wanted more than words. "I want you to come for me. Give it to me. I want everything you have."

He put the flat of his tongue on her needy clit as he eased two fingers deep inside her, curling up so he could find her hot spot. He pressed down with his tongue, rubbing while he massaged her. His fingers got soaked, his tongue tasting pure passion, and she shook underneath him.

He could taste her orgasm, feel it as she tightened around his fingers.

She bucked up against him, but he was far beyond play. This wasn't play anymore. This was necessary to his sanity. He had to have her in a way he'd never felt before.

He fumbled as he tried to get his slacks opened. He had to roll off her to work the zipper. How the hell to do this thing? He was better on his feet. He'd never had sex in a bed with his prosthetics.

131

"Ride me." He suddenly wanted to feel her hands on him, to watch her as she moved over him.

To give up a little control so he could feel her all around him.

Her face was flushed as she got to her knees. He fished a condom out of his pocket. He never planned on going to bed without getting inside her again. It would be a long time before a day didn't involve making love to her. Once or twice a day. As often as she'd allow him.

She stopped and stared for a moment and then her hands went to his chest. She flattened her palms on him, exploring him. She leaned over and kissed him.

He should take control, but it was right there to let her have some. If he gave her some leeway, he could see how much of this was about her wanting him versus wanting to be dominated. It shouldn't matter, but somehow it did. Somehow the idea that she was touching him and he hadn't ordered her to made his heart race.

Her tongue came out, running over his bottom lip. He couldn't help but shiver. He felt that touch all along his spine. He opened his mouth and let her in, his hands coming up to touch her skin. So warm and soft. He loved how she felt under his palm. He couldn't help but reach for her breasts. Her nipples were hard and he could pluck at them like berries he was trying to gently pick. All the while she was kissing him, her tongue delving deep to play against his own.

His cock was pulsing, but he wasn't going to give in. He was going to give her time, to let her explore in a way no woman ever had.

It was new to him, but he didn't want to consider that right now. He only wanted to feel. Feel her hands on him. Feel her mouth on his. Feel her wanting him.

"Can you taste yourself on me?" Sebastian asked when she came up for air.

She straddled him, her core over his abs. "I can taste arousal and you. I like it, Sebastian. I might love it."

She lowered her head again, this time kissing his jaw and his neck. Everywhere her mouth hit him, the skin felt lit from within. She moved down, her pelvis shimmying over his cock as she kissed her way down his chest. She licked at his nipple and the sensation fired to his cock. So hard. He was hard and wanting, and he needed her affection even more than the eventual orgasm.

How long had it been since a woman explored him? Worshipped him with her lips and tongue? Caressed him simply because she wanted to feel his skin under her hand?

He let her run wild, kissing his chest, working her way down. Her hands worked the buckle of his belt. She pulled it free of the loops and then went to work on the fly of his slacks. She ground against him. His dry cleaner was going to have a fun day, but he didn't fucking care. If they asked what kind of stain it was, he would smile and tell them it was the best stain of all. The Tiffany spot. He wouldn't care if they got it out. If anyone asked he would explain how he'd gotten it because there was nothing embarrassing about fucking Tiffany Hayes. She was a damn goddess.

She eased the zipper down and he was so thankful he was on his back because she tried tugging the slacks down his thighs. His cock had bounced free and that was all he needed.

It was time to take back a bit of control. He reached down and grabbed a soft fistful of hair. "Tiffany, it would make me so fucking happy if you would put that beautiful mouth on me. It's been a very long time."

She was staring down at his cock and there was zero sympathy in her eyes. Nope. There was lust there, and that was exactly what he wanted. She reached out and brushed her fingertips over him. "Why so long? I would think every sub in the clubs you worked in would be at your feet, ready to do your bidding."

It was time to be honest with her. "I've only really wanted one. Since leaving the Army, I've wanted sex from time to time, but I didn't want intimacy. I didn't want any one particular woman so I didn't want something so personal. I want you."

His words seemed to spark something in her. She wrapped her hand around his cock, pumping up and down as she leaned over and ran that hot tongue over the head of his dick.

It took all his willpower not to come then and there.

He groaned and gritted his teeth against the pure pleasure of her mouth as she started to work him over. He forced his eyes open so he could stare down his body to the place where his cock disappeared into her beautiful mouth.

So good. It felt so fucking good to have her tongue explore him. Close. He felt close to her. It went beyond the physical and to something else…something he hadn't felt in years. Need. He needed her.

He let his hand find her hair and tangled his fingers in it. He loved how soft she was. He also loved how she groaned when he lightly pulled on her hair. The sensation of the sound surrounded his cock. He pumped up into her mouth and she managed to whirl her tongue around him, taking more and more with each pass until his whole cock was surrounded by her heat.

He tugged on her hair, unable to take another moment without letting go. And he did not want to let go yet. He wanted the moment to last. "Ride me. Get on top and take my cock. I want to watch you."

She gave him one last lick and then let him go. Before she could grab it, he opened the condom and worked it over his cock. He wouldn't survive her doing it. He needed her too much.

"Let me help you out of these pants," she said, her hands moving to the waistband.

They were as low as they were going to go. "Not enough time. Don't make me stop and spank you. I want you. I want you now."

She straddled him, his cock nestling at her core, the damn thing standing straight up like it knew which way to go. Tiffany leaned over, her breasts brushing against his chest. "I won't make you stop, Master, but you should know I find every inch of you beautiful and sexy. I definitely love this part."

She rocked back against him and his cock thrust inside. Such torture. The head of his cock was right there, but he needed more. More of her. Now that she was so close, he couldn't think of anything but getting inside her again. He gripped her hips and thrust up.

Tiffany's body went taut, her head falling back as he took over. He held her waist, moving her up and down on his cock with ease. She was a gorgeous, curvy girl, but no match for his upper-body strength. She began to move with him. Her legs tightened and she ground down, taking every inch of him inside.

They moved together, finding the perfect rhythm. He forgot about everything but her. She was all that mattered in those moments. Giving to her. Finding his pleasure in her.

He watched how she moved, like a cat, graceful and sleek. Her breasts bounced, the nipples hard, her skin flushed. She was so gorgeous in her passion.

He couldn't take more, felt himself beginning to go over the edge. He wanted so desperately to take her with him. He let one hand lower, finding her clit and pressing down, circling around as he thrust his cock deep.

Her head fell back and she called out his name.

He let himself go, thrusting up inside her. His whole body stiffened with pleasure as he pumped up into her.

Sweet release. Like a champagne cork popping after years and years of waiting.

Tiffany fell forward and they were chest to chest. He put his arms around her, enjoying how warm she felt. He loved the way her hair spilled over him.

This was amazing. He'd never had this. The perfection of the after, the sweet solace of another body against his. Her body.

How nice would it be to sleep beside her? To wrap himself up in her for hours and know when he woke she would be beside him. He wouldn't be alone.

He was so fucking tired of being alone and he hadn't even realized it until he'd gotten close to her.

She was quiet for a long while and he reveled in it, stroking her and enjoying the peace he felt when he was close to her.

Finally, her head came off his chest and she gave him the sexiest half smile, her eyes heavy with the need for sleep. She looked tousled and tired and happy. "I think that was better than a scene."

"Definitely," he replied, holding her close. He wasn't sure he was ready to go back to his own bed.

She sighed and shifted to his side. "I think we should get you out of those pants and under the covers. We have a long day tomorrow."

She kissed his chest and sat up.

All his peace fled. His hands went to his slacks and he zipped up, condom and all. He'd have to deal with it and the mess it was going to make later. He wasn't about to get undressed around her. She'd said she found him beautiful, but she'd never seen past a glimpse of the ugly stumps of his legs, never watched him pull the prosthetics off, never heard the sickening pop. She certainly wasn't going to see the damn nasty wound he had right now.

She was his lover. He wasn't going to turn her into his nurse.

With maximum effort, he forced himself off the bed and onto his legs. The minute he put weight on his right side, the pain shot through him. Fuck. It wasn't healing, but there wasn't anything to do except take the pain.

"Thank you for the offer, but I prefer to sleep by myself. I'm afraid I snore." He would give her any excuse he could come up with.

She pushed her hair back. Her sex hair. She looked so adorable, oddly innocent sitting in the middle of her bed without a stitch of clothing on. "I don't mind. I sleep like a log. I probably snore, too. It's not a big deal."

He was so uncomfortable. Physically, mentally. How had he been so at peace only moments before and now he was a raging storm of emotion?

How easy would it be to take all of his clothes off? To allow her to take care of him. How nice would it be to dump his prosthetics and let his skin breathe? Would she still cuddle with him? He was sure she wouldn't turn him out. Her heart was too tender for that, but would she still want him? Still see him as the strong Master she craved?

"I said no, Tiffany. I made it plain in our contract that we would have separate sleeping arrangements. Don't turn this into a fight. I had a lovely evening."

He could see the way she flushed, but couldn't tell if she wanted to argue with him or if he'd hurt her with his cold tone.

She slid off the bed and started toward her bathroom. "All right then. Good night, Sebastian."

He turned and walked out, managing not to limp until he'd made it out her bedroom door.

He took the pain because he deserved it. When he made it to his lonely room, he realized he damn well deserved that, too.

CHAPTER TEN

"What do you mean you haven't seen him naked?" Deena smoothed out the pristine white tablecloth and stared at her over the table.

"Well, there was the once, but that was brief." She shouldn't have said anything but she'd kept it all bottled up for days. It had been three days since Sebastian had blown her mind in bed and then ripped her heart out of her body and stomped all over it.

Maybe not quite that bad, but he'd practically run out of her bedroom when she'd suggested they sleep together.

Deena glanced around, but they were alone in the dining room. The trainees were having a session with Eric about behavior and safety in the kitchen. Sebastian was backing him up. "Are you talking about the time he slept over at your place?"

Sadly, the only time she'd managed to catch her honey in his undies had been the night he'd driven her drunk butt home. She'd had sex with the man twice a day for the last few days, but not once had he taken his damn slacks off. "Yeah. And you know how he reacted to that. I thought once we started sleeping together that he would get over the whole nervous thing."

"I thought you said he snored."

Was she even listening? "No, I said *he* said he snored, and how many men do you know really care about the fact that they snore? Or even realize it."

Deena stepped back, looking critically at the table. "You have a point. So maybe he's just very self-conscious. Or a little prudish. Does he want you to keep your clothes on?"

"Oh, no. I'm not allowed to wear clothes at all." Not that she truly minded, but it seemed a bit hypocritical of him. "He pulled the Dom card and when we're at home alone I get to be all in my birthday suit and if I'm cold, I curl up next to him with a blanket, but he still looks under it every now and then like he wants to make sure I didn't manage to get dressed under the damn thing."

Deena's lips curled up. "Or he enjoys looking at you. So not a prude."

"He's a pervert. I can't even explain what he did to me in the wine cellar yesterday." It had involved some rope, a case of Malbec, and Sebastian's intensely creative mind. He'd managed to rig up a sex sling and he'd done some seriously dirty stuff to her. Thank god he'd gagged her first or the training staff would have gotten a full vocal concert. "He's amazing in bed. And when I say in bed, I mean all over the place. There's very little time spent in an actual bed. Until we go to sleep and then we go to separate beds."

Deena pulled the white cloth off. "Let's try the off-white. Does he think you can have a whole relationship where you never see his legs?"

Tiffany's heart clenched as she took the other side of the tablecloth and helped Deena recover the table. That was exactly what she thought. She wasn't a fool. This wasn't about snoring or preferring to sleep alone. This was about his legs. His stumps. He didn't want her to see him as anything but the elegant sommelier he would be with or without legs. Not that he would understand that.

That thorn was still in his paw and she wasn't sure how to get it out.

"I worry that he's planning on keeping me separate from whole sections of his life." She smoothed the tablecloth out and placed the candles in the center.

"I don't know how much he's trying to keep you out of," Deena

139

said quietly. "If you think about it, he doesn't have much of one. I think you've become the closest person in the world to the man. All he does is work and go home and go to Sanctum. He's made it clear he's not going to ignore you at work and you'll be his sub at the club."

"That leaves a lot," she replied. "I care about him. Hell, I've been falling in love with that man since the day I met him and he won't sleep with me."

"He seems pretty tender. I watched him with you earlier. I've never seen him so soft."

He'd stopped her in the kitchen not thirty minutes before as she and Deena had been gathering the different samples for the tabletop designs. He asked her to come to him and then wrapped his arms around her and he'd held her for a good minute and a half. Just held her. She'd put her head against his chest and listened to his heart beating. He finally kissed her forehead and then explained he had a training class with Eric and wouldn't see her again until dinner.

It made her feel so special. So adored.

It was the only reason she hadn't run. He'd basically done the same thing to her the morning after she'd asked him to sleep with her. He'd been up and making breakfast and he'd kissed her so sweetly she couldn't walk away.

It was then she'd realized this problem had nothing to do with her. It was all about Sebastian, but she wasn't sure he would ever solve it without a little help.

The question was what to do about it.

"He's very sweet. And he takes good care of me. He moved the furniture and set up my easel so I could catch the early morning light. Lately he's taken over breakfast because he realized I work best in the mornings. He'll put a cup of coffee in my hand and shove me toward the easel and I'll paint while he cooks breakfast. I love our mornings. We won't have those mornings if we don't live together."

"But Tiff, this relationship is pretty young," Deena pointed out. "Don't you think it's too soon to live together?"

Probably, but she worried if she wasn't right there, poking into his business and making herself a part of his life, he would distance again. "I think he needs me more than he knows. But yes, it's probably too early. You're right."

Deena walked around the table and gave her a long hug. "It's going to be okay. He's already come so far. When you go back to Dallas, you start simple. Have him drive you to and from work. Synch your work schedules. Convince him to go out with the crew for drinks. I'll bet he won't be able to stay away and before that man knows it, he'll be asking you to marry him because he's not stupid."

She pulled back and gave Deena a grateful smile. "I hope so because I'm not sure I can handle this kind of relationship forever. He does so much for me and he won't let me help him. Not at all. He gets nasty when I suggest helping him in the shower. Even when I was trying to be sexy about it."

"Nasty?"

She waved that thought off. "As nasty as Sebastian ever gets. His voice gets deeper and he frowns fiercely and tells me to mind my own business. I'm not good at that. I'm not good at that at all."

Deena's eyes narrowed. "What does that mean?"

She winced. Deena always was able to see through her. "I might have located his sister in Georgia."

A gasp came from Deena's mouth. "Tell me you didn't. You know how private he is."

Tiffany shrugged. "I told you I wasn't good at keeping my nose out of things when it comes to people I care about. I wanted to figure out why he doesn't talk to his sister anymore. So I left her a message. She totally texted me and told me to never contact her again."

Deena's eyes rolled as though she knew what was coming next. "But you did, didn't you?"

"I texted. That's way less stalkery than calling. That was the mistake I made the first time. I texted her back and explained that I was Sebastian's girlfriend and that he missed her and was working as a sommelier at a high-end restaurant in Dallas and he would simply like to know that she's okay. She texted back that he knew why she wouldn't talk to him and not to contact her again. She was big on that. So I hit a dead end there. I need another way to figure out the story."

"He's going to be so mad if he finds out," Deena chided. "Did you ask him about it?"

There was no point to asking him. "The man won't show me the bottom half of his body. Do you honestly think he's going to open his soul and tell me why his family collapsed?"

"Probably not, but then I have to admit I'm more like Sebastian than you in this situation," Deena admitted. "I would have been upset if I found out Eric had gone behind my back and contacted my mom."

She flushed with embarrassment. "Then I guess I should be glad he doesn't talk to her anymore. I'm not trying to hurt him. I'm trying to understand him."

"And if he doesn't want to be understood?"

"Everyone wants to be understood. What you're asking is what do I do if he doesn't want me to understand him. Everyone ends up opening up to the right person. What if I'm not the right person?" The question had been haunting her for the last several days.

"Then he's the unluckiest person in the world because you're pretty awesome." Deena turned back to the table. "I think you need to relax and let this play out. He's bending for you, right? He's not hiding the relationship at all. In fact, he gave Javi's brother a long talk about what he would do to him if he kept flirting with you."

Javi's younger brother, Gabriel, was one of the busboys. The kid was barely eighteen, but he was already following in big brother's footsteps. He was a flirt of the highest order, which was exactly why Tiffany took nothing the kid said seriously.

Had it upset Sebastian that Gabriel routinely told her how nice she looked—even when she knew damn well she didn't? Not that Sebastian didn't. He would stop and smooth back her hair and proclaim her to be the prettiest woman in the world.

Gabriel would tell her how nice her butt looked in her jeans.

"They're not even in the same league. Gabriel is a boy and Sebastian is an amazing man. I don't see anyone but Sebastian." That was the problem. She was in so deep with that man that she couldn't imagine her life with anyone else. Living with him had done nothing to quench her thirst. She wanted more and she wasn't sure how to go about getting it.

She wasn't sure love was going to be enough with Sebastian. No matter how much he needed it.

She had to find a way to make him understand it was all right to be vulnerable with her.

But in order to figure out how to do that she needed to know what had really started the problem. She thought it had something to do with what had happened to him when he'd gotten back home.

The door to the kitchen opened and Eric stepped out. He smiled at his wife, but it was a pained thing. "Are you sure we have to hire new people? Why can't we steal Sean's staff?"

Deena shook her head. "Because the Taggart brothers are excellent at revenge, or so I've heard. They'll get better."

"One of the new servers managed to trip on air, from what I can tell, and nearly set the kitchen on fire, and all she was doing was practicing how to put in an order. I still don't know how that happened." He sighed. "You still can't decide between white and champagne?"

Tiffany's cell trilled and she pulled it out of her pocket. "I like the white. We tried going with black, but the bread we serve is nice and flaky and makes it look super messy." She looked down at the number, more than surprised at what she saw. "Uhm, I'm going to step outside for a moment while you two figure it out."

They started arguing over white or off-white and Tiffany rushed toward the lobby. She swiped her finger across the screen to answer. "Hello?"

"He took his test? You said he was a sommelier. Is that just a title or did he actually take his test?" Ramona Lowe-Campbell sounded a bit sad and a whole lot curious.

Oh, she could work with curiosity. "Your brother is one of the youngest Master sommeliers in the country."

143

The woman at the other end of the line was silent for a moment. "He always had incredible instincts when it came to wine. Our father was so disappointed when he went into the Army, but I understood. He needed to see a little of the world before he settled down." There was a long sigh over the line. "So you're his new girlfriend?"

"I'm pretty sure I'm the only girlfriend he's had since he came home." She had to be careful. She didn't want to say anything that might put Ramona off, but she needed Sebastian's sister to understand what was happening in his life.

"Don't think he'll marry you. If he wouldn't marry Alicia, he won't marry you. You have to be careful because my brother changed over there. He got harder. I hope you don't fall for him because if he could leave the love of his life behind without a word, he'll dump you, too."

Yes, this was the mystery she needed to solve. She began to talk to the only person who might be able to solve it.

* * * *

Sebastian stared out over the sea of way-too-young faces. Had he ever been that young? A few weeks ago he would have said no, but lately he'd started to remember how good it felt to be stupid and young and crazy about a woman.

"Do you understand what you did wrong, Sally?" Sebastian looked at the college girl. She'd been hired to work as a server, but he might have to suggest the newbie move to a hostessing position at least for a few months.

Her eyes were wide as she looked up at him. She looked at him like he was a well-dressed monster who might eat her up if she didn't answer correctly. "I didn't yell that code thing when I moved through the kitchen."

She'd plowed through, trying to maneuver behind Javier, who was training the new line chefs in how Eric expected them to prepare his dishes. The whole kitchen smelled of tomatoes and garlic and basil since they were working on the marinara sauce Top served over certain pasta lunch dishes. It made Sebastian's stomach rumble. He was looking forward to sitting across a table from Tiffany and sharing the fruits of Javi's labor.

But only after he'd ensured Sally didn't nearly cause a kitchen fire because she was too nervous to call out.

"It's not a code. It's a precaution. When you are walking behind anyone who is handling food or drink or carrying a tray, you simply say in a firm voice, 'behind you' so they know not to step back while stirring a pot of ridiculously hot sauce that could have literally burned off his flesh if he hadn't been so quick on his feet."

Javier chuckled. "Don't you listen to him, honey. I was never going to ruin this face. I have incredible instincts, but I could have hurt you. Don't worry about it. You'll get used to how to work in a kitchen. Before long, you'll be shouting and won't even notice it."

Dear god, that kid would use anything as an excuse to get close to a woman. "And that, ladies, is your other real threat in the kitchen. Javier is a playboy and he will burn you, too."

Javi put a hand over his heart and managed to look deeply offended. "I can't believe you would say that. I'm a young man looking for love." He winked at Sally. "You looking, too? I think I saw some in the broom closet. We should go look. Leave no stone unturned. That's my motto, pretty girl."

Leave no woman unmolested might be a better motto. Though even as he thought the words, Sally was turning a nice shade of pink and giggling behind her hand.

Yeah, he had probably never been that young.

"Take a twenty minute break," he offered. The real job was coming up, but Deena was running that particular show. "When you get back, be ready for a rehearsal of lunch service. You'll be serving me and your service pro, Tiffany, and we'll be grading you on everything from presentation to quickness and knowledge of the menu and wine and bar choices."

There was a collective groan that went through the group, but

Sebastian ignored it.

God, he hoped they would be ready in a week. Soft open was in a week and he was worried they needed to replace at least two of the servers with more experienced employees. At least it looked like Eric and Javi had the line chefs working in tandem. He was absolutely certain the bar staff was ready. It was only a couple of servers he was worried about at this point.

He would sit down with Tiffany tonight and ask her opinion of what they should do. She had excellent instincts and this was her particular forte. He would put it all in her hands and she would figure out what to do.

It was nice to trust someone the way he did Tiffany.

What the hell was he going to do when they went back to Dallas? He wasn't sure he wanted to go backward. He wasn't sure he liked the idea of her not being around all the time.

Could he manage to convince her to live with him and maintain separate rooms? Could he handle that? He needed time off his legs, time to rest and breathe, and he wasn't about to do that around her.

Maybe it would be all right. Maybe she could handle being a part of his life but keeping some kind of distance.

Who the fuck was he kidding? She was the huggiest sub he'd ever met. She cuddled and needed affection and attention.

"Well, finally we have a winner." Eric strode in as the new recruits were heading to the break room. "We're going with champagne linens, copper candle holders, and white roses."

Thank god. The table presentation had been an issue for days. "Excellent. I'll have the servers set two tables if you would like to join Tiffany and me for lunch. I think it would help our servers to have two tables full of picky customers to deal with."

He planned to be incredibly obnoxious. Tiffany would almost certainly make up for him by being sweet, but he intended to give them a challenge.

"Sure, sounds like fun. I think Javi can handle lunch," Eric replied.

"It's already in prep." Javier wiped his hands off and joined them.

"The kitchen is ready. These guys are pros, but I have some questions about the servers. Mostly, though, I have to ask about the service trainer."

He wanted to ask about Tiffany? "If you're trying to imply that Tiffany has something to do with the quality of the server trainees, I'm going to take offense. She didn't hire anyone."

Javi held up a hand. "My question is far more personal. I know what a great job Tiff does. I'm not asking in a professional way. I'm asking as her friend. What the hell are you playing at, Sebastian?"

He had to do a double take because it wasn't every day he got called out. No one called him out. Not since he'd left Georgia for the last time. He'd kept his head down, his nose clean, and he never placed himself in a position where he could be questioned on a moral level. He hated being called into question. Loathed it.

"I think you should explain yourself." He couldn't help the fact that the words came out in an icy tone.

If it bothered Javier, he didn't show it. "Tiffany is a nice lady. She's genuinely kind. She's got no men here looking out for her. I would like to know what your intentions are when it comes to her."

Eric frowned. "Seriously, you're taking the moral high ground here, Javi?"

Javier crossed his arms over his chest. "Yeah, I am, because I know Sebastian is a hard case and though he won't mean to, he's going to break her heart."

"Why would I break her heart? I like Tiffany. We get along well together and I think when our contract is up we'll both want to sign a new one."

Javi pointed at him. "Yes, see, that's what I'm talking about. You plan to put her in a box marked *sub* and take her out when you want her. Can't you see that's not going to be good for her? Look, I've known her for years. We worked together at a restaurant before Top. There's a reason I've never hit on her and it's because she's like a sister to me. The problem is I know too many dudes like you and while I respect everything you've done for our country, you have to get right with yourself before you drag someone else into it."

"What is that supposed to mean?" He could feel his anger starting to well.

Eric held a hand out as though ready to come between them at any moment. "I think Javi is putting some of his own problems on you."

"I'm not. I'm taking what I know and applying it to the world around me." Javi's eyes drifted down. "That leg hurting you? You think I don't know the signs? My oldest brother came back with most of the left side of his body blown off. He came back to a beautiful wife and a three-month-old girl he'd never seen before."

He knew Javi's oldest brother, Rafael. He'd seen him at the VA a few times. He was a shell of a man. Sebastian was fairly certain he'd gone down a very dark hole. "I'm sorry about your brother. I don't know what he has to do with me."

"He wouldn't let Sonja help him. Wouldn't let her see him most of the time. Said he was a monster and she shouldn't have to live with him like that. The divorce came through a few months back and now my brother drifts around. I know you won't see it, but you drift around, too. You don't let anyone really know you. You never let anyone help you. You're favoring your right leg heavily. You tripped and caught yourself while you were running the servers through kitchen training. That was why I nearly burned myself. Not her. It was you. I would bet it's because you're spending far too much time on your prosthetics. Did you get a scratch or a cut that won't heal because you're so afraid of letting her see you as less than whole?"

He'd put extra padding in to ease the pain, but the scratch had opened up again. He'd knocked into one of the tables and he'd felt it.

Not that any of it was Javier's business. The way the younger man was talking to him was stirring up a mess of old emotions. "I'm fine and I'm not your brother. I wouldn't have left my wife and child behind."

Javi's jaw went tight. "That's not what I hear."

Eric straightened up, his shoulders stiffening. "What? Sebastian's never been married."

Javi's eyes met his, the knowing stare in them telling Sebastian he'd been doing his homework on him. "No, but he had a fiancée he left at the altar."

His stomach took a heavy downturn. No one knew about Alicia. He never talked about her. Never.

He'd given up a relationship with his family because he wouldn't talk about Alicia.

Javi's eyes had gone stubborn. "You didn't want her to see you as less than a man, did you? It's been years but you still don't accept what happened to you."

"Leave him alone, Javier," an unwelcome voice said.

He turned and Tiffany was standing in the doorway.

Javi frowned her way. "I know you have a thing for him, Tiff, but you don't know about his past. I looked into him when I found out you were living with him. I get it. You were doing Big Tag a favor, but I know you. I know you want him and you're going to get hurt. You need to understand that he's left women before. He left his fiancée and she was pregnant. He walked out on her and his family and never said a word to them again."

Humiliation swamped him. Now they all knew. The old accusations swept through him and there was nothing to do except get the hell out. He straightened himself up, refusing to be cowed. Even by the damn pain that pulsed through him. It was so much worse since he'd banged into that table. "Well, I didn't exactly walk away. I wheeled myself away. I did, however, leave as Javier has so kindly explained."

"I know," she replied.

He turned to look at her. Her cheeks were the faintest shade of pink and her eyes shifted away from him before she obviously forced herself to look back up. "What do you mean, you know? Did Javier send a report over to you? What did he do? Hire an investigator?"

"I didn't have to," Javi replied. "My sister's one. She asked a couple of questions. Apparently, you're still the source of a lot of gossip in your hometown."

"You know how people love to talk." He couldn't take his eyes off her. She knew. How long had she known? "Did he tell you about it today?"

She swallowed, a sure sign she was nervous. "Javi didn't tell me anything. I heard that you had a sister and I did some digging of my own. Why don't we go and talk? It's almost lunch. I'll pour you a Riesling and we can try to trip up the servers. And you can yell at me for not minding my own business."

He stared at her. What had she done?

Tiffany strode in the room, shedding any illusion that she was nervous about how he was going to react. "Come on, Sebastian. You know you want to do the last part. The yelling, that is. Or you can growl my way, but I think you should get off your feet and let me take care of you."

Take care of him? Like he was a pathetic thing that needed taking care of. He knew how quickly that could turn. He needed her to understand that he wasn't something soft and needy. "Javier is right. I had a fiancée. I went home to see her and I walked away from her. And, yes, Alicia was pregnant when I walked away. That's why my mother wouldn't speak to me for the last year of her life. I denied her a grandchild. Alicia had a miscarriage, but believe me she knew who to blame. She blamed me for Alicia losing the baby."

"I'm sure she did." Tiffany held out a hand.

"You had no right to call my sister." The enormity of the betrayal hit him like a punch to the gut. She'd gone behind his back and called his sister?

"I did. I care about you. That gives me the right."

"It gives you no right at all." He could feel the walls pushing in on him. She wanted to sit down and talk? What would she do? Gently break it off with him because she'd finally seen who he was? He wasn't about to sit back and allow her to take over. Not in this. She didn't get to pry into his life like this. She didn't get to walk in and bring back every bad memory of the life he'd left behind. "You broke trust with me. You're manipulating me again and I won't stand for it."

"She's manipulating you?" Javier asked, judgment plain on his face. "You're the one who ran out on your pregnant fiancée. Responsibility a bit too much for you?"

Shame burned in his gut. He could see his mother standing on shaking legs, looking at him like she wished she'd never had him.

You killed your father. Now you want to take this away from me, too.

"You back off and back off now." Tiffany moved between him and Javier. "He isn't Rafe and I won't have you bringing your personal baggage into this. I love you like a brother, but this is between me and Sebastian."

"He knocked up a woman and dumped her," Javier insisted.

Yes, there it was. All the judgment. He was the monster. Alicia was the well-bred girl from the right side of the tracks who made the mistake of falling for the middle-class monster. Everyone had known it would go wrong. Alicia had been guaranteed a beautiful future and he'd taken it all away from her.

"Or it wasn't his baby, dumbass," Tiffany shot back. "I am usually all about the sisterhood, but I know Sebastian. The man can't leave an order form unfinished. He's the single most responsible man I've ever met. He wouldn't leave his child. He came home, wounded and needing love and healing, and he found out his fiancée had cheated on him. So back off."

All eyes were suddenly on him. It didn't matter that she might understand. She'd disobeyed. She'd done exactly what he'd always been afraid she would do. There would be no careful distance with her. There would be no happy relationship because she would need far more than he could give her.

I don't need you anyway, Sebastian. What kind of a husband or a father could you be? God, I wish it had been you instead of Gary. Why did Gary die and you come crawling back home like the pathetic boy you've always been? Gary showed me what it meant to have a man in my life. I'm glad you know because the thought of actually getting into bed with you makes me sick.

151

He wasn't going to give Tiffany a chance to be disgusted with him. It took a special kind of love to deal with a man who needed help bathing himself. Hell, there had been times when he couldn't go to the bathroom without help. Weak. He felt a little weak. Like the room might start spinning.

"Eric, I'm sorry I'm going to need the afternoon off. I'm going to move my things to a hotel for the duration of the training period." He couldn't give up his job. It was all he had. But how could he work with her every day?

Tiffany turned to him. "You're moving out?"

She looked so hurt, but that was what he did. He hurt people. She would have found out sooner or later anyway. "Yes, I'm moving out. I explained to you that I wouldn't put up with these kinds of manipulations. Did you or did you not know I wouldn't want you to look into my past?"

She sighed. "I knew it, but we can't go on like this. We have to talk to each other more."

More. She wanted to talk more, but that wasn't what she meant. She would want to move herself into his world lock, stock, and barrel, and he would be devastated when she finally realized she wanted a whole man. She would want to get as close as she could and then she would find out how difficult he was, how hard he was to deal with.

He'd thought Alicia had ripped him apart. Tiffany would destroy him.

"Yes, you're right. We're not going on at all anymore." He needed to get away from her. He already wanted to call back his words, wanted to find a way out of the trap she'd put him in. It was already in his head to sit down and put forth her punishment and command her to stay out of his business, but to keep her.

It wouldn't work.

He stepped to his left, ready to get around her.

"Hey, I think you do need to sit down for a minute, buddy." Eric moved to his side. "You went a little pale there."

Javier was in his way. "Man, I didn't know. I'm so sorry. Why would you let everyone believe you did that? Did you not fight the rumors at all?"

Not once his mother had believed Alicia. And Ramona. His sister, the one who'd cried at his bedside and promised to do everything she could to help him, had turned her back on him, too. No. He hadn't tried to sway the town to his side. He'd called Macon and left. He'd rolled into Ian Taggart's office, broken down and alone in the world.

What do you want to do now? Big Tag had asked him.

He hadn't said what he'd wanted to say. Die. He wanted to go back to that moment when the world had exploded around him and not get up again.

I want to be useful.

He wasn't going to be useful to Tiffany. He would be a burden to her. He'd been a complete idiot to think this could work. Perhaps it could work with a woman who expected less of him, but the irony was Tiffany's sweet side, her giving soul was exactly what made him love her.

He couldn't love her. He couldn't be near her.

"Move out of my way." He tried to push past Eric.

"Hey," Eric said. "Calm down. I think something's wrong."

Everything was wrong. Every fucking thing in the world. He reached to shove Eric out of the way. That was the moment Tiffany stepped up and he caught her instead.

He shoved her, sending her back and making her hit the wall.

Horror rushed through him. He'd hit her. He'd hit Tiffany. "I'm so sorry, baby."

She brushed herself off and shook her head. "I'm fine, Sebastian."

He needed to get his hands on her, to make sure he hadn't hurt her. God, he didn't want to hurt her. No matter what he did, he hurt her.

He reached out to haul her up, but Eric got in the way. Sebastian lost his balance and his left leg banged against the prep table. His vision blurred, pain jarring through him, and he felt his leg give.

He crashed against the prep table, trying desperately to catch himself, but it was far too late. He managed to bang his elbow, another spark of pure agony shooting up his arm.

He heard Tiffany call out for him. Eric and Javier moved in, looming over him.

He could feel something wet. He managed to look down. Blood. It soaked his slacks.

Shit. He'd reopened the wound, likely made it much worse. He was going to need stitches, going to have to stay off it, and that meant crutches or worse.

Tiffany knelt at his side. "Baby, are you all right?"

There it was. There was the look he'd been trying to avoid. A sickening sympathy came into her eyes. She wasn't looking at him like a Dom anymore. She was seeing who he really was—a propped up man who could fall apart at any moment.

"Get out."

Her eyes widened. "What? Sebastian, you're hurt. We need to get that bleeding stopped."

"Get out. I want you out of the apartment. Stay with Javier. I don't care, but I don't want you there when I come home." He didn't have a choice. He couldn't move out on his own and he wasn't asking anyone for help. He turned away from her, unable to stand the way she was looking at him.

"Sebastian, stop this right now," she demanded. "Lie down and I'll call an ambulance."

She was so not doing that. "Don't you dare. Eric, give me a hand. I can drive myself. Better yet, do you have a needle and thread around here?"

He could sew the fucker up himself and not have to take the inevitable lecture. He could call some movers and leave her the apartment.

Eric rolled his eyes. "It's easy to see you're going to be an idiot."

Tears were rolling down Tiffany's face. "Don't do this. Don't do this to us. Please let me help you."

He knew how to manipulate her. She'd learned how to deal with him; well, he'd done the same with her. He could use her nature against her. "I'm not moving until you leave. I'll sit here and bleed out on this floor if you don't go away, Tiffany."

Her face went beet red, her eyes flaring with pure hurt. Yeah, he knew where to stick the knife in. She got to her feet, taking a step back. "I'm going to ask one more time, Sebastian. Please don't do this."

"Get the fuck out of here." He wasn't going to let her see him like this. Not broken. He would rather she hated him than pitied him.

She shook her head, wiping away her tears. Her jaw hardened and he could see the stubborn will on her face. "Have it your way, Master."

She turned and walked out.

And he was left with a gaping wound that was never, ever going to heal.

CHAPTER ELEVEN

Tiffany paced the dining room floor, her whole body vibrating with a mixture of rage and fury and a little bit of worry, and then more rage.

How fucking dare he.

Her lion was roaring. Now she knew what Beauty had felt like when the Beast had gotten pissed.

Stubborn man. Stupid man.

Was he all right? She knew he'd made it to the hospital. Eric had told her what he thought was going to happen, but she hadn't heard since then.

Her cell trilled and she looked down. There was a text message from Javier.

He's with the doctor now. Eric's staying with him. I'll come back and help move you out.

She frowned. Did they all think she was some wilting flower of a sub?

Not necessary. I'll handle things. Thanks for taking care of him.

"Hey, I heard something happened with Sebastian." Ally rushed across the dining room, her arms full of packages. "I'm dropping off some tools for the new pastry chef. Macon's coming in behind me. Is Sebastian all right?"

Sebastian was maddening. Sebastian was mean. He didn't deserve her normal sunny and happy persona. Not a bit.

"He's an asshole, but I think he'll be fine."

Macon strode in, carrying a large standing mixer, which he sat on one of the tables. "Eric called and said there was an emergency."

She waved it off. Eric was being a total drama queen. "Sebastian fell. He's been a stubborn ass for the last couple of weeks because apparently he cut his leg and hasn't been taking care of himself or allowing anyone else to take care of him. What the hell kind of Master doesn't let his sub do her damn job?"

Macon sighed. "I told you he still has some hang-ups. Do we know how bad it is? Is he going to have to be hospitalized?"

"No." Not according to Eric's call. Eric had told her that Sebastian would be off his prosthetics for a week or two to let the wound heal. Eric had gone back to her and Sebastian's apartment to pick up the wheelchair he'd tried so hard to never let her see.

He should have known that she snooped. She'd been the one to tell Eric where the damn chair was.

"Eric asked if Ally and I could help you pack up," Macon said quietly. He was treating her like she was a fragile flower, so upset by Sebastian's bark that she couldn't help but break down.

Still, she had to at least consider that he'd meant what he'd said. "He told me to get out of our apartment. Even before he fell, he'd told me I had to leave. He found out I tracked down his sister."

Ally nodded. "Good. What did you find out?"

"Hey," Macon said, his mouth a flat line. "You poked around in his past. I told you what I knew in confidence and I believe I also mentioned that he wouldn't like you putting your nose where it didn't belong."

"It does belong there and I was right to call her." The fact that Sebastian had allowed one woman's lie to keep him from his family was beyond frustrating. "Do you know why he no longer talks to his family? Because they think he knocked up his girlfriend and dumped her when he found out she was pregnant."

Macon's head shook. "What? I knew there was a fiancée, but I thought she left him."

"He left her because the baby wasn't his, but apparently he failed to mention that fact to his family." She took a deep breath. She couldn't give in to the anger she felt. It was far more important to decide on a course of action, and her time was running out.

"He didn't tell them?" Macon asked.

She sighed, weariness threatening to overwhelm her. Ramona had taken a little cajoling, but she'd told her the story. There had been bitterness in her tone, but also an undertone of loss. She was tired of hating her brother, likely tired of missing him. Like Sebastian, Ramona was an orphan. Though she'd married and had a child, it had been easy to figure out how much she missed the man she'd shared a childhood with. "From what I can tell, he tried to explain it to his mother, but she wasn't listening and he got stubborn. Apparently this Alicia person was the town sweetheart and everyone turned on him."

"And that was when he called me," Macon surmised. "He was in a bad place back then."

"Well, he's in a bad place now, too, because he's a stubborn asshole." He'd been a jerk and she wasn't talking about the fact that he'd accidently shoved her. That had been nothing. But the words had been something he would have to make up for. Groveling was in that man's future.

She simply had to convince him to do it.

Ally reached out, grasping her hand. "I'm so sorry, sweetie. You can stay back at your place and we'll drive you into work every day. I'm scheduled to help out here until the soft open."

"I told you, I'm not moving." This was war and the prize was Sebastian. Unfortunately, the opponent was Sebastian, too. The good news was her opponent was wounded and in no position to physically kick her out.

Macon's lips curled up. "You're going to give him hell, aren't you?"

She wasn't trying to. "I'm trying to give him heaven. I'm trying to show him he doesn't have to live like this. I might have failed at fixing his relationship with his sister. She's stubborn, too, but I can show him there's absolutely nothing wrong with asking for a little help. Can't I?"

Ally looked up at Macon. "Like I help you every now and then?"

Macon reached out and put a hand on her head, stroking her hair. "Yes, though Sebastian needs it even more. Helping him shower and keep his wound clean is going to be important. The apartment isn't built for a wheelchair and he's going to be in his for a week or two. He does need help, but I think he isn't going to want it from Tiffany."

"Well, that's sad because I'm all he has." She needed to make that plain to everyone. The plan coalescing in her brain wouldn't work unless she outflanked her opponent.

Macon shrugged. "I'm a busy man. Obviously Eric has a lot to do."

Ally seemed to catch on. "I'll call around and make sure everyone knows you're taking care of the situation."

Tiffany steeled herself because she was going into battle.

* * * *

Sebastian was beyond tired as Eric wheeled him down the hall toward the apartment he'd shared with her.

Had she struggled with the easel? It was heavy and a little unwieldy. He'd wanted to see what she was working on, but she'd claimed it wasn't ready for viewing yet.

How would she feel when she found out he'd convinced Eric to put two of her paintings up in the lobby and Sean was purchasing another for the dining room in Dallas? They'd bought all three from the gallery that Tiffany showed her work at. He'd meant to make it a surprise for the soft open. He'd been able to imagine how happy she would be, how she would run up to him and throw her arms around him. Now she likely wouldn't even look at him.

It was going to be the last gift he could give her.

"How exactly are you going to get around?" Eric asked.

"I'll manage." He'd done it before. He could do it again. After

Alicia's lies had cost him his family, he'd gone for a couple of weeks with no help at all. It had been hell, but he'd managed somehow. He would deal with all of it because he deserved this. After the way he'd hurt Tiffany, he deserved all of it.

He fished his key out. Best to start dealing with the new reality right now.

"I can stop by and pick you up," Eric promised.

He had a lot to deal with. "It's all right. I can take the bus. They have a wheelchair rack and they drop off a block from Top."

Eric sighed, a frustrated sound. "Please tell me you're kidding. You needed stitches. You don't need to bang around on a bus."

Only two. For a man who'd needed four different surgeries in a six-week period, it was nothing. He had a folder full of instructions, prescriptions for antibiotics, and pain meds he wouldn't actually use. "It's not anything for you to worry about. I appreciate the fact that you got me to the hospital, but I'll be fine in a day or two."

He was never going to be fine again because she wouldn't look at him the same way. She would never smile his way or look up at him with eager eyes. She wouldn't call him Master in that sweet tone of hers, wouldn't turn that saucy mouth on him.

Fuck, he was going to miss her.

He managed to get the key in the door and turn it. He struggled to open it. He hated the fact that Eric had to move into the doorway so it opened wide enough for him to get the wheelchair through. Eric was carrying his legs.

God, he was such a freak. At least Tiffany didn't have to see him like this.

He wheeled himself through and then stopped.

Tiffany was standing in the middle of the room, her pretty face frowning his way. She loomed over the room, her arms crossed under her breasts.

Eric stopped beside him.

"I thought you would be gone by now." He had to play this cool. He wanted nothing more than to turn around and wheel himself right back out of the apartment. "Do you need additional help?"

His tone was properly chilly. He couldn't afford to look any weaker than he already did.

"No, I'm fine," she replied, her voice cold as well. She kept her eyes steady on him. "Eric, why don't you give those to me and then let Sebastian and me have some alone time. We have some things we need to work out."

"Don't you dare." Panic made an appearance. It started low in his gut. What was she planning? What the hell was her game? "Tiffany, you will leave now or I'll have to do something neither of us wants me to do."

Tiffany took a deep breath, seeming to forcibly settle herself down. "Sebastian, are you worried I'm going to treat you like a helpless invalid? Are you so afraid I'll see you in a different light that you're willing to burn down everything around you to keep me at arm's length?"

That was pretty well put. "I want you to go. Do you not understand that?"

"Sebastian, is there any way that you think you might be able to love me?"

This was it. He could cut this shit off at the pass and never have to deal with her again. That one tremulously worded question gave him the out he needed. He'd miscalculated with her. He hadn't expected her to see him as a challenge. "It won't work."

It was all he could manage. He couldn't look at her and break her, couldn't say those final words that would make her hate him.

"That's not a no," she said with a long sigh. "So this is all about you being too stubborn for words and not accepting help from anyone."

He was fully aware that Eric was standing there, his head swinging back and forth like he was watching a tennis match. He hated it, hated the fact that Eric was standing with his prosthetic legs in hand and he was relegated to this hated chair looking to all the world like an invalid.

And yet she was here. She'd given him an in. Was he really so stubborn that he would shove her away for the crime of seeing him fall,

161

seeing him at his lowest?

Maybe, just maybe he could salvage this, but first he needed to get her out of here so he could rest and try to heal. Hell, he might heal faster if he knew she was waiting to resume their relationship.

"Tiffany, if you'll leave now, we'll talk again in a few days and perhaps we'll negotiate a new contract. I do have feelings for you, but this can't work if you don't respect my authority."

"Oh, Sebastian, you lost all rights to your authority the minute you became too vain to take care of yourself." She was standing there, her arms crossed over her chest, a look of monumental disappointment on her face.

So that was her game. He'd hurt her and she'd come here to get a little of her own back. She was going to have her scene and then storm out, likely letting him know how much he was missing. Too vain? That was a ridiculous claim. "If you're no longer interested in maintaining a relationship, you should leave. I notice you haven't moved your things out. I'll wait in my room and Eric can help you with packing."

"I can?" Eric sounded a bit chilly himself.

Tiffany's whole face turned, her smile becoming a gracious thing as she moved to Eric. "Not at all. Eric, I can't thank you enough for helping my stubborn boyfriend. It's my turn to take over. I'm so sorry you had to give up an afternoon of your precious time to do my job. I'll take those now."

"I told you what I wanted." Why wasn't she listening to him?

She didn't bother to look his way, simply took his freaking legs from Eric and walked back to his bedroom.

"I think Tiff's gone insane." But there was a smile on Eric's face.

"I need you to remove her." He didn't want to do it, but he couldn't have her staying here. "Haul her out of here physically if you have to."

One brow arched over Eric's eyes. "Really? I think I'm done taking orders from you today. I'm a little sick of watching you fuck up everything in your life."

"Yes, I think we're all sick of that." Tiffany was back. Her blonde hair was up in a ponytail, her gorgeous body in a T-shirt and jeans that clung to her every curve and reminded him of all the ways he hadn't had her. He'd never once slept beside her, his arms wrapped around her, bodies tangled. He'd never have that with her.

"Then you should feel free to leave." She thought she was sick of dealing with him? She had no idea what it was like to be in this chair, unable to do even the simple act of tossing out a volatile ex-lover.

"Oh, baby, have you not figured it out yet? I'm not going anywhere. You want me gone, get rid of me yourself. Eric, I'll take his phone, too. Wouldn't want him calling the cops on me, would we?" She held out her hand.

He watched in utter horror as Eric passed it over to her. "Good luck, Tiff. Call if you need help moving him around, though he's actually got incredible upper body strength. He can manage a lot. He'll need someone in the shower with him for a few days. The doctor's orders are all in this bag along with his meds and some extra bandages. Keep the wound clean and he needs to go back in a week."

"I'll take care of it. Thanks." She took the bag from Eric.

Eric looked down at him. "She's giving you another chance. I would take it if I were you."

Oh, would he? Well, Eric wasn't the one stuck in the chair. Eric didn't understand what life would be like for her if she did stay with him. Eric wasn't the one who would mourn her when she was gone. "If you walk out that door and leave me with her, you can find another fucking som. Do you understand me?"

Tiffany's eyes rolled and there was a sad shake of her head as she looked back at Eric. "I'll have him back at work in a day or two. If you need something from him before then, call me. You can also send Javi with food if you need wine pairings. Send me a list of the foods and I'll tell you what he'll want to try with each course."

"Thank you. I can send sample plates over tomorrow night." Eric turned and walked out, closing the door as he left.

And he was alone with Tiffany.

"Since when do you know what I'll select to try with a dish?" Now she was taking over his job, too?

"Let me see. I believe the dish Eric's working on tomorrow is the rib eye. You'll want the 2013 Lafite and the 2012 Balmont Cabs to test for the high-end pairing. And I've got three in mind for a Zinfandel pairing. All rich in tannins and high in alcohol volume. I'm also going to ask them to bring in a Malbec. I know it's not traditional, but Malbecs are all the rage and we have to stay on the cutting edge." She put one hand on her hip. "See, I listen. And I know you far better than you know me."

He couldn't argue with that. She'd hit it on the nose. He could only shrink back into the real argument. "I don't want you here."

"Well, honestly, right now I don't particularly want to be here, but some things we suck up and take, Sebastian. That's what couples do. We don't run out on each other when the going gets tough or when one of us turns into an emotionally tight-fisted asshole." Tiffany held up his phone. "You can have this back when you earn it. Mean men don't deserve cell phones. Are you hungry?"

He was confused. So damn confused. There was a part of him that wanted to hold a hand out to her, to bring her close and not let go. He knew how that would end. "What the hell are you doing? I don't want you here."

"I know what you're afraid of," she said, her tone calm. "You're afraid that I'm going to treat you like a poor little cripple. Good news, baby. I'm not going to do that. I'm going to treat you like the overstimulated toddler you're acting like. When you want to act like the kind, loving adult I know you are, we can renegotiate."

"We didn't negotiate in the first place. Wait. You know we actually did and you seem to have forgotten who the Dom is."

"The Dom broke our contract so as far as I'm concerned, there's no contract at all between us. If you want to kick me out, you're more than willing to try. See, I'm not treating you like a precious invalid I have to take care of. I'm being a massive bitch because that seems to be the only way to talk to you about this. Here's how this is going to go. I'm going to wheel you into the bedroom. You're going to rest up and

I'll cook us both some dinner and read up on the meds the doctor sent you so I'll know how to take care of you."

"I can take care of myself." But the words were starting to sound stubborn even to him.

"No, you've proven that you can't. How long have you known you needed to be off your feet?"

"It doesn't matter." He didn't have the will to truly say what he needed to say to get rid of her. Hell, he wasn't certain it would even work at this point. She seemed to have some wild need to prove to herself that she could handle this.

And what if she can? a hopeful voice whispered deep inside. *What if she really, by some miracle, loves you? Love hadn't been enough for Alicia and that started long before you lost your legs. Tiffany isn't Alicia. She's more. She's better.*

"The fact that you had to see a doctor today tells me that it did," she replied. "Did you do this because you didn't want me to see you in a wheelchair?"

He felt his whole body flush with shame. He shut down that stupid voice and got back to reality. "You are not my nursemaid."

"No, I'm your girlfriend, though I'm worried that doesn't mean the same thing to you that it does to me." She moved in closer, getting down on one knee in front of him. Her eyes softened as she looked at him. "The worst happened, Sebastian. I'm looking at you in a wheelchair and do you know what I'm thinking about?"

"I don't want to know."

She moved on like he hadn't responded at all. "Mostly I'm thinking about how pissed off I am, but underneath all of it, I'm so happy to be done with this bullshit. I want us to get through this so we can be normal."

He seized on that very naïve statement. "There's no normal here. Do you understand that? This isn't normal. This is hell."

Her eyes rolled in a way that made his hand itch to smack her pretty ass. She stood over him. "Don't be ridiculous. And you mistake me. I wasn't talking about you being a normal man. There's no such thing. There are no normal people. Everyone is different. There are normal behaviors. Like sleeping together. Like caring for each other. Like loving each other's bodies. I know you think you're some monstrous thing, but you forget that I have seen you."

Oh, he forgot nothing. He could still remember how she'd stared at him. "Yes, you've seen it so you should thank me for being polite and not forcing you to see more."

"You don't see yourself the way I see you. I've dreamed about you. In my dream you come to me and you're my strong, confident Dom. You don't need clothes because there's no place for them between us. You understand that I think you're gorgeous and that I crave every inch of you. I don't care about the parts that are no longer here. They mean nothing to me. I love you the way you are today. In my dreams, you let me help you when you need it because you would never dishonor my place in your life. You give me your strength when I need it. In my dreams, you love me enough to love yourself. Maybe that won't happen. Maybe you spent every bit of your love on a woman who wasn't worthy of you, but I'm going to get you through the next few weeks. When you're back to being healthy, you can choose which man you want to be. The one who hides or the man I love. Until then, sit back and relax. I'm in charge now."

She started to move behind him. He caught her wrist, twisting it lightly in his hand.

"I can make you let me go. I can hurt you."

She stood there calmly. "You won't."

Her wrist was fragile in his hand. He could break it and break her at the same time.

He let go. His will seemed to be a weak thing around her.

As she moved around to start to push the chair, he knew it wouldn't matter. None of it would work so perhaps he should be selfish and take what he wanted for as long as she was willing to give it.

CHAPTER TWELVE

Tiffany walked into the living room and bit back a frustrated scream. Sebastian was still sitting where she'd left him. He'd growled her way the first time she'd tried to help him back to the bedroom. Such a grouchy lion. He had to be totally retrained, so she'd turned on her heels and left his ass there.

She'd spent her time making the changes she needed to make including moving all of Sebastian's things into the bigger of the two bedrooms. Now his clothes were hanging next to hers, all his toiletries lined up by his sink. It finally felt right to her.

She'd read his meds and planned out their meals around them. She worried she might have to force the pills down Sebastian's throat.

Of course, just the fact that he was still sitting there was kind of a win. She'd been afraid he would roll himself out of the apartment and to a hotel somewhere.

She hated how defeated he looked, his face blank and eyes staring out at nothing.

"Are you ready for dinner? I made tomato soup and grilled cheese. I know it's pretty plain, but you need to eat something so you can take your antibiotic." She kept her tone even, attempting not to give him any real emotion to feed off of.

If he heard her, he didn't show it. He simply stared off in the distance.

"Sebastian, please. I'm not going anywhere. I'm here until you're well again and then I'm sure you'll be strong enough to kick me out." She stopped, looking over at him, but he didn't turn around.

"Why did you call my sister?" His voice sounded rusty, his usual deep honey sound failing him.

She moved to the couch, sinking down to the arm, the closest she could get to him without kneeling at his side. "I wanted to know why you're always so sad."

"How did she sound?"

Finally something they could talk about. "Good. Angry at first, but then she called me back and she wanted to know about you. She asked a lot of questions about your career. Did you know she got married?"

He didn't look her way, but his hand tightened on the arm of the wheelchair. "No. I hadn't heard. Did she marry Tyler Grant?"

"I don't think so. She called her husband Johnny. Is that a nickname?"

His lips curled up ever so slightly. "John Campbell. Good for her. Tyler was her high school sweetheart, but Johnny was her best friend. Tyler was the high school quarterback, and Ramona was nothing but another trophy to him. I hoped they would break up when Tyler went away to college, but he blew his knee out the first semester and came running home. Johnny really loved her. I'm glad she figured that out. Do they have any children?"

"A little boy." She had to hold back the tears that threatened. It hurt her heart that Sebastian had to ask if he had any nieces or nephews. "He's two. His name is Ethan, after your dad."

"Good for Ramona." He put his hands on either side of the chair, finding the wheels. "I think I'll turn in."

She blinked back tears as he managed to turn himself around. Away from her. It seemed like he was always turning away from her. This couldn't work if Sebastian was telling her the truth. If he really couldn't find a way to love her, all of this would have been for nothing.

Not nothing. She would get him through this. She would be a friend to him even if he didn't want her as a lover.

Still, as he started toward the bedroom, she couldn't let him go without asking the question. She needed to know. He might not answer her, but she had to ask. "Did you love her very much?"

It hurt to think that Sebastian had already found his love because she was fairly certain that she wouldn't love anyone but him.

He stopped, the chair wheels gripped firmly in his hands. "Alicia?"

The name came blandly out of his mouth, but she could see the tension in his body.

"Did you love her?"

"I loved her since I was a child." His voice had gone low, so low she had to lean in to hear him. "Her parents were the wealthy patrons of the town. Her mother and mine would work together. Our family restaurant catered for her often. While our mothers would work, she and I would play in the gardens of her house. We were best friends for a long time. I think that's why she chose me. She'd gotten very hurt by a high school boyfriend. She never told me what happened, but I think I was a safe place for her."

The rich girl and the working-class boy. How often did he think of her? Every day? Every hour? Was she the ghost who clung so tightly to him?

"I was planning to marry her," he continued. "I knew her parents didn't approve, but she was strong willed. Sometimes now I think that I was her way of rebelling. Other times I wonder if there wasn't a darker reason for her accepting my proposal. I went into the Army over my parents' strong objections. I needed a way to take care of her. That's where I met Gary. He didn't have any family left so when we had leave, he would come home with me."

She got a sick feeling in the pit of her stomach. An instinct that none of this turned out well. "Was he the father of her baby?"

Sebastian swung the chair around, meeting her eyes for the first time in hours. "Why on earth would you think that baby wasn't mine? Make no mistake. Alicia was pregnant when I was injured. I'd been home on leave not six weeks before."

"And you brought Gary with you."

His eyes narrowed as he stared at her. "Why would you question that the baby wasn't mine?"

"Because you wouldn't have walked away from your child."

He leaned forward, his eyes hard. "Perhaps I realized that I wouldn't make a good father since I lost my legs. Perhaps I didn't want that child burdened with a father who can't walk, can't play with him, can't be anything but a source of pity."

"God, Sebastian. Right now I have no idea why I feel the way I do about you. You're not a source of pity, but that's an argument for another day. I know that child wasn't yours because no matter how self-absorbed you are, you wouldn't have left your kid to fend for himself. Even if Alicia didn't want you anymore, you would have stayed close for the kid. So I have to assume Alicia was a complete bitch and you allowed her to cost you your family. Why, Sebastian? Why let her get away with it?"

"Because she didn't want me." The words burst from his mouth like a bomb exploding. "Do you know what she said to me? She said she wished it had been me. She said she sat down and cried and prayed she could wake up from her nightmare when I came home and he didn't. She'd known him for all of three days when she hopped into bed with him. I found that out after he was dead, of course. My dear friend and my fiancée would hop in the sack together every time we came home. Do you know how I knew the baby wasn't mine?"

The truth hit her like a punch to the gut. "Because you never touched her."

"Because she convinced me to wait until I could honor her properly. Like she was some kind of Southern belle from another century. But I was the dipshit who loved her so I honored her. I never once had sex when I was a whole man."

She felt her hands fist at her sides. "You are whole. The fact that you don't have legs doesn't make you less of a man, but your self-pity does. Look around you. No one pities you but you. You let everyone believe the worst of you because of your pride. What the hell would you have done if she hadn't miscarried? Would you have allowed that child to believe you were rejecting him?"

"It didn't come to that."

She didn't understand him at all. "Why didn't you tell your mother the baby wasn't yours?"

He ran a hand through his hair. "I did tell her. She didn't believe me. What did you want me to do, Tiffany? The woman had lost her husband and then she'd had to see her son come back like this. She wanted that child more than anything and nothing I said could sway her. Alicia was the town princess. Who the hell would believe me? So I left and I ended up in England where I thought seriously about drinking myself to death, but I found something I was good at. I found a place where I could provide service. You don't need my services, do you, Tiffany? You've manipulated me at every single turn."

"Services. I hate that you call it that. Do you have any idea how much better my life is since we moved in together? I know I'm chaotic. I can't help it. I'm built this way, but suddenly I have this amazing peace because I don't have to worry about forgetting important things or being late because I lost track of time. I know that sounds like a little thing, but you've rapidly become important to me on a fundamental level. My life is better because I have this man who cares about me enough to take care of me. The trouble is he won't let me take care of him and I need that, too. I need the exchange in a way I never thought possible. I went into D/s to play and have fun and suddenly I want nothing more than to honor my contract and my Dom and he won't allow it." She was suddenly so tired. Weariness blanketed her and it was all she had to simply stand up. "I need you, but I'm starting to think that the you I thought existed was someone I made up in my head. I'm going to eat something. You can eat or not, but the meds are supposed to be taken with food."

She turned and walked to the kitchen, the world blurring behind her tears.

Had she made him up in her head? Had one day's kindness been enough to make her fall in love with an illusion?

Like she was on autopilot, she made a plate for herself. She wouldn't taste the food, but she would eat it. She needed something to do before she tried to figure out how to get through the next few days with some kindness.

When she turned, Sebastian was in front of the table. "I am not self-absorbed."

He looked as tired as she was.

She moved a chair so he could slide in and set the plate and bowl in front of him. "You are. Totally self-absorbed."

She started to turn, but his hand shot out, gripping her wrist.

"I thought I loved Alicia and when she turned on me, I wanted to die. I realize now that I worshipped her like a little boy. It wasn't love. There was nothing complex about the emotions, no real drive to have her beyond the fact that I thought I should. I say I honored her by not touching her sexually, but those are her words, not mine. I wasn't trying to dishonor you."

Silly man. "There's nothing wrong with sex. Even if it is just an itch you need to scratch. There's nothing truly dirty about it."

His hand gripped tighter. "You were not an itch."

That was good to know. "I'm glad. You weren't for me, either."

"If I was devastated by a woman I didn't truly love, how much could one I did hurt me?"

She managed to turn her palm over, offering to hold his hand instead of being trapped by it. That was what he needed to understand. He didn't have to trap her. She wanted to be here with him. Wanted it so badly, but he still needed her patience. "That's the trade, baby. Love can lift us up or it can crash us right down. Nothing good comes without risk. I love you, Sebastian. You can believe me or not. You can return the feeling or not. The one thing you can't have is absolute certainty that you won't get hurt. I can almost promise that you will. I could die. I could find myself in your position. What if I had an accident and lost my legs? Would you turn away from me because I wasn't whole anymore?"

His fingers threaded through hers and he was suddenly holding on like he was afraid to let go. "Never. I would never leave you. I would…" He took a deep breath. "I would do anything I could to help you because that would be my place. It would be my right."

That was exactly what she wanted to hear. "Why are you taking my rights away from me?"

He pulled his hand away, but didn't move from the table. "I don't want to lose you and what you're going to have to go through in the next few days…I don't want to lose you."

"Then eat your soup." She wasn't going to push him any further tonight. She would have enough trouble getting him into bed.

He started to eat, slowly at first and in silence.

"This would pair well with the Grenache we got in yesterday."

Tiffany got herself a plate. Normalcy. She'd meant what she said about there being no normal people, only normal behaviors. This was sweet, blissful normalcy. "Tell me all about it."

"Well, you know they're some of the most widely planted grapes in the world. Grown in hot and dry conditions," he said quietly. "Spanish, mainly. I spent some time at a vineyard there."

He proceeded to talk and for the first time in hours, she felt a real spark of hope.

* * * *

Two days later, Sebastian stared up at Tiffany and wondered when she'd lost her damn mind. "I can shower by myself."

She put her hands on her hips, a sign he'd come to know as pure stubbornness. "You can't put your legs on. Am I supposed to dump you in and hope for the best?"

He pulled all his patience together. They'd survived the first night. He'd managed to get into bed without her help. He'd done it while she was changing into her pajamas. He hadn't argued about sleeping with her—even though he'd wanted to. He'd lain there stiffly, staring up at the ceiling as she'd fallen asleep beside him.

But waking up that first morning with her cuddled up to him, her hair covering his chest and her breasts snuggled against him had made it all worth it. She'd been warm and soft and he'd wanted so badly to roll over and pin her down. He'd wanted to take her then and there and be done with it all.

He hadn't that first morning and he hadn't this one either. They'd been polite and calm, but he could feel the tension between them. Tension that would only get solved by getting inside her.

What if he did it wrong? What if he was awkward?

Technically, he might have had sex with more partners than she had. When he'd been at The Garden, he'd been determined to prove he could. But she likely had far more experience than he. He'd never taken a woman without his legs on, never pressed his body down on hers and forced her to take his weight. Never rolled in bed for hours with her.

He'd had sex but no intimacy.

Shit. He was really afraid of intimacy. If there was anything he'd come to learn about himself in the last two days, it was that fact. Having to depend on Tiffany was both wonderful and awful. Wonderful because she took care of him with a smile and no sign that it bothered her at all. Awful because he was waiting for her to get tired of it all.

The master shower was large and had no door, just a pretty tiled wall. He glanced in and his shower seat was already there. It would feel good to get clean. He hated how he had to do it though.

And he hated disappointing her, but he wasn't ready for this. He'd slept with her. After he'd gotten cleaned up, he would have to allow her to help bandage the wound again. She'd seen it, of course, but only a bit of his right stump. Only what was necessary to apply the ointment and keep the wound clean. Now she would see him in all his glory.

But at least she wouldn't have to bathe him like he was a child.

"Get me close enough to the shower seat and I'll get myself there." He would then hang his robe on the wheel chair and handle everything himself. She already had the shower water nice and steamy.

She moved the chair into place. "If you insist. I'll be back in a minute."

He took a deep breath. At least she was being reasonable. He shrugged out of the robe he'd managed to put on earlier. She'd promised to lay out some clothes for him. He would prove to her how independent he could be. That would help. He would show her that she wouldn't have to sacrifice so much for him.

Thank god Sean Taggart believed in luxury. It was simple enough to hoist himself up and onto the seat.

It just wasn't very comfortable.

But the water felt good. It didn't quite hit his chest though. He would have to make do. He leaned over, trying to reach the soap. It was barely out of reach.

Suddenly, perfect pink nipples were right in his line of sight as Tiffany leaned over, grabbing the soap. They were right there. He could pop one in his mouth and suckle at will.

"Were you looking for this, babe?"

Fuck. He was hard as a rock. His cock was jutting up, aching and needy. She was naked. Completely beautifully naked and he realized what a long time it had been since he'd seen her like this. He'd indulged in hurried sex with her, shifting her skirt aside, keeping them both on edge.

He was naked with her. Nothing at all between them.

She was so beautiful.

"Look at that," she said, her lips curling up. "I'm looking at your naked body and my nipples are hard. I'm not running, Sebastian. As a matter of fact, if you check, you'll find I'm already getting wet and it's not about the water."

He couldn't help but look down at his legs. Where they used to be. How long was he going to allow this to hold him back? How long was he going to let what happened with Alicia beat him?

"I don't like how they look. It's not how I see myself."

Tiffany knelt down, getting lower than him so she could look up into his eyes. "I don't know how you looked before, but I love your body. I love it because it means you survived."

Her hands were on his legs and he shivered at the feeling. No one touched him there except impersonal doctors. No long, loving caresses of his flesh. No affection. God, he was hungry for her and it was making him reckless.

He stared down at his ruined limbs. His left leg had been amputated below the knee, his right almost entirely gone. He had some thigh left, but both legs ended in stumps, the surgical scars showing how hard it had been for the doctors to save him.

Her fingers brushed over the small wound that caused so much damn trouble. Two stitches. It was all he'd required. It was one small scar in a battlefield, but that one tiny scratch might save him.

"Tell me how this happened."

He didn't like her ordering him around. Something about being naked with her made his instincts flare. "Excuse me?"

Her head dropped down to a more submissive position, but not before he saw the way she smiled. Like a kid given the keys to the candy store.

Was it manipulation? Or the desperate plea of a sub to her stubborn Dom? He wasn't sure it mattered anymore.

"Could you please tell me how it happened, Master?" Tiffany asked, her hands moving over the skin of his legs. She didn't avoid the stumps, didn't gingerly move around them so she didn't have to touch the spot where he'd been sewn up. She embraced them in a way he never had.

It felt so good.

"I fell in the shower one morning and then I banged into one of the tables at Top and reopened it. I lost my footing. I didn't realize until later that the scratch had opened a wound. When you get closer to the stump, the skin becomes less sensitive."

It didn't feel that way now though. His skin felt alive for the first time in forever.

"So if you'd taken care of it and spent some time in the chair, you would probably have been all right?"

"Probably." He watched as she reached over and grabbed the bottle of body wash.

She pumped soap into her hands and then she was working it over his body. She started with his hands, taking one in hers and working her way up the arm. "I would like for this relationship to work. I want it very badly but for it to work, you have to trust me."

It felt so good. So damn good. She moved to his side, soaping her way up his other arm, not missing an inch of skin. He would be so clean when she was done. He'd made do with quick wash downs, but Tiffany was going to make sure he was thoroughly cleaned. Her hands were strong, working across his muscles. Between her touch and the heat of the shower, he felt the bunched up, overworked muscles begin to relax. "I do trust you. So much more than anyone else."

She got to her feet and started to clean his shoulders, massaging them as she went. "I don't know about that. I had to kidnap you to get you here."

"I could have left." The door had been right there and he hadn't taken it. Yes, she'd had his phone, but he could have easily made his way to Top and someone there could have called him a cab.

Yet he'd sat in his chair, staring at the wall and wishing she would come back.

"Why didn't you?" Her hands moved down his back.

He let his torso shift to give her better access. When her thumbs moved on either side of his spine, he couldn't hold back a groan of pure pleasure. "I knew if I left that it was over and no matter what I said, I didn't want this to be over. I didn't want to leave you. I wanted things to go back to the way they were, but I wasn't willing to leave you."

She leaned over as she washed the small of his back, her breasts brushing against him. "I don't want things to go back to the way they were. I want to move forward. I want times like this. I know you're scared that I'll run away in horror, but I won't. I've wanted this ever since the first time I saw you."

"You didn't know about my legs then."

"I didn't care about them then. I don't care about them now with the singular exception of how much of your life revolves around hiding them." She ran her hands up his neck, the soap facilitating the massage. While it was arousing, there was so much more to the way she was touching him.

It felt like affection and caring and…it felt like love.

"I don't want to, but you have to see what they've cost me."

She sighed behind him. "They cost you nothing. You gave them for your country. You gave them to keep people like me safe." She moved in front of him and dropped to her knees, putting her hands on the object of her speech. She soaped up his legs, being careful around the wound, but paying particular and loving attention to the scars that marked his loss. "She cost you. Alicia. Put the blame where it belongs. Her lies cost you up front and then your pride did the rest. I pray that your pride doesn't cost us both. You need a change of view, Sebastian. You need to start seeing the world through my eyes because I see so much clearer than you."

"Do you? Tell me then." He had to try something because she was right. He didn't want to lose her. He couldn't stand the thought of going back to his lonely apartment, his solitary existence.

"You didn't want me in here because you saw me bathing you as a chore." She moved between the stumps of his legs until they were touching her on either side. If it bothered her in the least, she didn't show it. She simply went to work on his chest. "I see it as a way to serve my Dom, my partner, my lover. I see it as a way to get close to him because I love being close to him. And in some ways, I see it as something you earned by being brave. You knew what could happen and you still went into the Army. You earned a stunningly beautiful woman putting her hands all over you."

When she put it like that… How much of his misery was about perception? How much could change if he allowed it to? "I want my turn."

"Your turn?"

She had to understand that if he was going into this with her, he wouldn't be the only one offering his body up. "If I earned the most beautiful woman in the world putting her hands on me, I get to put my hands on her."

She stopped and he could see tears sheen her eyes. She started to say something and then fell silent.

He wasn't so self-absorbed that he didn't know what had gone through her head. He reached for her hand. "Sit with me."

She looked down at the chair. "Can I?"

He put his hands on the sides of the chair. If she'd prepped it properly, the suction cups at the legs would hold it all in place. The shower chair was built for a large man and quite frankly if they fell, they fucking fell. If they fell, they would do it together and he would laugh and be embarrassed a little less than the last time and he would let her help him up.

She would be careful with him. She would have read all the instructions and tested it because Tiffany, while reckless at times, was very loving and thoughtful.

Without another thought, he lifted himself up and repositioned his body so she could sit on his lap. The seat never moved. He did it with ease because one of Damon Knight's conditions for training him as a Dom was that he also trained him physically. He was strong because his mentor wouldn't allow him to be anything else.

He was safe because Tiffany was careful with him.

It was good to have people who cared about him.

Never, not once, had Alicia done something to make his life easier. That had been his job.

He'd given that woman years of his life. What did he owe the smart, sweet sub who was willing to fight for him? Who was willing to fight even him to bring them together? Didn't he owe her a little trust?

"Sit with me."

She gingerly got to her feet and placed herself on his lap, her arms going around his shoulders. It was awkward at first, but she seemed to find a comfortable spot. "Like this?"

She was going to kill him. His cock was nestled under her ass and he was hard as a rock, but he needed something more than sex. He needed this quiet intimacy. Sex was great, but he'd never once had this with another woman. He held her close, resting his head on her shoulder and just breathing her in.

"You are the single best thing to ever happen to me," he whispered to her. "Don't ever compare yourself to Alicia. She was a childhood dream. She was who I thought I should be, but I think it's far past time to let all of that go."

She cuddled close, holding onto him like she wouldn't let go. "You don't have to be anyone but you with me. I want to be your safe place. You can put on whatever airs you want to the rest of the world, but I want the real man."

"And if I'm not sure who that is?" That was his real fear. He'd held onto the pain and the past for so long, he might not like what was on this other side.

"I am." She kissed his cheek, above his eye, on his forehead. Each butterfly touch felt like a benediction. "I know who you are even if you don't. You're brave and afraid at the same time. You're incredibly smart and profoundly stupid. You're so sure of yourself sometimes and a ball of insecurity at others. You're almost always kind. Despite everything, you try to help the people around you. You're human and you're everything to me."

And she was reckless and careful. Brilliant and sometimes tactless. Crass and yet more of a lady than he'd ever seen.

For so long the world had been flat. Good and bad. Light and dark. He was whole and then not. Life had been simple, but hadn't he learned so much about complexity? Sometimes a thing had to be destroyed to become something new, something more beautiful than it had been before.

He'd clung to the vision he'd had at the age of seventeen. A young wine could taste good. There was nothing wrong with it, but something unique happened when a grape was placed in barrels and aged, put through a crucible of time.

I'm not a submissive, but I understand what they go through. Some people need the pain to find themselves, to find pleasure. They transform it into something new. It's our duty and our joy to help them.

His British mentor had been talking about D/s, but perhaps there was more. Perhaps his own pain, his tragedy could be a trigger to propel him to something more. Something better.

Or perhaps it was simply the woman in his lap and her boundless heart that could make him want to be a better man.

"I miss my sister," he admitted quietly.

"I know you do, baby." Her arms tightened around him.

There in the quiet of the shower, surrounded by her warmth, he finally started to talk, to tell her everything.

CHAPTER THIRTEEN

Tiffany looked over at the man she was absolutely certain she was going to love until the day she died.

Sebastian was trying. He was currently attempting to do the dishes in their too close for a wheelchair kitchen. Watching him struggle was going to kill her. She wanted to barge in and take over, but she had to be patient with him.

Only hours before they'd cuddled together in the shower and he'd really talked to her about his life before and how he'd lost it. When they'd come out of the shower, he'd allowed her to dry him off and help him get dressed.

He hadn't tried to get her in bed. That hurt a little, but she was being patient. After all, this was only day three.

"Damn it." Sebastian's deep voice broke through the quiet of the apartment.

She rushed in. "Are you okay?"

His eyes narrowed as he turned her way. "I'm fine. I nearly dropped the damn plate. It fell in my lap and now my slacks are wet."

She grabbed a dishtowel and handed it his way. "I don't mind doing the dishes."

"You cooked. I clean."

She held her hands up. "I know you like to keep the scales balanced, but this place wasn't built for a wheelchair. You know the world doesn't have to be perfectly even. I could cook and clean until you're back on your feet and you could make it up to me in other ways."

He stubbornly swiped the towel over his slacks. "What other way did you have in mind?"

"Sex. You could do dirty sex stuff to me." Maybe she should have gone a little more subtle, but sometimes Sebastian needed a push.

He sat back in the chair. "Are you sure you want that? We could wait until I'm out of the chair. It shouldn't be more than a few days until I can get in my legs again."

"The doctor said at least a week, probably two." She did not want to have this fight with him. Not after how lovely the afternoon had been.

"That's not so long."

She took a deep breath and started to turn to walk out.

He reached out, his hand nabbing her wrist. "It isn't that I don't want you. You had to have felt how much I want you."

She had. He'd been so hard in the shower. She'd understood how awkward it would have been to make love then, but she'd expected him to order her to bed afterward. "I know you want me, but you don't trust me. You can say it all day long, but you're still expecting me to run. You still think I'm going to change my mind."

"I'm nervous that I won't be able to properly top you from this chair."

"You did it with subs at The Garden."

"It wasn't the same," he insisted. "I wasn't having sex then. It was fairly simple to top submissives who had come to me for exactly that purpose. You're different. You need me to be stronger than you in some cases. You need that little edge of threat to make it exciting."

"That's not true."

"I've watched you in the club." He turned the chair so he could properly glare at her. At least that was how it seemed to her. He was giving her that Dom stare that let her know she was in for a lecture. "You're reckless. You offer yourself up for some of the more extreme play."

He'd misunderstood. "Play, yes. I like to try things. I do like to push my limits, but I didn't have sex with any of those Doms."

"Because you decided you wanted me."

"Yes." How could he make that sound like an accusation?

"Tiffany, I'm considered one of the rougher Doms in Sanctum. Wade and I are the only two Doms who have worked professionally."

"That doesn't mean anything."

"You like a firm hand in the bedroom. You like a firm hand in life. I've been quite rough with you over the few weeks of our relationship. Do you know why I took you home that night?"

She knew exactly what night he was talking about. It had been that awful night a few days before her father's surgery. "Because Chef asked you to. I know the story. Deena told me. It was the night she and Eric really got together, but it almost didn't happen because I was so drunk."

"You don't know the whole story. I told Chef I would take you home. I wasn't about to allow anyone else to take you. I also was upset that you were in a position where someone could take advantage of you. I'm not saying it would have been your fault. It wouldn't, but that doesn't make me less upset that it could have happened."

"Sebastian, it was a party at Chef's house. I knew almost everyone there. It was not an issue."

His mouth firmed. "When I found you, you were pushing away one of the busboys. He was trying to grope you."

She barely remembered most of that evening. It hadn't been her finest moment. She felt her cheeks heat with pure embarrassment. "I didn't lead him on or anything."

"I didn't say you did. I never thought you did. It was his fault. I explained the situation to him and then I took you home. I intended to offer my services to you the next morning when you were sober and clear of mind and yes, those services would have led to sex."

She felt her eyes widen. "Are you kidding me? Why didn't you ask me? I would have said yes."

"Because you cried that night," he admitted. "Because I took you back to your place with every intention of putting you to bed, sitting up and drawing up a contract and presenting you with it in the morning. Instead, I held you for the longest time while you cried and told me about your parents and how you miss your father."

"So I scared you off." It hurt that they could have been together all this time.

"I came to the hospital a few days later. I sat with you. I felt more needed that day than you can imagine. I tried to see myself as something more than a Dom to you and I couldn't because I always knew I would still need this damn chair. The funny thing is now I see I might very well be a decent partner for you, but I'm not sure you'll be able to see me as a top after this."

She felt her hands fist at her sides. "You have to be kidding me."

"Forget I said anything." His hands went to the wheels again.

She wanted to scream. "No, I can't forget you said anything. Sebastian, this is ridiculous. You can't do the dishes. The sink is too high. Find something else to do if you absolutely have to. Do you understand how ridiculous it is to say I'm not treating you like a real Dom when I'm offering you service? I'm offering to literally wait on you hand and foot. You say you're the baddest Dom in Sanctum? Well, here I am being twelve kinds of subby and you reject me at every turn."

"Yes, you sound so very submissive. This is exactly what I'm talking about."

She stopped. She wasn't being patient, wasn't trying to figure him out. He'd bent this morning. He'd let her in and she needed to do the same for him. "I started in the lifestyle because my friends were doing it. I'll admit it. I enjoy the hell out of it. It's more arousal than I've ever had, but it still didn't tempt me into uninvolved sex. I've had four sexual partners and I've cared about all of them. I'm an emotionally based lover."

"Who has very likely chosen every lover for what he could give you," he shot back. "I suspect you always chose the alpha male in the group."

Maybe, but couldn't he see that he belonged to that group? He was a quiet top, but definitely a top. "I chose you. I don't know why we have to question that."

"I'm not trying to question you beyond the fact that I'm worried I can't give you what you need."

"I only need you."

He looked down, his eyes on the floor. "You say that now, but I'm not sure where we'll be a few weeks from now. You know I can't physically force you to obey me."

Did he understand D/s at all? "I have a safe word, Sebastian. You can't force me to do anything. It stops everything."

"I know I wouldn't actually force you. But tell me you don't like the idea that the safe word is merely a ploy, that I couldn't force you at any time at all. You like the knife's edge. You push boundaries. Tell me I can push yours. Because I can't. I can't follow you in this chair. I can't force you. Not ever."

He couldn't force her but it had little to do with the chair and everything to do with the man he was. "I'm okay with that. Whatever you think I need, I don't need any more than you can give. Will you please let me do the dishes so we can go to bed where you very likely won't do anything interesting?"

His lips curled up in the sexiest snarl. "You are asking for it."

She kind of was because patience sucked. Still, she turned to the sink. "I just want to get this done so we can watch some TV and enjoy the rest of our evening. Unless you've recently decided to not be a complete OCD freak who can't enjoy anything until the kitchen is bleached and cleaned?"

He frowned. "I'll go and sort through the god-awful amount of mail Deena dropped off for you earlier today."

She watched as he turned the chair toward the living room. Deena had been out at Top Dallas the day before and stopped by her apartment and Sebastian's place to bring them mail. He'd already gone through his, though apparently all his billing was online at this point. If he wanted to sort through all the crap she got, he was welcome to it.

She turned back to the dishes and shook her head. Somehow he'd still managed to do most of them. Overachiever.

How did she get him to believe she didn't need anything but him?

He was right about one thing. She did enjoy rough play. He could still be rough. He'd been rough all week with her. The fact that he used a wheelchair from time to time didn't make him soft.

He had very little imagination. Smart as hell, but no imagination.

That wheelchair could play into some seriously filthy scenarios if only he would stop viewing it as something to hate.

"Do you ever pay your bills on time?"

She could hear the frown in his voice. She didn't have to turn to know he'd gotten a little crease on his forehead. "Mostly. Sometimes I get involved in work and I forget. I had a roommate for a while. She was good at paying the bills on time."

"Perhaps you should have tried to keep her because according to this your electricity is about to be turned off."

She groaned. She had forgotten that one. "I lost the last bill. I think I used it to mix blues together. I couldn't get the right shade so I was playing around, but obviously I can't do that on the canvas."

"Obviously."

Yeah, he was likely never going to understand her on that one. "So I thought I would wait for the next bill and pay them both at the same time. I'll send it off. It's no biggie. I'm not even at the apartment right now so my sister would say I'm helping the earth by turning off the electricity. And I couldn't keep Heidi. Her best john finally forked over the cash to make her a permanent mistress and they left for New York. I tried to tell her that there was no such thing as a truly permanent mistress, but she had stars in her eyes."

He was quiet for a moment. "Please tell me you weren't living with a prostitute."

Well, she hadn't known Heidi was on the game when she first moved in. "Okay, I won't tell you."

A long sigh issued. "I'm taking over paying your bills. You'll need to give me the passcodes to your banking accounts. I'm going to set everything up to pay online and I'll monitor that your bills get paid in a timely manner."

Yep, he was so not dominant. She turned to him, putting down the sponge she'd been using. It was time to turn this around on him. "I don't think that's a good idea. I wouldn't want to be a burden to you, Sir."

He shook his head. "It's far more a burden if I'm worried you've forgotten to pay a bill because you're too busy painting or finding new objectionable roommates."

She only wanted one roommate, even if he was a prissy, gloriously gorgeous asshole. "But I have so much fun finding new roommates. I'm interviewing a few drug dealers next week. I'm hoping to upgrade my cable subscriptions. Also, you know how I like to live on the edge. Never knowing if the meth lab is going to explode makes for fun days."

"Tiffany, I am serious."

She shrugged. "Then let me move in with you."

There was a gleam in his eyes as he replied. "All right. I'll have you moved out of your place and into mine before we go back to Dallas. Knowing what I now know about your neighborhood, I'll feel better if you move. I live closer to your father, anyway. He'll be thrilled to know you're moving uptown."

Whoa. What had just happened? "How do you know where my father lives?"

Did he turn the faintest shade of pink? "I might have formed a friendship with your father."

"When?"

"I called him the day we moved in together to get the full story of your stalker. I knew I wouldn't get it from you, so I talked to him. He's worried about you and I think him knowing that I am taking responsibility for you makes him feel better."

Now she was fairly certain she'd turned beet red. "Please tell me you didn't explain D/s to my father."

His lips curled up in the most honest smile she'd ever seen from him. "I didn't have to. He asked if I was going to top you. He's known about it ever since he figured out you got a membership to Sanctum."

If she'd been holding a dish, she would have dropped it. "How the hell did he find out about that?"

Sebastian shrugged and went back to sorting through her mail. "People in the lifestyle talk, sweetheart. You should know that. You're one of the biggest gossips at Sanctum." He looked up, giving her a stern glare. "We'll work on that problem, too."

It wasn't gossip. It was finding out interesting facts about her friends and talking about it without said friends necessarily being there for the conversation. And what? "My father was not in the lifestyle."

A satisfied look came over Sebastian's face. "Now this is what it feels like to know something Tiffany Hayes doesn't know. It's nice, actually. It's a warm feeling right there in my chest. Yes, I could get used to this."

He was such an ass. "Tell me. Sebastian, if you don't tell me right now I'm going to…"

That look in his eyes made her stop. It was dark and when he spoke, his voice had gone low, and she realized she was playing at the edges of his tolerance. "You're going to what, my darling? I would think about what you say next."

And he said he couldn't top her from that damn chair.

She knew damn well he was annoyed and it was up to her to soothe the savage beast. She rather thought the splinter had come out of his poor paw in the shower today, but he still had some healing to do. She moved around the bar and dropped down to the sofa beside him. "I was going to say that if you don't tell me, I'll cry."

His hand came out, knuckles brushing over her cheek. "Sure you were." He sighed as he stared at her. "Have I told you how beautiful you are today?"

"You might have mentioned it once or twice." She gave him a smile and reminded herself that patience was the word of the day. "I think you're pretty, too, Sir."

"I prefer Master," he replied quickly. "I like the way you say it. I know that goes against what we talked about, but I do want to try with

189

you. I need you to be honest with me about how you feel when we start to play again. I'm going to want more control than you might be willing to give me. I know Deena and Eric simply play, but I need more."

She knew that. She also knew that there were things she would love to push off on him so she didn't have to worry about them. Things he would enjoy doing for her. She wasn't organized. He loved to file stuff and kept careful and copious notes not only on every wine he tasted but on household stuff like scheduling when to change the air filters. She hadn't known they had to be changed. Which could explain a lot about her apartment.

"Top away, Master. Though I'll never be happy with you picking my clothes." She didn't like the thought of that. Some submissives let their Masters select everything from food to clothing to scheduling out their days.

His hand moved over hers and he tugged at her gently. "Sit with me."

Her heart warmed instantly. This was exactly what she wanted. Sebastian needed affection and now he was asking for it. Well, he was asking for it the only way a Dom would. She moved the mail to the side and sat down on his lap. Such a comfy lap. Well, except for the rod that suddenly poked at her backside. "I like sitting with you."

"I like sitting with you. I think I like this more than having you at my feet." He frowned. "I can't actually feel you at my feet since I left them behind in Afghanistan."

He could joke, too, it seemed. She chuckled. "I like being closer to you."

His arm wound around her waist, holding her in place. "You can't imagine how good it feels to be close to you. It's addictive. You're addictive. So if I can't get out of this trap you set for me, we should at least negotiate terms. I won't ever take control of your creativity. Your clothes, how we decorate, your work, those are all your purview. You will likely want to redo the apartment or whatever space we decide on and I'll happily give it up to you. I'll control everything that requires precision."

She could handle that. "But I reserve my right to poke you when I think you aren't taking care of yourself."

"I promise, I'll handle it with grace."

There was one thing she couldn't handle. "Please tell me my daddy isn't a Dom."

He smiled and there was no way to describe it as anything other than brilliant. "I will not tell you that your father was a Dom. I don't want to lie to my sweet sub."

She shuddered. "Please tell me my daddy wasn't a sub."

He leaned in and whispered in her ear. "Like father, like daughter. He's very happy to know you've got a Dom looking out for you and now I'll be sure to keep him up to date." He dropped his head close to hers. "Does it bother you knowing your parents were together that way? He hasn't practiced since the day she died if that makes you feel better."

She wasn't selfish. "I'm glad they were happy." But she was also a reasonable human being who didn't want to ever think about her parents having sex. Of any kind. "But they never did anything at Sanctum, right? Sanctum wasn't around back then."

"Rest easy, darlin'. They played at an older club." He kissed her cheek, his hand slipping under her breast. "I like your father. He's a very nice man. I'm afraid of your sister. Not the fluffy one. The crazy one in France."

She couldn't wait for her sisters to meet Sebastian. V would adore him and Berry might stop looking at herself in the mirror long enough to realize how cool he was. "She's a sweetheart, though she will lecture you on your dry cleaning practices."

"My suits aren't going through a washing machine," he insisted. "Those are custom-made suits. The earth will have to suck it up."

And she loved how he wore them. "V would never advise you to clean them in a modern washing machine. She might give you a rock to go down to the river and beat them with, but only if she was certain it wouldn't harm the wildlife."

"Tiffany?" His voice had gone low again. Deep and dominant.

How could he even question his abilities? The sound of his voice alone made her shiver. She was ready to spend the rest of the night playing. All night long. "Yes, Master?"

"Is that a letter from the Department of Corrections?"

Shit. She scrambled off his lap and had that letter in her hand in a heartbeat. She definitely didn't want him involved in all that. "I'm sure it's nothing. Don't worry about it."

She should have gone through that damn mail, but she'd forgotten about Bobby's upcoming parole hearing thingee. It was nothing to worry about, but she didn't want it to come between them right then. The last thing she wanted was Sebastian lecturing her on her previous choice of boyfriends.

He held a hand out. "I think I'll decide whether it's important or not. Give me that letter."

This would likely be a very bad time to tell him it was her mail and he should take his hands off it. She'd just agreed that he was pretty much in charge of exactly that and somehow she was certain he would take offense.

"Yes, think about it," he encouraged her. "Run it through that creative brain of yours and you'll come to the right conclusion. Otherwise, this evening is not going to go well for you."

Damn it. She handed it over. "His parole hearing is coming up. My dad made sure the Department of Corrections would inform me of any changes in his status but that was all he could manage to get them to do. Bobby threatened me, but he also apologized and he's done therapy time. I think Dad's making a big deal out of nothing."

Sebastian opened the envelope. "He threatened to kill you before they took him off to jail. He shouldn't be up for parole at all. He should rot there for the rest of his life and I'm calling an attorney in the morning. I know your father has money, but Chef has connections through his brother. I'll have a protective order on you before his parole board hearing. I think we should send someone, too. Not you. I won't give him the pleasure of seeing you, but perhaps sending a McKay-

Taggart representative to speak on your behalf would help."

"Why would someone speak on my behalf? What am I saying?" He was so serious about something that hadn't really touched her life in years. She barely remembered what Bobby looked like much less that he'd once threatened her.

Sebastian sighed, obviously attempting to be patient with her. "You're saying you want the man to do every single second of the time he was sentenced to do. No parole."

That seemed harsh. Especially if he was really sorry for what he'd done. "Don't you think people can be rehabilitated?"

"No," he replied with no patience whatsoever. "Rehab is for injuries. Prison is for assholes. Assholes are always, always assholes."

He and V were so not going to get along. She foresaw many political arguments in their future. "The last time he communicated with me, he said he'd gone through AA and needed to work through his steps."

"He can work through his steps from prison," Sebastian insisted. "When is the hearing?"

She shrugged. "No idea."

He huffed a bit, a deeply irritated sound. "So this is the first letter they've sent you?"

"Think so." Or there might have been another. "Maybe this is the second. I didn't actually read the first one. It was a lot of lawyer stuff. Boring. And unnecessary. Lots of people going to jail are pissed. It's a natural reaction. Do you want another glass of Pinot?"

There went her happy sexy time. At least she still had wine.

Sebastian stared at the letter and then back up at her. "This letter isn't about his parole hearing. It's about his damn release date. Which was three days ago."

"And yet I'm still alive." He was making a mountain out of a molehill. A criminal molehill, but a molehill nonetheless. "There's nothing to worry about. I'm not even living at my apartment anymore. I'm out here where no one can find me."

"Unless he was watching your place and followed Deena back

here." Sebastian pushed back and turned the chair toward the kitchen. "I'm calling Ian Taggart. I want to know where this man is. And I'm definitely calling your father. He needs to understand why you won't be able to sit down at the next family dinner. Or perhaps ever again."

Yeah, he could totally top her from the chair.

There was a knock on the door. "Sebastian, you're making a big deal out of nothing. I told you Bobby Len wrote me a couple of times and at the end he explained that he was in AA and wanted nothing more than to make amends. It's apparently one of the steps."

"You'll meet with him over my dead body," Sebastian swore. "And don't you dare answer that door."

But she'd already opened it. The doorknob had turned and she was struck dumb by the man standing in her hallway.

Bobby stood there, so much leaner and more muscular than he'd been before. He looked meaner, too.

"Hello, Tiffany. Miss me?"

She hadn't. She really, really hadn't.

CHAPTER FOURTEEN

Sebastian went perfectly still as he heard the door open and a deep voice speak. It chilled him though the room was perfectly warm.

"Hello, Tiffany. Miss me?"

Son of a bitch. He quickly moved to the back of the kitchen. From his vantage, he couldn't see where Tiffany and her erstwhile, soon-to-be-dead stalker were, but that meant they couldn't see him either. From here he could either charge straight into the living room or work his way around the hall and come from behind.

"Hey, Bobby. Wow, you dropped a ton of weight," Tiffany was saying. "You look scary, but good."

Why wasn't she slamming the door in his face?

"Well, prison will do that to you, sweetheart," Bobby was saying. The door slammed closed. Unfortunately, that asshole was on the wrong side of it. Sebastian could hear the heavy thud of boots against the hardwood floors.

That did not sound in any way like a man who was coming to ask for forgiveness. It did not in any way sound like a dude who was trying to check off some kind of penance list. If the man who was currently stepping into his living room was marking off a list, it was a revenge tally.

"This is Taggart."

Sebastian looked down at the phone in his hand. Damn it. He

moved into the hallway as quietly as he could. Luckily Tiffany didn't believe in silence. There was music playing. It wasn't loud but it would likely cover the sound of him moving to a place where he could get his message out.

"Seriously, do you think I don't have caller ID? I know it's the wine dude so if this is some kind of prank call, you're twenty years and a load of technology too late. Also, you woke me up from a nap so I might send a missile your way. Don't think I won't do it."

God, that guy was such an ass at times.

"So I'll ask again, did you miss me, babe?" Tiffany's stalker asked his question a little louder this time.

Sebastian could see them in the mirror over the small fireplace. Tiffany had her back to the hallway and Bobby was standing in the middle of the living room, his predatory form looming over Tiffany's.

Please don't let him have a gun. He couldn't see the man's left hand. It was right out of the frame of the mirror.

"How did you find me?" Tiffany asked. For the first time she sounded halfway scared. At least she had the tiniest bit of sense.

"I followed the brunette. You weren't at home so I had to track you down, but then I think I told you I would."

"I am hanging up now and sending the missile your way. Sorry about the wreckage, but a nap is a nap," Tag was saying over the line.

There was nothing like a potential killer in one's house to get the old adrenaline up. He put the phone to his ear and kept his voice low. "Ian, Tiffany's ex-boyfriend is here and I'm fairly certain he's about to murder her."

"Shit. Charlie, baby, send the cops out to Sean's place in Fort Worth." Big Tag's voice came strongly back on the line. "Did he bring friends?"

"No, but I'm in the chair." Of all the fucking times to not have his damn legs. This. This was why he didn't get involved. He couldn't help her. He was a fucking coward hiding out in the hallway. She was likely scared out of her mind and he was skulking back here because he couldn't walk in and save her.

"Awesome. Stealth. I like it. Is he a talker? You know the monologueing kind of mother fucker who puts his victim through a ridiculous lecture that makes them long for the sweet release of death?" Taggart asked.

What the fuck was he going to do? He couldn't get to the revolver he kept in a locked case by his bed. He would have to wheel himself by the living room. "They're talking. Well, he's talking. I'm going in. At least I can give her a chance to run."

"She won't run," Taggart replied. "She's in love with you. Women are weird when they're in love. They get all protective and shit. You need a plan, soldier. If he's talking then he very likely wants to take his time with her, make it last. That means you have a few minutes. Take stock. What do you have on hand that you can use to kill the fucker? Or to distract him. Charlie says the police are three minutes away. She's trying to get Javier on the line right now. He's in the same building as you but apparently some chick answered and she didn't sound sober. What are your assets?"

He had a fucking cell phone and no goddamn legs.

Soldier. Taggart had called him soldier. Sometimes he forgot. He forgot that he'd been a soldier. He'd gone into the service for financial reasons. For rational, logical reasons. And then he'd gotten there and discovered he was more than the dweeby kid who'd followed his father around and daydreamed his life away. He'd discovered discipline was more than a word to scare kids into behaving.

He'd learned he could do great things when he put his mind to it. When he stopped being afraid and did his job, he could work some miracles.

It hadn't all been bad. Most of his time had been good. He'd loved the camaraderie. He'd loved waking up every morning with a purpose.

How had he forgotten how much he'd loved it? How had he allowed the end to tarnish all the things that came before? And all the good things that had come after.

If he hadn't gone in the Army he wouldn't have found the focus and discipline to follow his dream. He would have married Alicia and never met his adorable, sexy ball of chaos who was going to get her ass smacked if they both survived this.

No. When they survived this. When.

Three minutes wouldn't guarantee them anything. That asshole could take her hostage. He could still hurt her. The police could only ensure that he didn't get away. They couldn't promise to save her.

That was up to him.

"Sebastian, you can do this," Taggart said, his voice as steady as his former CO's.

One bad day. He'd had one bad day and it didn't have to ruin the rest of his life. But this one—oh, if this one turned bad, his life might be over because she was the one. She was everything he'd never thought he wanted in a woman and everything he absolutely needed to be whole.

He didn't need his damn legs. They were incidental and he could see that now.

He needed her. Only her.

"I have a corkscrew in my pocket. I would go back into the kitchen for a knife, but the block is too close. He would see me so it's me and the corkscrew. It's fitting since it's my favorite tool. I have a decent line of sight on him. Everything else will be pure luck and willpower. Thank you, Tag. For everything. You take care of her if anything happens to me."

"Understood, but you're a badass and he's a fucker who could barely handle minimum security prison. Take him out."

He hung up the phone. He wouldn't need it.

Or maybe he would. After all, a smart man could do amazing things. All he had to do was try. He'd spent the last few years hiding away, taking very few risks.

It was time to take the biggest of his life.

He wheeled slowly toward the living room and prayed he would be in time.

* * * *

She was surprisingly calm once she realized Sebastian wasn't going to come charging out to save her. That had been her moment of pure panic. She'd seen the knife in Bobby's hand and envisioned him gutting Sebastian with it.

"Bet you didn't think you'd see me again." Her ex stared at her like she was a deer he was about to skin and mount to his wall.

"I have to admit, I didn't think you'd be dumb enough to show up on my doorstep." She'd thought he was so smart, sure of himself. He'd been a twenty-four-year-old in charge of his own brokerage firm. Of course she should have known it had all been a scam. Still, it had required some brainpower, and he was showing none of that now.

His hand curled around the knife. It was a nasty-looking thing that most people would have used for hunting, though she supposed he was kind of hunting her. "I told you I would be back for you."

She couldn't help but roll her eyes. Fear was there, but Sebastian was in the back of the apartment and he would wait until the time was right. He would come in and save her. There was no way he didn't do that. It was odd, but she'd never trusted anyone the way she did Sebastian. He was solid no matter what his wounded psyche might tell him. He was also strong as hell and obviously way smarter than her old boyfriend. All in all a real upgrade. "Everyone knows you made that threat."

He shrugged, the knife still glinting. "And I wrote to you many times explaining about how I only want to see you to make amends. Tell me you didn't believe me."

"Of course I did. I'm eternally optimistic and I get the feeling I'm going to pay for that later on today." Her Master was going to be so pissed when they got through this. "But you should know that everyone who knows me knows that if I die after the man who threatened to murder me gets out of jail, they should probably give you a look. Also, I'm not planning on letting you kill me."

He took a step forward. "I'm not giving you a chance. And I've planned this out perfectly. I've got ten people who will swear I'm at a family dinner right now. Unlike you, you little traitor, my family sticks together."

"And my weird work family is totally paranoid, so while you might have some people willing to lie for you, this building has so many cameras you won't have been able to avoid all of them." Anger thrummed through her. How dare he? He had zero right to invade her space. She'd done the right thing. He'd been a bad person. "You know you could have done your fairly easy time and still had a life."

"I don't have a life," he snarled back. "They took everything from me. They took all my money. All my power."

What a pathetic shit. She was going to have such a talk with Sebastian. He'd lost everything and still made a life for himself. He'd lost his legs and his family and his view of himself and he'd still found a way to survive.

The man in front of her didn't have half Sebastian's strength.

"You're going to go back to jail if you don't get out of here." It would be best if she could scare him away and never have to put Sebastian in harm's way.

"I didn't see any cameras." He glanced back at the door as though trying to figure a way out of the trap.

"There are a bunch. They're placed throughout the building." She almost felt sorry for the asshole. There really were carefully placed cameras just about everywhere. He might have avoided some of them, might have kept his head down, but there was zero chance he wouldn't have been caught by at least one security cam.

"My boss's brother owns a security firm." She kept her voice quiet, soothing. Anything to keep him from using that knife. Where would Sebastian come from? Not the kitchen. He would probably come from behind, from the hallway where he would be able to maneuver more freely.

She needed to turn them around. If he came out of the hall right now, Bobby would see him.

"I hate you." Bobby's face had gone red, his hand twitching.

Now she was afraid. Adrenaline flooded her system. *Please don't let him hurt Sebastian.* She couldn't lose him now that she'd finally found him.

"I did what I thought was right." She shifted slightly to her left. He'd been mirroring her movements. If she was careful maybe he would continue. "You were hurting people."

His eyes flared but he took the bait, moving to shift around her, keeping her in his sights. "Old people. They were dying anyway. They didn't need that money the way I did. Stop moving right now. I swear, Tiffany, I'm not going back to jail. And if I'm going down, I'll take you with me."

She put her hands out, ready to try to hold him off. "You won't get away with it."

He held up the knife. "Oh, but it's going to be worth it, bitch. This time I'm really going to deserve it because I'm going to gut you. I'll make you wish you had never been born."

There was a horrible thudding sound and Bobby's head snapped to the side. Had that been Sebastian's phone?

That was when Sebastian moved in. He hit Bobby with more power than she would have thought a wheelchair could have. As Bobby groaned and fell over, Sebastian launched his big body out of the chair and onto her attacker.

She watched as something silver flashed out of his hand and he managed to use his ridiculous upper body strength to flip Bobby over and get him in a tight hold.

Was that a corkscrew?

Bobby had dropped the knife when Sebastian had apparently launched his phone like a brick. She moved in and kicked it to the side.

"Do you understand that I have a corkscrew to your jugular vein?" Sebastian had her ex around the neck, the silver edge of the corkscrew pressed hard against his neck. "It will take some strength to shove it through the skin, but I possess more than enough and I want nothing more than to see your blood all over this floor because that woman is mine and you threatened her. Tiffany, love, would you like me to open this boy's jugular vein and let him bleed out?"

She actually thought about it. He was a jerk. But she did have something of a conscience. And besides, after this he would go to a bigger, better prison likely with way more opportunities to teach him valuable lessons. Sebastian really liked those slacks. Blood didn't easily come out of linen. "No. I hear sirens. Let him live, babe. He'll have fun in max. We can get that, right? Big Tag knows the district attorney, right?"

"I believe he does." Sebastian sounded so fierce and those sirens were getting closer. "All right then. Don't move and you live. Move the slightest bit and we'll have a problem, you and I. I'll open you like a bottle I don't give a damn about. Just try to breathe."

Damn that man was sexy.

CHAPTER FIFTEEN

Sebastian signed the document the police officer handed to him while Big Tag slapped him hard on the back.

"You almost killed that dude with nothing but a cell phone and a corkscrew," Big Tag was saying. "You win employee of the week. Sean, I think we should totally have a program at the restaurant for employees who creatively handle crime."

The police officer gave him a smile and a little shake of his head. "Good luck, man. If anything at all happens with McMurtry, we'll let you know. He's obviously violated parole so he's going back to prison, but he'll have a new trial based on what happened today."

"Damn straight," Sean Taggart said. "And my wife thanks you for not murdering that man on our rug."

Oh, but he'd thought about it. Sebastian had thought seriously about killing that fucker when he'd called Tiffany a bitch. When Bobby had talked about gutting her, he'd nearly seen red. She was his. Fucking his. No one got to touch her. He'd had another crazy caveman moment and it had felt oddly good. He'd always prized himself on being a modern man, but he wasn't when it came to his blonde ball of chaos. She was all his and she was going to stay that way. She should get used to it.

He'd walked away from Alicia. She'd been his whole life for years and he'd turned and walked out on her. He'd walked out on everyone.

He wasn't sure he would ever be able to do that with Tiffany. He could be angry with her, pissed as hell, and he would still tie her tightly to his side.

"No, V. He didn't kill him. He only threatened to kill him," Tiffany was saying into her phone. She looked far too calm and perfect for a woman who had almost been horrifically murdered. "Yes, I agree with his choice. Yeah, well, pacifism kind of gets tossed out the window when someone tries to knife you. Bobby was awful. I thought about kicking him in the crotch. No, Sebastian's not a brutal man warrior and you're not protesting him at Thanksgiving. He's my boyfriend."

He was going to be her husband one day, and his new family was an interesting one.

"Are you really okay?" Sean asked. "You don't need to see a doctor? The cops said you obviously took a rough fall when you took that idiot down."

"I'm all right." The EMT had already checked him out and declared he was fine. It wouldn't have mattered. He wasn't going to be moved from his plans for the evening.

He owed his sub some time alone.

"I've calmed her dad down," Sean explained. "He's still insisting on cutting his vacation short and catching a flight back from France so you'll have company in a day or two."

Luckily now they had an extra room. "I can handle her dad. I just pray he doesn't show up with her sisters."

The door banged open and Javier rushed in, still buttoning his shirt. "I'm here. What happened? Britney told me Charlotte called and Sebastian was being murdered. Or maybe it's Brianna. I can't remember. She was half coherent. It was a crazy night."

Ian shook his head. "You're too late and it wasn't Sebastian being murdered. It was Tiffany."

Javier's eyes widened, but when he looked over at Tiff, she merely smiled, waved his way, and then went back to defending the American jurisprudence system to her sister.

Javi shook his head as he looked back at Sebastian. "What happened? Did Sebastian kill him?"

"Why does everyone assume I killed the man?" Perhaps his reputation as a gentleman wasn't as sparkling as he thought.

"Because you're a badass, man," Javier said with a nod. "Look, I might be worried about you breaking Tiffany's heart, but that doesn't mean I don't respect the hell out of you. You lost both legs and almost no one would be able to tell because when you walk in a room, you're the tallest man there, one who quietly commands respect. But you're pretty much doing that right now and you're in a chair."

"I wouldn't mess with him," Sean agreed. "But then I've seen what he can do with a corkscrew. Were the cops telling the truth? Did he pee his pants when you threatened to pop his neck open like a bottle of Merlot?"

"That was an exaggeration. It was mostly tears and pleading and then my sweet submissive threatened to kick him in the balls while giving him a lecture on how violence is killing our polite society. Thankfully the police arrived before I decided to turn the corkscrew on myself." When his girl wanted to, she could give quite the talking to.

She wasn't going to be talking much tonight.

"Your sub?" Javier asked, one brow over his eye.

"Mine. Always mine." The younger man should understand that. He said he only had interest in Tiffany as a sister, but he should know that Sebastian was going to be the final authority figure in her life.

Sean slapped a hand on Javi's shoulder. "You're a shitty fake big brother. Don't you know that siblings always come first? Ian's walked out on plenty of sex because I was in trouble."

"He cock blocked me my whole senior year of high school," Ian said with a sad shake of his head.

Javi's smile dimmed. "Yeah, well, I was always the little brother. Guess I have to learn some things. Are you really going to take care of her?"

Oh, he had plans. "I'm going to marry her at some point, but I'm definitely taking care of her tonight."

"Care, as in holding her tenderly and making sure she's emotionally all right?" Sean asked.

Big Tag held his stomach. "My respect is going down."

"Care, as in teaching her to take her own life and safety seriously from this day forward. Care, as in teaching her exactly who her top is." Sebastian looked over where she was shaking her head and whispering into the phone again. "But I think I might need some help. After all, every soldier needs his backup, right?"

It was another thing he'd forgotten. It was good to have friends.

"Respect rising. You have a game plan or are we winging it?" Big Tag asked.

"Oh, I have a plan. I'll need help with the setup and then I'll take it from there. Are the police all gone?" He wouldn't want any misunderstandings.

"Yes, but I think we're going to have to pry that cell phone from her hands," Sean pointed out.

"That's the least of her worries. I'm going to need some handcuffs, two pairs to be exact. I need to be able to twist her back and forth. I want all access but she needs to understand that I mean business." She liked it rough. He could give it to her. He would give her everything she needed because no matter what had happened in the past, he was her man now.

"Oh, I can MacGyver something for you," Javi promised.

It was good to have friends.

* * * *

"I'm perfectly fine, but if you want to come over and check on us, you're more than welcome," Tiffany said.

"I can't believe he followed me. I feel so bad. I should have sensed something, shouldn't I?" Deena sounded the tiniest bit tortured over the line.

After she'd hung up with her sister, she'd immediately gotten a call from Deena. She was so grateful for the distraction because Sebastian had seemed pretty fierce.

Tiffany glanced over and Sebastian was still talking to the Taggart brothers, though it looked like Javier had left. She hadn't actually seen him leave, but he wasn't in the living room anymore. She was happy their company hadn't left yet. Sebastian had to be annoyed with her. Or he would be angry with himself. Either way, it was a talk she would prefer to avoid. If she kept him busy with company for a few hours, she could claim she was far too tired to talk and get him in bed. Once he was there, she could make him forget his annoyance/self-consciousness. "It wasn't your fault, sweetie. You're not some super spy. You don't know when someone's tailing you."

"But he could have killed you," Deena said. "What if Sebastian hadn't been there?"

"But he was. I'm okay. Sebastian's okay. Come on over and we'll have a glass of wine. I'm sure Sebastian knows what pairs well with a murder attempt."

Suddenly a big hand pulled the phone from her. She looked up and Ian Taggart was holding the cell. He put it up to his ear.

"No time for guilt, Deena. Your friend has been a bad, bad sub and you know what happens to bad subs. Unless you want to help Sebastian do nasty things to her. Because I might wait around for that. I wonder how fast Charlie could get out here."

"I think this is going to be a private party, brother." Chef was standing right next to Big Tag, their massive bodies making a wall she couldn't get through.

Yeah, if Bobby had been half as smart and ruthless as the Taggart brothers, she likely would have been dead by now. A little thrill of fear ran through her, not because she thought the Taggarts would hurt her, but this definitely had something to do with Sebastian.

Had he decided she was too much trouble? Was she about to be escorted out of his life?

Or was he planning something else?

"You can talk to her tomorrow." Big Tag hung up the phone and set it aside. "Tiffany, I need to ask you a few questions before we get started."

Where was Sebastian? She couldn't see him now. "I'm not leaving him. I know he's mad, but I won't let you haul me away. I might look all soft and fluffy but I have moves, too."

She didn't. She had no moves, but sometimes men could be intimidated by confident women.

Not the Taggarts, though. She supposed when one of them was married to the most beautiful woman Tiffany had ever seen and the other had married a gorgeous woman who knew how to kill a man a thousand different ways, one got used to confident women.

They simply stood there and gave her stares that would send any sub with a sense of self-preservation running away. Unfortunately, she had to fight for her Dom. "I'm sorry, Sirs. What was your question, Master Ian?"

She gave him his honorary title because it suddenly felt like they were in the club.

"Tiffany, do you accept Sebastian as your Dominant partner? Will you wear his collar and attempt to honor him as he intends to honor you?"

She felt her eyes widen. "This is a collaring ceremony?"

"Sort of," Chef replied. "But I think you can expect something more romantic after Sebastian's had some time. He simply doesn't want to go further this evening until you agree."

"Because this is a shitty collaring ceremony." He wasn't having her dragged away. But a girl still had her standards. She might be willing to run away to Vegas and marry him, but a collaring ceremony was a serious freaking event and one that should be carefully planned and considered. "I'm not even in fet wear."

"Oh, he's going to fix that very quickly, brat." Big Tag shook his head. "If you think the evening went poorly before, you haven't even thought about what that Dom intends to do to you. I wouldn't complain about his lack of romanticism."

"Too late." Sebastian was sitting in his chair outside their bedroom door. "I already heard her very disappointing rejection."

She shook her head. "Not a rejection. No. I didn't reject anything. I was simply stating that a submissive waits all her life for the right Dom to collar her and maybe she expects something a little more romantic."

"Tonight isn't going to be romantic," Sebastian promised, rolling into the living room. "I've given myself enough time to calm down and think your punishment through, but I will not allow you to disregard your safety ever again. You are the most precious thing in the world to me and I won't allow you to harm yourself through blatant disregard and complete idiocy."

Well, she took exception to the idiocy part, but then again he'd called her precious and he was still here. "Are you really going to offer me a collar?"

"I'm going to offer you everything I have, Tiffany, but you should think about what that means."

"Yes." She didn't need to think at all. She crossed the distance between them and dropped to her knees. "Yes, Master."

"Such a reckless brat." But there was a smile on his face. "Are you satisfied, Master Ian?"

Big Tag nodded. "I am."

"He wanted to make sure this partnership is real before he walks out the door." Sebastian's hand moved over hers, drawing her up.

She knew exactly what he wanted. He hated that damn wheelchair, but he seemed to like it when she shared it with him. She moved up and curled into his lap like a happy kitten. This was right where she wanted to be. "It's very real, Master Ian. I should know. I've been plotting and planning it for months."

Both Taggarts smiled.

"Yes, I think you'll find out your Master has an answer for that as well." Big Tag winked her way.

"Come on, brother," Chef said. "Let's leave the youngsters to their fun."

"Youngsters?" Big Tag was complaining as he started out the door. "I'm not old. You're the old one. Don't you know getting your balls snipped twice ages you? I'm the baby now."

Chef groaned. "I have no idea why I put up with you."

The door closed behind them.

"Should I lock it?" She didn't really want to leave his lap.

"Javi will take care of it when he leaves." Sebastian turned them around, his arms easily handling the extra weight.

She was fascinated with his arms. So masculine and yet he hid them beneath layers of pristine suits. He maneuvered them through the hallway and back to the bedroom they'd shared the night before. He only cursed a few times because the hall was a bit narrow. It didn't mean a damn thing to Tiffany. All that mattered was being here with him.

"I'm so sorry that happened." She let her head rest against him. She was likely going to get a nasty spanking, but she could handle that. Sebastian would need the play, too. They would play hard and then go to sleep in each other's arms. Something he'd said before finally registered. "Javi's still here? I thought he left."

He stopped in front of the door. "He stayed behind to help me with something. Tiffany, I can't pick you up and carry you across the room tonight. I might be able to do it when I'm back on my feet, but I'll always be somewhat off balance."

"You managed fine. I like it right here, Master."

His hand moved over her thigh. "I need you to understand that when you pull a stunt like you did today, I will go to any length I must to make you understand the seriousness of the infraction."

She sat up. "I didn't pull a stunt. It was his fault. I wasn't the jerk carrying the knife."

His eyes went positively glacial. "I called the DA's office. They show that they not only sent you a notice of his parole hearing, they sent it via courier so you would have to sign for it. Did you sign for anything in the last month?"

"Maybe." She wasn't good at keeping up with the boring stuff. "But I still didn't ask to be nearly murdered."

"Were you afraid?" He reached up and touched her hair, brushing it back. "Did you think I was hiding until the police showed up?"

Was he high? "I wasn't really afraid because I knew you would save me. It's what you do. And then I was afraid because I realized he might hurt you instead of me. And then I was oddly turned on because you taking him down was totally hot. Then I was afraid again because I thought you might kick me out for being too much trouble."

He took her chin in his hand and forced her to look at him. "Not ever. Understand this. I may spank that pretty ass of yours. I might get angry, but I won't walk away. Never." His lips curled up into the sweetest smile. "But you might when you see what I have planned for you."

Her body heated at the thought. What had he done? "Please tell me you're not sharing me with Javi. Because I don't know that I like that idea."

His hand smoothed under her shirt and he cupped her breast right before he pinched a nipple. Hard. Just the right side of pain. "I won't ever share you."

That tweak had her heating up faster. "Good, because I won't share you either. You're mine, Master."

"And you're mine. Mine to pleasure and punish, and you're going to get both tonight."

The door opened and Javier stood there holding a set of keys. "There's not a lot I can't do with two sets of handcuffs and some bungee cord. She should be able to move at your command but she'll damn straight know she isn't leaving your bed until you're ready to let her go. And I made sure there's a way for her to reach the phone if she needs it."

"I need to reach the phone?" She looked around the room. Their bedroom had been transformed. At some point Javier had lit the candles that had only been decorative until now. The candlelight threw the whole room into a romantic glow. The bed was turned down and there was something attached to the headboard. Had that hook always been there?

"Sweetheart, we're playing some pretty heavy bondage games this evening. If I should fall and can't..."

211

He was putting in fail-safes to protect her. "Anyone can fall, Sebastian. Any top in the world can have an accident. I'm just happy my Dom is always thinking of me and my safety."

"I have to. You welcome prostitutes into your home and forget to mark down when your stalkers are getting out of prison," Sebastian replied.

Javi snapped his fingers. "I knew I'd seen Heidi somewhere."

"Thank you for the setup help, Javier. We'll see you tomorrow." Sebastian held out a hand, but the tone of his voice told Tiffany that he was through with all joking for the evening.

Javier shook Sebastian's hand. "Tomorrow then. 'Night, Tiff."

"Javier." Sebastian's call stopped Javier in the hallway.

"Yeah?" He didn't turn around.

"Taggart was joking, you know. You're a good brother. Not everyone wants to be saved. If you like, I'll talk to Rafael."

Tiffany's eyes filled with tears. How far he'd come in a few short weeks. This was the man she knew he could be. Open. Loving. Kind.

Javi's shoulders slumped but he still didn't turn. "Thank you."

When she heard the door close and lock, she turned to Sebastian. "That was a kind thing you did for Javier."

Sebastian sat in that chair differently than he had before. His shoulders were squared, his chest larger and his eyes hawkish on her. A king on a throne now. "I realized something. I am my brother's keeper. I forgot that for a long time. It can hurt to get involved, but that hurt is far better than the numbness I've felt for the last few years. Take off your clothes."

That was an easy request to honor. "Yes, Master."

His lips curled up as he sat back, watching her pull the shirt over her head. "I think you should be naked as often as possible. You would like that, wouldn't you, my lovely exhibitionist?"

The minute she felt the air on her skin, she sighed. She shoved the yoga pants she was wearing off her hips. "I do. I know it makes me weird, but I like how it feels. I like to paint naked. I think better that way, but I so rarely do it because I also need the morning light and that leads to one of two things. Complaints from the neighbors or unwanted attention from them."

"Well, we'll have to build a fence around our house that's high enough we don't worry about the neighbors."

"We have a house?" She liked the sound of that.

"I suspect we will. Apartment living can be confining and I want a house I'll feel comfortable in. The halls in apartments are typically too small to comfortably move around in. Knees, please. I think a lovely apology to me is in order before we get started with the punishment."

That punishment word was ominous, but she was willing to go along with it. She dropped to her knees in front of him. "I'm so sorry I forgot about the parole board hearing, Master. I won't forget again."

His eyes narrowed. "How the hell many others are there going to be?"

She gave him a brilliant smile. "None. Absolutely none." She thought. She was pretty sure that dude in California wasn't ever getting out. Probably. "I was talking about when Bobby goes on trial for nearly murdering me. I will hand over everything to you and I will be the best of submissives."

He chuckled as though he found the idea highly entertaining. "Somehow I doubt that. Do you understand why I'm punishing you?"

Because he was a freak who needed to let off a little steam, and she was wound pretty tight so she would enjoy it. She wasn't going to say that. There were protocols to be followed. "Because I put myself in danger and you won't have that."

He reached out and stroked her hair back. "Such a smart girl." The hand in her hair twisted and his mouth took on that faintly cruel and entirely sexy twist it got when he was ready to go hard core. "I'm also doing it because you scared the shit out of me, Tiffany. I'm doing it because you belong to me and because what I'm going to do will bring me great pleasure."

What he wasn't saying was how much pleasure it would bring her, too. "Yes, Master. I want that for you. I want to make up for disturbing you this evening."

"You disturb me every single day and never apologize for that. Come here." He held out a hand and helped her up so she could move into his lap once more. "Have you ever heard of a phantom limb? It's a thing that happens to most people who lose an arm or a leg. We're so used to them being there that we wake up and still feel them. You can feel an itch you can never, ever scratch, and it can threaten your peace, to say the very least."

She smoothed a hand over his face, the beginnings of a beard lightly scratching her palm. His hands moved over her skin as though he couldn't help himself. Another joy of being naked. He seemed to find touching her soothing, and there was nothing she wanted more than to be a peaceful place for Sebastian. "I'm so sorry. When you feel that way, tell me and I'll try to help."

He shook his head. "That's not my point. I lost more than my legs. After what happened when I got home, I cut out another part of me, the part that connected to people. I cut it out and never intended to use it again. I eased the ache with minor connections and thought I was feeding my soul. And then I felt that phantom itch when I saw you. Except it wasn't really a phantom. It was more like an awakening because I don't think you can truly lose that part of yourself. It simply sleeps until the right time. You're my right time, love. You're the right woman."

"I haven't lost the way you have, but I have drifted through life," she replied. "I always wanted what my parents had. I didn't actually realize how similar it was until recently, but I thought it wouldn't happen. My father always told me that I would know when I found someone I was willing to really fight for. He didn't tell me I would have to fight you, but I knew you were the right one, too."

"Let's see how you feel after tonight, my love." He leaned over and kissed her, melding their mouths together. His tongue dominated hers, turning the kiss carnal in an instant. Heat sang through her, lighting up her body.

No one could make her so hot, so fast.

He broke off the kiss and turned them toward the bed. "You will place yourself on the bed and wait for me. This might be awkward. I've never done this before, never played like this."

Never played without his legs. "We'll be fine. And if it's awkward, we'll laugh and make it work anyway. There's nothing we can't handle, nothing I can't handle as long as you're with me."

"Keep that in mind. Up you go."

She climbed on the bed and the candles weren't the only things the men had set up while she'd been on the phone. A good portion of Sebastian's kit was laid out neatly on one side of the bed. Her eyes widened at the sight of a rather large butt plug and a tube of lube.

"Please tell me that's regular lube." It wasn't like she hadn't been plugged before. That was a fun Saturday night at Sanctum.

"Good girls get regular lube," he replied.

"Can I point out that I was merely forgetful? It's part of my artistic temperament."

A sadistic grin slashed over his handsome face. "You can try but every second buys you a bit more of the ginger lube. You're lucky I neither had fresh ginger in the refrigerator nor the time to carve a plug. I assure you this is going to be easier on your little asshole than real ginger. Big Tag did offer to run out and get some. Should I call him back?"

Nope. The last thing on earth she wanted was Big Tag consulting on her punishment. That would go poorly for her. Her Master already seemed to have a creative mind when it came to punishment. "I'm good."

She scrambled on the bed.

"Lie back, put your hands over your head."

She'd seen the handcuffs. There were two sets, one directly attached to a hook in the bedframe. A silver cord stretched out binding another set of cuffs. The cord looped between the center of the free cuffs and back up to tie to the side of the cuffs not attached to the hook. It was an odd setup, but she was willing to go with it. "Should I bind my hands?"

"Don't you touch them. That's for me to do. Obey me. Lie back

215

with your hands over your head."

She wasn't sure how he was going to plug her if she was facing front, but he obviously wasn't going to explain and he didn't want any help. It was definitely one of those times when a sub had to give over and let her Master have his way.

She laid back on the crisp, clean sheets and waited.

Then looked up because she could hear Sebastian moving. When she looked at him, he was shrugging out of his shirt, folding it. The muscles of his chest and arms moved as he then eased up from the chair.

So much strength in his body. She had to wonder what he'd been like before, but it didn't really matter. He was perfect now. He hauled his body up on the bed. It was awkward, but she didn't move to help him. He could manage, wanted to. And she wanted the joy of watching that magnificent body as he moved to join her.

He rolled over her, his body pinning hers down. His legs were still encased in the slacks he'd put on earlier in the day. She could feel the cool metal of his belt buckle against her belly. Something about the dark look in his eyes as he let his body slide over hers made her breath hitch. It was the first time he'd ever given her his whole weight and she was deliciously pressed down into the mattress.

"This feels good," he said, lowering his mouth to her neck. He kissed her there, working his way up to her ear. "You're so soft. I love how soft you feel against me."

She loved how hard and masculine he felt. "Can I touch you?"

He shook his head. "Not yet. That isn't punishment, love. That's me knowing my own boundaries. If you touch me, I'll forget all of my plans and fight my way inside you. I want this to last. I want you to remember tonight forever."

She was sure she would, but she didn't argue with him. His hands moved up, brushing against her sides until he reached her wrists. Cool metal wrapped around her and she heard the snick of the cuffs snapping shut.

"This is where it gets fun," he murmured against her lips. "Well, fun for me."

He pushed back and rolled off her.

She missed the weight of him, but felt him move beside her. He undid his belt and struggled briefly before shoving out of his slacks and boxers. He tossed them to the side.

How could he ever think he was anything but the hottest man alive? He managed to balance on his knee, looming over her. His body was so beautiful. All she wanted was to touch him. He was a work of art, but she intended to honor him by being as good as she could be.

Not that she could touch him. He'd very effectively cuffed her to the bed. He'd laid her out and now he could do whatever he wanted to her. She was at his mercy and she hoped he had none.

He reached down and grabbed the ridiculously large plug that wasn't actually as big as he was, but seemed silly anyway. "I'm going to need you to flip over, sweetheart. Flip over and then draw your knees up, ass in the air."

"Kind of handcuffed here." It hit her suddenly. He'd improvised. "That's what the two cuff setup and bungee cord are for."

"Yes, so stop thinking and do as I say. I can always get a bigger plug. This one is large. Have you met extra large?"

She didn't want to. She flipped her body over, the cuffs moving with the cord easily. What wasn't so simple was pulling her legs up under her. She needed more yoga or something. She wiggled and squirmed until she finally got into position. "Is this okay?"

She prayed so because she was about as open as she was going to get. Her knees were under her belly, splayed wide so she could feel the air on her pussy and that part of her that was about to get tortured.

A big warm hand was on the small of her back. "It's perfect. You're perfect."

"If I'm so perfect I wouldn't be getting a ginger plug up my backside."

"That's not true," he argued. "The fact that you give me the opportunity to play with you this way makes you perfect. Who needs a well-behaved sub? Give me a sweet-natured brat every single time.

This might be a little cold at first, but it's going to heat up quite quickly."

She felt him part her cheeks, felt the chill of the lube against her. It wasn't anything she hadn't felt before. Yep. She could handle this. She'd done the crime. There was no denying that. She hadn't wanted to deal with Bobby so she'd ignored it and he'd nearly killed her and...oh, god, the pressure.

"Take a deep breath," Sebastian said.

She filled her lungs, fighting the urge to move away from him. This wasn't her first rodeo. All that would do was piss off her Dom and start the process over again. He rimmed her and she could already feel the ginger going to work.

A loud smack split the air and she felt fire lick at her as Sebastian spanked her ass with one hand. "Don't you try to keep me out."

She bit back a curse because that wouldn't do her any good either. She had a safe word, but she wasn't about to use it. Not now when they were so close to everything she'd ever wanted. So what if her asshole was on fire. "It burns."

"Let it settle in." He worked the plug, massaging her sensitive flesh. "It's like any other sensation. There are different levels. Don't fight it. Experience it."

This particular level seemed to be discomfort. Lots of crazy discomfort. She held on to the cuffs, her spine straightening as he pushed the plug in and pulled it out, gaining ground with each pass.

Finally it slid home and she could feel the hard burn along her flesh. Breathe in and out. She could take a couple of minutes and then she would scream out her safe word and end all of this.

"Hold that plug or we'll have trouble."

When she turned slightly, she watched as he grabbed the hand sanitizer he'd placed with the rest of his toys and cleaned his hands. He was surprisingly well balanced on that one knee. She concentrated on him, trying to forget the burning. It was worse when she clenched. When she relaxed, it was fainter. She had to remember to breathe.

His body was so lovely. Exactly what she remembered from the brief glance she'd gotten of it that morning so long ago. His butt was a muscled mass of perfection. His legs were like a statue, carved beautifully but broken somewhere along the way. It didn't take away from his beauty. One leg had been lost four or five inches below the knee and the other halfway up his thigh. And still he moved with a certain hesitant grace. One day he would be so comfortable with her, he wouldn't hold back at all. He would throw himself around because falling wouldn't matter. She would catch him. Though not today since she was totally not going anywhere. Javier's cuff system was getting a workout.

She could feel tears squeezing from her eyes. "How long does it last?"

"If I told you, it wouldn't be torture." He leaned over and grabbed a wand. It was pink and shiny and she wasn't quite sure what he was going to do with it.

The uncertainty made her quiver. The fact that her ass was on fire did something for her, too. This was what she needed. She would feel incomplete without this intimacy, without testing herself and exploring all the possibilities of her sexuality, but it was so much better because he was going to be her guide and her partner.

"Let's see if I can get your mind off it for a bit now that you've taken your punishment with such beautiful grace. Hold on tight to that plug. I'm going to flip you over. If you lose the plug, I'll have to start all over again."

That would kill her. Although he was right about the burn. It hurt, but then the aching went somewhere else, making her so aware of her core. She could feel her pussy getting wet, feel the burn turning into a heat that needed release.

"Be still and hold on tight." He was behind her again, but she could feel him, feel his hands on her, feel him moving into place. "Are you ready?"

His hands were on her hips.

He was going to kill her. She clenched down, determined to make it through this punishment so they could get to the good stuff. "Do it."

She took a deep breath and held on tight as Sebastian flipped her over in one neat move.

Suddenly she was looking up at him and he was holding that slim wand in his hand. He loomed over her and any thought that might have lingered that he couldn't top her in a perfectly nasty, sexy, sadistic way was utterly obliterated. There would be no locking away of her masochistic self. Sebastian's sadistic streak could match her.

And then she felt the cool bulb of the vibrating wand between her legs. He moved it over her pelvis and then she wasn't thinking about the burning anymore.

"Do you know what I can do with a flick of this wand? All I have to do is turn it on and what do you think will happen?" Sebastian asked, his voice rich with arousal.

His voice wasn't the only thing. That gorgeous cock of his was straining. Long and thick, she couldn't take her eyes off him. "Please, Sebastian. Please. I hurt and ache."

"Only if you've learned your lesson." He rubbed the head of the wand over her clit, but still didn't turn it on.

She nodded, the ache too much to deny. She couldn't play anymore. She needed him. "Yes, Master. I won't ever do it again. Please."

His thumb flicked the button and all she could think about was the buzz that hummed over her clitoris.

He pressed down and between the throbbing in her ass and the pulse of the vibe, she couldn't hold out a second longer. Her whole body went taut and she screamed out her orgasm. He held the vibe tight, riding out the wave.

She floated down, her body still humming. He held the vibrator a moment more, just enough to get her to twitch and squirm as she started to respond again.

He pulled it off, the vibe going silent as he put it away. He picked up a condom and rolled it over his cock. "You remember how I said this wouldn't be romantic?"

She didn't care. Her body was thrumming with the release and now she wanted more. "It's all right. I can handle hard-core Sebastian."

He picked up one of the keys. "But I think I need more." He released her hands and stared down at her. "You're so beautiful to me. You make me want to be better, to be more."

She shook her head and reached for him. He didn't need to be more than he was. He simply needed to allow his instincts to rule. "You only need to be here with me. I love you, Sebastian. I'll say it until you believe it."

He lowered himself between her legs, covering her body with his. "I love you. I never thought I would say those words again. I damn straight never thought I would mean them. I need you to understand that I've never loved a woman the way I love you."

She reached up and wrapped her arms around him, not even caring anymore that he'd been so mean to her poor backside. "Then don't you ever hide or hold back from me again because I love every inch of you."

He moved between her legs, his cock entering her in one long thrust. His eyes closed and his face took on a look of pure pleasure. "You feel so good."

She was sure she was super tight. She felt tight. The plug pressed in even as Sebastian started to move inside her. So full. She'd never been so full.

He gave himself over, leaning down and kissing her as though he had to fill her in every way possible. She held on to him, giving him everything she had. His cock thrust in and out, his pelvis grinding down on her clitoris, and it wasn't long before she went over the edge again.

Sebastian stiffened over her, holding himself tight to her as he came. His whole body relaxed and he pressed her back into the mattress.

"This is better," he whispered. "Better than all the rest."

She held him close. It was the best because this time the pairing was right.

CHAPTER SIXTEEN

Three weeks later, Sebastian looked up at the painting with a deep sense of satisfaction.

"It looks good here, doesn't it?" Eric stood at his side.

The large canvas dominated the previously bland wall forming the focal point of the dining room of Fort Worth's Top. It was done in shades of blue, the strong form of a man coming out of the whirl of fascinating colors. It was stunning. Like the artist.

And like the artist's muse, the man stood, but had no legs. He didn't need them. He was held up, made strong by the love that surrounded him.

"It's perfect here." If he didn't stop thinking about it, he was going to get ridiculously emotional. Better to think about other things until later tonight when he could get her all alone and show her how he felt. "But I'm shocked at how much that damn gallery took. She barely saw two thousand off that painting. They took forty-five percent of the price. I'm finding her another gallery."

Eric's eyes had gone wide. All around them the new staff was bustling, getting ready for the open that happened in less than ten minutes. But Sebastian and Eric had wanted a moment. "That's the best gallery in the city. I think you might want to talk to Tiffany about that particular part of her career."

He would, but he thought she could do better. Perhaps he could work a deal. Anything for her. She was going places and he was going to be the man who supported her while she got there. "I only want the best for her."

"Have you thought about selling them here? Or doing our own gallery nights? Deena loves interesting community outreach. We could have a wine and cheese and art night."

All of his favorite things in one place. "I'll talk to her about it. It could be fun. There's Chef."

Sean and Grace Taggart walked out of the kitchen. Chef was dressed in an impeccable suit, while his wife looked stunning in a cocktail dress. Grace had an infant in her arms while Sean was escorting his daughter. Carys Taggart held her father's hand and looked around the restaurant with wide green eyes.

Sean extended his free hand. "Eric, Sebastian, the place looks great."

Grace smiled, patting baby Lucas's back. "And the crab cakes are amazing."

Chef grinned. "Javi might have given us a tasting plate. It's a phenomenal menu."

He'd gone with a classic Chardonnay. It paired beautifully, the fruity notes bringing out the flavor of Eric's perfectly cooked crab.

Tiffany stepped up. She was wearing her uniform, dark slacks, crisp white shirt, her blonde hair in a sedate bun, but he knew what she looked like when her hair was wild and her eyes were only for him.

And she knew every part of him and somehow, someway, still loved him.

For that he was eternally grateful.

He reached for her. It was easy now. If she was in a room, he wanted to be close to her. If she wasn't in the room, he was thinking of her. All roads led right to her.

She eased into his arms. "Good evening, Chef." She smiled at Eric. "And Chef. We're almost ready to open the doors, but I was wondering if I could steal Sebastian for a moment."

She could steal him any time.

"Is our guest here?" Eric asked.

Tiffany nodded. "Yes. I'd like to introduce him."

"I would love to meet your guest." He frowned. The soft open was for friends and family, a way to ensure that the staff was truly ready. "Did your sister come over from France?"

Not that he didn't love her family. Her father had stayed with them for a few days and Sebastian found the man delightful. Even her wanna-be supermodel sister was bubbly and bright, but he was a little afraid of the other one.

Tiffany started to lead him toward the front of the restaurant. "Nope. She's not coming in until the holidays, but she's decided to protest you for not handling my stalker in a nonviolent fashion. Don't worry. She's also going to honor your military service with song. So it won't be weird or anything. No, this is another sister of mine. Or she will be one day."

Sebastian stopped.

Ramona stood in the lobby, her husband beside her. There was a young child in Johnny's arms. His nephew. He had a nephew.

His childhood came back in a wash of love. All the years… they hadn't been bad. They'd been wonderful and he was through with holding it all in.

"Ramona?"

She looked up and ran toward him, tears pouring from her eyes. "Bas. Bas, please forgive me. I was angry and lost and I'm so sorry."

He opened his arms to the only other person in the world who remembered what it meant to be loved by his parents. Ramona hugged him tight. "It's all right. We all made mistakes."

Ramona sniffled and stepped back. "You look so good."

If he looked good, it was only because he had a gorgeous woman on his arm. "So do you."

Johnny stepped up and held out a hand. "Sebastian, I can't tell you how good it is to see you. This is Ethan, your nephew. Ethan, this is your Uncle Sebastian. I told you about him."

"He's a hero," Ethan said quietly, his eyes wide.

Ramona nodded. "Yes, he's a hero."

Sebastian held out his hands and Ethan eagerly came into his arms. "I don't know about that, but I do know that I'm happy to meet you. This lady is going to be your Aunt Tiffany."

Tiffany smiled. "I will be once your uncle properly asks me. I'm getting at least one amazing proposal out of him."

Oh, she was. She was getting one tonight. He was never letting that woman go. He would ask her to be his forever during dessert, while they were surrounded by their friends and family.

By his family.

"Let me show you around," Sebastian offered. "Ethan, this is the best restaurant in the south. Don't let anyone tell you otherwise, but once your grandparents ran the best one."

He started talking about his father and mother for the first time in years with nothing but love. There was no place for anything else. He was too full.

Later that evening he would propose. He'd already picked the perfect champagne. Light and sweet, but with great substance. Like his future wife.

It was the best. That was what she deserved.

AUTHOR'S NOTE

I'm often asked by generous readers how they can help get the word out about a book they enjoyed. There are so many ways to help an author you like. Leave a review. If your e-reader allows you to lend a book to a friend, please share it. Go to Goodreads and connect with others. Recommend the books you love because stories are meant to be shared. Thank you so much for reading this book and for supporting all the authors you love!

Sign up for Lexi Blake's newsletter
and be entered to win a $25 gift certificate
to the bookseller of your choice.

Join us for news, fun, and exclusive content
including free short stories.

There's a new contest every month!

Go to www.LexiBlake.net to subscribe.

MASTER BITS AND MERCENARY BITES
The Secret Recipes of Topped
By Lexi Blake and Suzanne M. Johnson
Now Available!

Top restaurant has become the hot spot in Dallas for elevated comfort food—and a side of spicy romance. Run by executive chef Sean Taggart, Top is the premiere fictional destination for gourmet food. Join creator, *New York Times* bestselling author Lexi Blake, and Southern food expert Suzanne Johnson as they guide you through the world of Masters and Mercenaries via the secret recipes behind the food served in Top.

But what would a gourmet meal be without some company? Spend an evening with your favorite characters from McKay-Taggart as they celebrate the special moments that make up their happily ever afters. Learn how to make Sean's specialty dishes and Macon's desserts while exploring the private lives of the characters who make up the world. From Charlie and Ian's next demon spawn to a change in path for Simon and Chelsea, these are the times that bind us together, the moments that make us a family.

Good meals, good times, good friends.

Bon appétit!

* * * *

Ian went to grab the dog's leash. Bud started up his pee-pee dance, his massive body twisting and turning as he ran after Ian. His big paws thudded against the brand new hardwood he would never have spent that god-awful amount of money on had he realized a dog would pee on it.

He looked back Charlie's way. "You know there's a whole forest out back for him to go in. He should be a free-range dog. Aren't we taking away his dogness by putting him on a leash?"

Charlie frowned his way as she refilled Kenzie's cup. "Yes, he's the mighty wolf dog, Ian. I watched him run away from a bunny the other day."

He grabbed the leash. "See, if he had to go out and hunt, he wouldn't be such a shitty guard dog. Don't even say it, you two. Say good words. Not Daddy words."

Charlie put a hand to her belly. "I swear this one will come out giving the world the finger and cursing."

Bud whined, running back and forth in front of the door. Ian sighed and attached the leash. He stepped outside and Bud took off, barking and jumping against the leash until he managed to drag Ian out onto the lawn where he immediately squatted in the middle of Charlie's azaleas and started to take a crap.

Yep. This was his life. Watching the dog crap. He was so building a fence. "You know you were supposed to be a guard dog. You were supposed to be a raging, feral beast who would take out anything in your way."

Sort of like Ian had been at one time.

He'd been the bane of intelligence agencies. He'd been Dr. Death, raining down justice and protecting America.

Now he was a dumbass with a mortgage, a dog who seemed to be a bit constipated, two tiny chaotic things, and another on the way. No one even let him kill people anymore.

It was a never-ending cycle of waking up in the morning and seeing their faces, taking care of them, going to work, coming home, and going to bed with his wife.

It was kind of fucking awesome.

Sure, his younger self would likely tell him he'd sold out and he was a pathetic version of himself, but his younger self had been stupid as shit. His younger self thought a great time was following a known terrorist around for three weeks so he could find the cell. His younger self had needed a freaking shower, some decent food, and a comfy bed.

And a dog who didn't take his time with the poop.

"Come on, Bud. Pinch off, man. We've got shit to do today." Well, he did anyway. He was sure Bud would have a full day of licking his private parts and waiting for the girls to drop food. Bud seemed forever optimistic that one of these days the girls or Charlie was going to drop a ham in front of him.

A butterfly landed on the bush next to Bud and that was when he went into protective mode. He barked, the deep sound threatening to anyone who didn't know what a wuss he was, and he pulled hard at his leash.

Hard enough to make Ian stumble and damn near break his toe on the garden gnome Alex had left as a joke. Hard enough to send Ian crashing down to his knee, pain flaring and making him curse.

Bud twisted again and Ian tripped over the riding ladybug thing Kala liked to push around the yard. He landed flat on his back, looking up at the sky.

Taken down by a freaking ladybug. And his back was spasming. The pain flared through him and he could feel his lower back seizing like a motherfucker.

Bud suddenly blocked out the sky, his big doggie face staring down.

"Don't you dare."

It was too late. Bud licked his face and Ian realized he shouldn't have gotten up that morning. Nope. He should have stayed in bed and then he would be warm and happy and not having his face licked by a gargantuan mass of body odor and a tongue that licked its own ass from time to time.

God, if he didn't die from breaking his spine he was going to catch some dog disease and waste away. Right here. Because he wasn't sure he could move. "Bud, I need you to go get Charlie. Go on. Run and get her." He let the leash drop. Bud simply sat down beside him. "Go get Charlie, boy. I think she's got a ham for you. Go on."

Bud laid his big head down on Ian's chest.

Now he had a sleeping mutt and a garden gnome that was

practically up his ass. He could feel the pointy cap thing attempting to violate him.

"Ian? Ian, I need you."

Thank god. His wife would laugh her ass off, but at least she would be able to maybe help him up.

"Ian, I think the baby's coming."

Yep. It was that kind of day.

SATISFACTION
A Lawless Novel, Book 2
By Lexi Blake
Coming January 3, 2017

The sizzling second novel in a sexy new contemporary romance series featuring the Lawless siblings—from *New York Times* bestselling author Lexi Blake.

Brandon Lawless is a man on a mission: obtain the information that will clear his father's name. He's willing to do whatever it takes—even seduce his enemy's personal assistant, the beautiful and innocent Carly Hendricks. But with her beguiling smile and captivating intelligence, Brandon soon realizes he doesn't want to deceive Carly, he wants to win her over—both in the boardroom and the bedroom.

Then a twisted crime leaves Carly vulnerable and Brandon finds himself reeling. The stakes of his mission are now life or death—Carly's life. And Brandon realizes he's lost his heart to an amazing woman and his plan must succeed, because the stakes are no longer just revenge, but a once in a lifetime love.

* * * *

Patricia looked back at Bran, a faint smile on her lips. "Of course. I'm not a monster. You should take a nice long lunch. We'll have to work a bit tonight. Have you thought about bringing your friend to our little art show? Do you enjoy art, Bran?"

He had the most glowing smile. "I don't know much about it, Ms. Cain, but I do enjoy a party, and I know if you're in charge it's going to be an amazing one."

The woman actually blushed. "Well, then you should definitely come. I'll make sure there's an invitation waiting for you." Bran nodded. "Thank you so much. Any excuse to spend some time with my girl." The smile that lit Patricia's face dimmed a bit. "Of course. I'll expect you back in, say, an hour and a half, Carly. Brandon, it was lovely to meet you. You remind me of someone I knew. A long time ago."

Bran frowned. "Hopefully it was someone you liked."

"Yes," she said quietly, her eyes looking him up and down before she turned away. "Someone I liked quite a bit."

She walked away, her heels never making a sound against the hardwood.

Had Patricia-freaking-Cain hit on her boyfriend? Maybe there was some Alabama redneck still left in her, because she kind of wanted to throw down right now.

Bran's hand found hers, tangling their fingers together. "Let's go someplace quiet and have some lunch."

He squeezed her hand as though reminding her that they were in this together.

As partners. Not as boyfriend and girlfriend. This wasn't some grand romance and she didn't need to protect her man. He wasn't her man. As far as she knew, he might want Patricia's attention. It might make it easier for him to get what he needed if he was sleeping with the boss.

Was that why he'd really gotten close to her? Had she been a stepping-stone to the place he'd wanted to be?

That was when she realized he wasn't squeezing her hand. His hand was shaking.

She turned to him, moving close and taking his free hand in hers so she held them both. He hadn't enjoyed the attention. It had made him sick and scared and he needed her.

His face was perfectly blank, but he'd been shaken and she needed to do something to bring him back. He'd let her cry the first night they'd met. He'd held her then and eased her fears. He'd slept on her couch and dealt with the security stuff.

What could she do for him? She couldn't say anything, couldn't verbally give him any comfort while they were standing in her office.

She could rush him out, but she needed him to know she was here with him.

"Kiss me."

He stared down at her, his eyes focusing for the first time since Patricia had walked away. "What?"

Yes, now she had his attention again. And it wasn't only his. Patricia had stopped at her door. Out of the corner of her eye, she could see her boss standing there with one elegantly manicured hand on the door. She was watching and Carly needed her to understand something.

"Kiss me," she whispered. "I'm so happy to see you. I need you to kiss me. I missed you."

His eyes flared and his lips curled up, and she was utterly mesmerized by the way he lit up. His hands moved from holding her own to coming up to her face, where his fingertips skimmed along her jawline before cradling her cheeks. He was gentle, but she could feel the strength in those hands.

His mouth descended and she expected a brushing of his lips over hers. There it was. A soft meeting of their lips. It was nice. She was about to pull away when his hands tightened ever so slightly and his mouth demanded more.

He drew her in, his body against hers as he settled in.

Her hands moved at first to balance herself against his body, and then she could feel him, feel his muscles through the thin cotton of his shirt, feel the heat his body gave off.

Suddenly it didn't matter that she'd begun this as a way to calm him down. All that mattered was the fact that his mouth moved on hers, tempting her, teasing her. Heat flashed through her system and she could feel her whole body softening under his kiss.

She followed him, opening for him and allowing his tongue to invade. She shivered against him as he took her mouth. She'd been kissed before but not this way. Not in the sweetest, melt-against-him way that made the rest of the world seem to fade into the background.

He was calm and in control when he kissed her one last time and sighed as he pulled away. "Let's go find somewhere quiet to eat."

ABOUT LEXI BLAKE

Lexi Blake lives in North Texas with her husband, three kids, and the laziest rescue dog in the world. She began writing at a young age, concentrating on plays and journalism. It wasn't until she started writing romance that she found success. She likes to find humor in the strangest places. Lexi believes in happy endings no matter how odd the couple, threesome or foursome may seem. She also writes contemporary Western ménage as Sophie Oak.

Connect with Lexi online:

Facebook: https://www.facebook.com/lexi.blake.39
Twitter: https://twitter.com/authorlexiblake
Website: www.LexiBlake.net

Sign up for Lexi's free newsletter at www.LexiBlake.net.

Made in the USA
Middletown, DE
30 November 2016